"This is a memorable and stunning and pitch-perfect debut and one you should grab forthwith. I can't remember a first novel this good in a long, long time." ED GORMAN

'WHEN HE TURNED to face the starkly lit post office interior, Eddie, balaclava stretched over his face, was striding towards the head of the queue, hand dipping into his pocket. The woman at the front, staring at her feet, didn't notice the man wearing the dull yellow balaclava. She didn't notice when he pulled his hand out of his pocket and pointed a doctored Brocock Orion 6 pistol at her. Behind her, some of the other customers were beginning to back away. Somebody said, 'Jesus.' Somebody else moaned.

Robin grimaced. He hated this part. He picked up his bag and moved away from the door."

two-way split

allan guthrie

POINTBLANK

Set in Sabon

POINT*BLANK* is an imprint of Wildside Press
www.wildsidepress.com
www.pointblankpress.com

edited by JT Lindroos

For more information contact Wildside Press

ISBN: 0-8095-5651-0

For my wife Donna

PART ONE

*F*OUR MONTHS and twenty-two days after he stopped taking his medication, Robin Greaves dragged the chair out from under the desk and sat down opposite the private investigator.

After all this time, everything still seemed normal.

As the PI shuffled through a stack of papers he'd scooped out of a plastic tray, Robin glanced round the office. It didn't take long. A desk, the chairs they were sitting on, a filing cabinet, a plain grey carpet with a rectangular indentation to the left of the doorway (a heavy piece of furniture had once stood there, he guessed)—that was it. Behind the PI, a framed certificate hung at an angle on the wall and, above his head, a bare bulb dangled from the ceiling. The only natural light came from a single tiny window on the right.

Well, Robin thought, here he was. About to find out, at last. That's what he wanted, wasn't it?

Hands hidden beneath the desk, he started to tap out Bach's Italian Concerto on his thighs, fingers making little slapping sounds against his trousers. The PI glared at him for a second or two, then returned to the serious business of scrutinising his papers.

Robin winced as a twinge in his wrist momentarily paralysed his fingers. When the stabbing pain passed, he locked his hands together and squeezed them between his knees. He took a deep breath. As much as he wanted to know the truth, part of him would have preferred to remain ignorant.

The PI coughed. After a while he coughed again and began placing each sheet of paper, individually, back in the tray from which, only moments before, he'd removed it. When he'd finished, he stood slowly, as if his knees needed oiling, and approached

7

the grey, three-drawer filing cabinet crammed in the corner of the room. He tugged at the middle drawer. It didn't budge. He opened the top drawer, fiddled with a catch on the side, shut it and tried the middle drawer again. This time it slid open.

He started flicking through dozens of green suspension files, tongue darting in and out of his puckered mouth as he sought the information Robin had requested.

Robin stood. "Mind if I smoke?"

"Yes."

Robin shrugged and walked towards the window. A fire escape fragmented his view of a pebble-dashed brick wall four feet away. Hardly the finest vista in Edinburgh. He tapped his fingers against the windowpane, listening to the deep drumming sound, wondering why it was so unlike the tinkle glass makes when it breaks. "You going to be long?" he said.

"Be with you in just a second."

Robin wedged his hands in his trouser pockets and bent his knees. With his head craned back just far enough to be uncomfortable, he could see a sliver of grey sky. He ambled back to his chair, took his hands out of his pockets and rubbed his left eye with the back of his wrist. For a while he sat motionless, observing the PI. Then a muffled cry came from outside, where a crow was perched on the far railing of the fire escape. It shuffled to the left, stopped. Another two steps, stopped again. It looked straight at Robin, opened its beak and squawked.

If it was trying to tell him something, it was wasting its time.

The PI slammed the drawer shut and turned, gripping a white envelope between his finger and thumb as if it was a soiled tissue. He lobbed the envelope onto the desk.

Robin trapped it beneath his palm and let his hand rest there as he gazed out the window, watching the crow fly away.

"Go ahead," the PI said. "Open it."

The envelope was unsealed. Robin reached inside and removed a handful of photographs.

"You wanted proof." The PI sat down.

Robin said nothing. Did he really want proof? Did he really want to know? The skin over his cheekbones prickled as if he'd been out in the sun too long.

Proof. Photographs. He couldn't look. Didn't want to see them.

Don't look. Don't do it. Don't. Oh, shit, you've done it now.

The first photo. A couple getting into a taxi. By itself, proof of nothing. He let out a long breath. They could be going out for a friendly drink. The fact that his hand was on her elbow was, well…you could easily read too much into something perfectly innocent.

This was Robin's first visit to *Eye Witness Investigations*. He didn't know the private detective's name and he'd never asked. He didn't care. His solitary prior contact with the PI had been over the phone.

Robin had said, "I need you to watch someone."

The PI replied, "May I ask why?"

"I want to find out if she's…seeing anybody." Robin hesitated. "Can you do that?"

"I can do that."

"How much?"

"Three hundred a day."

"Give me proof within seventy-two hours and you get fifteen hundred. You need a deposit?"

The PI said, "That won't be necessary. Just give me your name and a contact number."

"The name's Robin Greaves. I'd rather you didn't phone me, though. I'll get in touch with you."

"Let me write this down." The PI broke off for a second, then said, "What's her name?"

The sound of gunfire blasted through the paper-thin walls of Robin's sitting room. He would have jumped if it weren't for the fact that by now he was used to his elderly neighbour watching Westerns on his TV with the volume cranked up. God, this was hard. Finally, he spoke. "Carol," he said. "My wife." He gave the PI their address.

Within seventy-two hours, he'd said. He couldn't complain. He was getting the service he'd asked for.

He slapped the picture face down on the desk. His palms were sweaty. In the next picture the photographer had snapped them from behind, catching them holding hands.

"I'm sorry," the PI said.

Who did he think he was? Why was he fucking sorry? When Robin looked at the third photo he noticed his hand was shaking. The picture showed the couple entering a nightclub. The next shot, in which they were laughing, had been taken as they left. In the fifth, Eddie had his arm around her. In the sixth, Carol had her fingers tucked in his back pocket. There were ten photographs in all. The remaining four showed the same scene: his wife and her good friend Eddie in the doorway to his flat, joined at the neck, the chest, hips, his arms twisted around her, her eyes closed.

He tucked the photos back in the envelope.

"Happy?" The PI coughed again. "Or maybe that's not the right word. Satisfied?"

Happy? Satisfied? Who was this joker? Patches of black spotted the edges of Robin's vision.

The PI stared at him, grinning.

Robin imagined leaping across the desk, ramming the heel of his hand into the bastard's nose, then standing back and watching the blood stream out of it. He imagined the injured man staggering to his feet, groaning behind the hand cupped over his very probably broken nose, shirt collar a red band around his throat. Robin took out his wallet and counted fifteen hundred pounds in fifties, the last of his money, withdrawn from the bank less than an hour ago. He bent forward.

The PI leaped backwards with a yell. His hand fell from his face, tracing a dark red curve on the pale wallpaper behind him. He leaned against the wall, snorted, spat into his hand. His mouth sprang open and his stained teeth chattered. He blinked several times, then said, in a thin, sticky voice, "What was that for?"

Robin took shallow breaths. He dropped the money into the plastic tray on the desk. His lungs were full of pebbles. He ferreted in his jacket pocket and found his cigarettes and disposable lighter. He stuck a cigarette to his bottom lip. Had he hit the poor man? Surely not. But there was no one else in the room and the PI hadn't assaulted himself, had he? Robin lit the cigarette. "I'm sorry," he told the cowering figure, stuffing his cigarettes and lighter back in his pocket and picking up the envelope. "I don't know what—"

He had to leave right this minute. Who knew what would happen if he stayed?

10:25 AM

*W*inter in Scotland was far too cold to walk around bare-chested. That's why Pearce wore a t-shirt. His fists clenched, relaxed and clenched again. His forearm muscles writhed under his goose-pimpled skin. He smacked his hands together.

Who wanted to live in a tower block? Last time he ventured into this area was over ten years ago. A housing scheme roughly six miles west of the city, Wester Hailes was the dumping ground for single mothers, the elderly, the unemployed, winos, whores, students, foreigners, crazies, ex-cons, junkies, and dyke social workers. The properties were damp. The heating didn't work. There were problems with the plumbing. The lifts kept breaking down.

Ten years ago Wester Hailes was Edinburgh's drug centre. Junkies congregated from all over the city to share needles in the dozens of abandoned flats.

As Pearce's sister had said, "The views from the top are pretty cool. Get high to get high, you know. You got the Pentlands to the south. You ever seen snow-capped mountains through a heroin haze? And on the other side, sometimes I see the struts of the Railway Bridge wriggle just like my veins after I've jacked up."

Last time he was here he arrived too late. Dislodged from his sister's arm, a syringe nestled against the skirting board. She lay on her back, naked, her only view a web of cracks in the ceiling. She'd been dead for two days.

Maybe things had changed, like they said, although it needed more than a bit of re-cladding to convince him. At street level the multi-storey blocks shortened his horizon. He felt hemmed in, imprisoned. He rubbed his palms on his jeans.

An upturned shopping trolley propped open the door of the building he was looking for.

"Hey!"

He craned his neck. On the top floor a teenage boy in a grey hooded top was leaning over the balcony, waving. He held something in his hand. Without warning, he let go. Pearce stepped to the side. The object struck the ground a couple of feet from where he'd been standing, bounced once and rolled to a stop. A syringe. Clear plastic split down the centre, plunger depressed, needle snapped off in the fall. He tossed the trolley out of the way and ducked through the doorway. So much for change.

Staircase to the left. *Sprinting up the stairs. Out of breath. "Muriel!"* Lift straight ahead, door yawning at him. Chest tight, lungs burning, he stepped inside the lift and its scarred, steel-grey mouth swallowed him. The door shut with a clang that made sweat break out on his forehead. Stale air filled his nostrils. His hand shook as he pressed the button for the eighth floor.

He had arrived too late. *Stop it.* He had failed to protect her. *Forget it. She's dead. I wasn't looking out for her. Stop it. Think about something else. Concentrate on the job. Do what you're here to do. Concentrate on the old man.*

The old man was called Willie Cant and his mother had gone to school with him. They'd even kissed once, she told Pearce. She asked him not to be too hard on the old guy. Pearce looked down at the steel toecaps of his light-brown boots. They could cause a bit of damage. He wouldn't use his feet, then. The lift grumbled to a halt and the door struggled open.

Two teenage boys blocked Pearce's path. Fifteen, sixteen years old. The one wearing the grey hooded top pointed a knife at him.

Pearce felt nothing at all. He said, "Move."

The teenager's hand was unsteady. He glanced at his pal, and grinned. His teeth were yellow.

Pearce took a step to the side and the youth mirrored his movement. "Out of my way," Pearce said.

"Where's the party? Are we invited?"

Pearce's eyes probed the boy's. Dull brown. No sparkle. Lots of movement. The silence lengthened. In a little while, the one without the knife spoke and the voice startled Pearce. It belonged to a girl.

"Let's piss off, Ross," she said. "This guy's weird."

Pearce's eyes darted over the contours of her light brown jumper, then back to Ross. "Listen to your girlfriend," he said.

She had started to move. She was tugging Ross's sleeve. Her hair was as short as Pearce's.

Ross licked his bottom lip slowly, carefully, as if his tongue was an expensive lipstick. Somewhere below, a dog started to bark. Ross lowered his hand and his tongue shot back into his mouth. "Next time," he said, faking confidence, and wheeled around.

Pearce watched them disappear up the stone staircase. The girl shouted something he didn't quite catch and forced laughter ricocheted off the walls. Cant's handwritten name was taped on top of the garish pink paintwork of his front door. The letter *a* had been scored out and replaced with a *u*. Pearce felt the corners of his mouth twitch. He slipped a fingernail under a burst paint blister, which peeled off like boiled skin.

He slammed on the door with the heel of his hand. "Open up." He waited a minute, watching the second hand of his watch complete a full circle, before hammering on the door again. Then he waited another minute, precisely. "Last chance, Cant."

From the other side of the door a quiet voice said, "What do you want?"

Okay, let's see. I want to pay off the grand I owe Cooper. And I want Mum to get another job. It's not safe working there these days. To Cant he said, "I think you know."

The old man whined, "I don't."

"Open up."

After a moment, Cant whispered, "I don't want to hurt you."

"That's very kind of you," Pearce said. "Now open the door."

Silence.

"Open it."

The old man's voice rang out: "Bugger off."

Following Joe Hope's advice, Pearce tried a different approach. "My mum remembers you," he said, pressing his ear to the door.

"Hilda Pearce. When she knew you she was Hilda Larbert. You were at school together. Ring any bells?"

A slight pause. Then, "What are you going to do?"

"Open the door. We'll talk."

"Tell me what you're going to do."

"You're making me angry. Open the door, Mr Cant." He waited. "You can do it."

"Tell him he can have his money tomorrow."

"I won't discuss business through a closed door."

"Tomorrow. I promise."

Pearce took a deep breath. Fuck Joe Hope's advice. What did he know? He was nothing more than one of Cooper's hired thugs. Pearce flicked a switch in his head and instantly words rattled out of his mouth like bullets out of a machine-gun. "If you don't open the fucking door right fucking now you piece of shit there's no way I'm going to be accountable for what happens to you, you with me on this, you understand or do I have to explain it all again?" He waited a moment, took a step back, aimed to the right of the handle and kicked the door with his heel. His boot went straight through the wood and stuck there. He hopped a couple of times until he regained his balance. Splinters scuffed his boot as he dragged his foot back out.

He dug his hand in his pocket and pulled out a pair of surgical gloves. They fitted like an extra layer of skin. He wriggled his gloved hand through the hole and fumbled for the key. His fingers caressed the empty keyhole, slid up the door and turned the knob on the Yale. Locked. He flicked the snib downwards and tried again. The door opened, but only as far as the length of chain allowed. He leaned against the door, tearing the chain out of the wall.

Cant's flat smelled of dried vomit. A puff of dust rose from the carpeted hallway as Pearce stepped into the old man's home. Coffee-brown stains flecked the left hand wall. The right was shelved. Two shelves. A dead plant on each.

The old man had fled.

But he had to be here somewhere. Pearce walked to the end of the hallway. The door facing him was shut. There was another door to his left, open a crack. He kicked it.

A single bed was jammed against the wall. He lifted the quilt and glanced underneath. Dozens of identical socks—grey with parallel strips of red diamonds—littered the floor. He lowered the quilt and reached the wardrobe in two small steps. Brass handles. Dark wood scarred in a dozen places. He opened both doors. Empty, except for a solitary coat hanger and more socks. The right hand door squeaked when he closed it.

His eyes swept the room one last time. Turning, he stepped into the hallway and grabbed the handle of the other door. It clicked and swung open with a groan.

Cant was pressed into the far corner of his living room, upper body gently rocking. He didn't look up. Pearce traced the grain of an unvarnished floorboard with a critical eye. Living room segued into kitchen with only a tattered patch of linoleum indicating the change. He shook his head. Grime coated the kitchen surfaces. A tower of dirty dishes sat next to the sink and more dishes swam in a basin of filthy water. The open drawer by the sink was where, presumably, the old man had found the bread knife he was cradling against his chest.

Pearce would never live like this. He'd die first. He found himself wondering what his mum had seen in Cant. Well, who could tell with kids? Would she still have kissed him at school had she known he would end up in this pitiful state? Probably. Mum was all heart. Always had been. She understood why he'd had to kill Priestley.

"Fifty quid." He fixed his eyes on the old man.

Cant's lips were moving. He was mumbling. Praying, maybe. For all the good it would do.

"Due yesterday," Pearce continued.

Cant stilled for a moment, then started rocking and mumbling again.

Pearce moved towards him.

"No closer," Cant cried out. His bony fingers squeezed the handle of the knife, his knuckles pale, the skin stretched across the back of his hand. His shoulders heaved as he gulped air in desperate mouthfuls. "No closer, you bastard." He wiped his nose with the back of his hand. His eyes met Pearce's briefly, then lowered to gaze at the floor.

"The way I look at it," Pearce said, "I'm doing you a favour. You'll be looked after in hospital. Free meals. No bills. And by the time you get out you'll have saved enough to pay back Mr Cooper."

"Oh, no," the old man said, and started moaning. He fell to his knees. "Go away." He dropped the knife. "Please." Eyes shut, he rolled over onto his side and drew his knees to his chest.

Pearce picked up the knife. He carried it into the kitchen, returned it to the open drawer and slammed the drawer shut. He yawned and said, "Excuse me," into his cupped hand as he ambled back over to Cant. He prodded Cant's scrawny arm with his toe.

The old man's eyes snapped open. His arm recoiled and he tucked it between his legs. His dark eyelashes fluttered. A thick thread of drool joined the side of his mouth to the floor.

"I'll give you another twenty-four hours," Pearce said. "But fifty pounds won't be enough." He rubbed a thick finger across his chin, enjoying the rasping sound it made. "You've defaulted on a payment. That's a ten pound fixed penalty. My time's another ten. Interest, that's another ten. And another twenty, say, for not breaking anything. What's that? A hundred?"

Cant looked up. He sniffed, propped himself on an elbow. "You're a nice guy," he said.

Pearce nodded, eyeing Cant's socks. Grey, with red diamonds.

10:44 AM

"*P*ish." Kennedy was holding a cup of coffee in each hand and his phone was ringing. Directly ahead of him, residue of Edinburgh's volcanic past, Salisbury Crags formed a jagged wall high enough to obscure the massive mound of Arthur's Seat. Just looking at it made him dizzy. He tried to find somewhere to deposit the paper cups. "Pish," he said again. If only the drinks dispenser hadn't been repossessed. He bent down and set the cups on the ground.

Expecting the caller to hang up just as he answered, he dug his mobile out of his pocket. "Kennedy," he said.

He was wrong. The caller said, "Where are you?"

The voice sounded familiar, even if it was strangely nasal. He asked, "That you, boss?"

"Course it's me. Where are you?"

"Across from the office."

"He should be leaving the building now."

"Who should? You developed a heavy cold since I went to get the coffee? Either that or you're wearing a nose-plug. Oh, God. You haven't taken up synchronised swimming, have you?"

"Shut up and listen."

"Since you asked so politely."

"About five ten, five eleven. Short dark-brown hair. Padded black jacket. See him?"

The grocers beneath the office had spawned a canopy when it changed owners a couple of months ago. Two wall-mounted heaters kept the crates of vegetables that littered the pavement from freezing. Today's special deal was on cabbages: two for the price of one. Kennedy couldn't manage to eat a single cabbage before it went off, let alone two. He had the same problem with bread. Even small sliced loaves were too big. In fact, half the food he bought went stale or rotted and ended up in the bin. If only you could buy individual bread slices. Or pairs, in case you wanted a sandwich. Maybe it was time he bought a freezer.

He'd have to get paid first, though. Or get a new job. He'd just about had enough of this one. God, he was bored.

His boss's voice again: "Do you see him?"

To the left of the grocers, six narrow steps led to a salmon pink door. It was shut. "No." As he spoke, the door opened. "Wait. Got him, I think. Dark green trousers?"

"Yeah. Don't hang up. Get in the car and follow him."

"What about your coffee?"

"Fuck the coffee."

"I would, but I don't fancy the blisters."

"Not funny. Now fucking move."

Kennedy left the coffee on the pavement and crossed the road. "He's getting in his car. Want the registration?"

"Read it out."

He read it out. "Who is he?"

"Robin Greaves."

"Isn't he a client?"

"He was."

Robin Greaves's metallic green Renault Clio squealed away from the kerb.

"He's off. Speak to you in a minute." Kennedy dropped the phone onto the passenger seat. He let a couple of cars pass, then tucked in behind a silver Nissan Micra. Driving one-handed, he picked up the phone again and said, "Wasn't Greaves's wife involved in a bit of extra-marital?"

"Yeah." His boss sniffed. "I showed him the pictures."

"How did he take it?"

"He broke my fucking nose."

"Fucking hell!" Kennedy bit his lip and rocked with silent laughter. After a while he cleared his throat and said, "Broke it, eh? No shit?"

"No shit." After a pause, his boss said, "And your sympathy is duly noted."

He wanted sympathy? Kennedy said, "I'm very fucking bloody sorry. Sir."

"Don't be an arsehole, Kennedy."

Neither man spoke for a while.

Kennedy's boss finally broke the silence. "When he gets where he's going, phone me."

"Shouldn't you go to the hospital and get your nose fixed?"

"I'm staying right here. And, Kennedy? I don't need your bloody advice."

The line went dead.

Robin Greaves led Kennedy through light traffic towards town, then headed east down Leith Street. Construction work was underway at Greenside. The shell was now in place and already it was brown with rust. In yesterday's paper some journalist had suggested that the sixty screens offered by Edinburgh's eight existing cinemas ought to be enough for a city with a population of less than half-a-million. Building a new multiplex at Greenside, so claimed the writer, was a scandalous waste of money. Kennedy wouldn't have worded it quite as strongly, but he agreed that it did seem excessive. Bizarrely, though, the dickhead had gone on to complain about Edinburgh having twice as many bookshops as Glasgow. Which gave a new slant to the whole article. Kennedy chucked the paper in the bin, since the journalist was obviously from the west coast and therefore everything he said was unadulterated pish.

Greaves turned off Leith Walk, Kennedy following two cars behind. Greaves parked in Iona Street, got out of his car and entered a block of flats in a tenement where scaffolding had spread in rectangles like ivy with an instinct for geometry. Kennedy was impressed. The scaffolders had done a hell of a job. Kennedy had no head for heights. When he painted his ceiling last month, he'd almost fallen off the stepladder.

He found a place to park and called his boss. "How's the nose?"

"Where is he?"

Kennedy peered through the scaffolding and read the number off the door.

"Ah, he's returned to the nest," his boss said.

"Probably could have worked that out for myself. The set of keys gave it away." There was no reply. "What do you want me to do?"

His boss said, "I'm thinking."

With the phone still held to his ear Kennedy got out of the car and crossed to the doorway where Greaves had disappeared. "You still there?" he said into the phone.

"Yeah."

On the left of the doorway a row of buzzers ran down the wall, and opposite each buzzer, protected by a clear plastic cover, was a name. Sixth from the top, beneath Hewitt and above Law, was Greaves. Kennedy said, "Looks like our man lives on the second floor. Want me to pop up and say hello?"

"Keep out of sight for the moment. And keep an eye on him until I tell you otherwise."

"If he leaves his flat?"

"Follow him."

10:57 AM

*P*earce had been living in his mum's spare room for the last two months. It didn't amount to much, but it was home, and it was a big improvement on what he'd been used to for the last ten years.

One night, relaxing with a can of Tennants, listening to his mum's Burt Bacharach CD, he'd told her about Julie. It took a lot of nerve.

She said, "How can you have been so stupid?"

"Stop it, Mum." He looked at her and his shoulders slumped and he said no more.

She released a big fat sigh. She said, "Come here, you great pillock. It's so good to have you back."

He had known Julie for two weeks. Retrospectively, it might have been too soon to get engaged and, certainly, his mum thought so. But, at the time, it seemed like a good idea. How gullible could you get? He had never had any luck with women. *You want to get engaged, Pearce?* Nothing better to do on a Saturday morning. *Yeah, Julie, but what's the catch?* Julie wanted a diamond ring and she'd seen one she liked in Jenners. If he could put up the money she'd pay him back when the banks opened on Monday.

"I won't let you pay for your own ring," he said.

"I want to. In fact, I insist. Besides, you can't afford it."

He thought about it for no time at all. "You're right," he said. "I don't have that kind of money."

"What about your friend, Cooper?"

"Cooper isn't a friend. I don't want any favours from him."

"You scared of him?" She touched his bare arm.

Pearce went to see Cooper, borrowed a grand and bought

Julie's ring. They parted after lunch, at one thirteen, and that was the last time he saw her. They'd arranged to meet later that evening but she didn't show up. When he dialled her mobile it was switched off. He left a message. Soon afterwards, he visited the address she'd given him, a semi-detached in Gilmerton. When he got there the owner claimed he'd never heard of her. Pearce described her: tiny, slim, fragile, dark-haired, pale. The owner shook his head. Pearce checked he had the correct address and the owner said yes and closed the door. Pearce tried her mobile again and left another message.

On Sunday he went back. This time the owner wasn't so help-ful. He refused Pearce's request to have a look around, so Pearce shoved him out of the way and started hunting for Julie. The television blared in the sitting room. Otherwise it was empty. In the kitchen, a pot of soup simmered on the cooker. Upstairs, he glanced inside both bedrooms. No Julie. He already felt foolish enough, otherwise he'd have checked under the beds. One last place to look. He knocked on the bathroom door and, when no one answered, he walked in. He pulled back the shower curtain, just in case she was hiding in the bath. She wasn't.

He apologised to the owner for his intrusion and promised he wouldn't be back again.

He postponed seeing Cooper for a week. By that time any last hopes of his fiancé's miraculous reappearance had vanished as surely as the thousand-pound engagement ring. If he waited any longer he knew Cooper would send someone to look for him, so he went to Cooper's house and told him what had happened.

"Stitched up," Cooper said. "By a wee girl, eh?" He shook his head. "Lost it, did you, Pearce? Inside?" He pursed his lips. "What did you have in mind?"

"I thought, maybe, I could work off the debt."

"Let me think about it." Cooper showed him the door.

Two days later Pearce got a call. Cooper said, "Here's the deal. Your debt currently stands at two grand."

"Twelve hundred's what we agreed."

"We're discussing a compromise here. You want to argue with me or do you want to hear how you might be able to keep your legs?"

Pearce said, "Go on."

"You've already missed your deadline and you're telling me the girl, your security, has done a bunk with the ring, which was your sole asset. Therefore, your financial situation has changed. Accordingly I have reviewed our initial arrangement, the consequence of which is that you now owe me two grand. However, I'm prepared to let you work it off. Isn't that good of me?"

"How much are you going to pay?"

"What?"

"I want to know how long it's going to take me to pay it all back."

"That's up to you. This isn't Burger King. You don't get paid an hourly rate, same as I don't pay your fucking national insurance and neither of us pay any tax."

"So how do I pay you back?"

"Commission. You earn twenty percent of what you recover. I'll deduct that amount from your debt. So the more you get out of my clients the happier, and richer, we'll both be."

"None of these people, your *clients*, have any money, Mr Cooper."

"It's surprising how often they can *find* money."

"Shit."

"You think so? We must use different dictionaries. Tommy Gregg, now he was a shit."

Everyone knew about Tommy. He'd mouthed off about how he wasn't scared of Cooper. One night, Cooper and one of his thugs visited Tommy's flat armed with a coffee grinder. These days, Tommy walked with a limp.

"This is the only offer you're going to get," Cooper said. "It's generous and it's non-negotiable. Difficult to believe, but Tommy used to fancy himself as a hard man." He laughed. "See him now, Pearce. If I told him to suck my dick, the dirty toeless cripple would be down on his knees with his tongue hanging out like a hundred quid an hour whore before I got my fucking zip down. You wouldn't want to end up like that, would you?" He paused for a moment. "So what's your answer?"

Pearce said, "Okay," and Cooper said he'd see him tomorrow. One of his lads would show him the ropes.

When Pearce told his mum she said, "Don't do it. I'll lend you the money."

"And where are you going to find two grand?" he asked her.

"I suppose I could borrow it from Cooper."

"Right, Mum."

Pearce dug in his pocket and pulled out the list Cooper had given him. Four names, four addresses, four debts. The first on the list wasn't at home. Cant had been second. The woman, Ailsa Lillie, was number three. She owed Cooper three hundred quid. Pearce wondered how much she'd borrowed. Hating this job already, he checked the street number, folded the paper and put it back in his pocket.

Cars slalomed down Easter Road, weaving between lay-bys and traffic islands. Buses stuttered along, threading through gaps in the oncoming traffic towards the next stop or pedestrian crossing. He squeezed through a gap in the queue at a cash machine, nearly treading on the tail of a dog tied up outside the neighbouring newsagents as he did so. At the first break in traffic, he crossed the road.

Ailsa Lillie's building was next to a bookies. The exterior wall was black with soot and traffic grime. The outside door was open, but he pressed the buzzer and waited. No harm in being polite.

10:58 AM

There they go again. Bang. Bang. Fucking bang.

Robin couldn't sit in his flat doing nothing, not with that racket driving him mad. For at least a week now his almost totally deaf neighbour had been watching back-to-back John Wayne movies with the volume turned all the way up. Robin usually retaliated with a CD of a late Beethoven string quartet, or something with a prominent brass section—Janacek was good—or a Baroque opera played so loud the windows rattled. Often he'd sing along at the top of his voice. But not today. Today was different.

Two hours to go. He was tense. Couldn't stay cooped up. Had to get out.

As if being a tenant again wasn't depressing enough, their flat wasn't as nice as the old one. They no longer had a separate kitchen, for instance, and on the rare occasions either he or Carol cooked, the smell permeated the furniture in the sitting room. The couch would stink of fish or steak or bacon or whatever for days. A granny carpet—flowers, in pinks and purples—covered the floor. The piano had been moved once too often and badly needed tuning. Didn't matter, though, since he hardly ever played it. Five minutes now and then, maybe once a week, if the pain wasn't too severe. Once his Robinson upright might have been a musical instrument, but these days, it functioned primarily as a piece of furniture.

If he was going out, he'd better fetch the bag.

Maddening striped wallpaper covered three of the bedroom walls. Despite the illusion of depth created by the mirrored wardrobes running along the remaining wall, the room looked crammed. On the dresser, squeezed in the space between bed and door, stood twelve framed photos of Carol. Watching himself in the mirror, he knocked them onto the floor with a sweep of his arm.

How could she do this to him? He couldn't believe she'd let Eddie touch her.

Observing his movements in the mirror as he shuffled forwards, he moved his right hand slowly, as if waving underwater. *Conducting, of course. Who was asking?* Yeah, he'd carry on as normal. *An orchestra. What else?* Pretend he didn't know. Raising himself on his toes for an imagined upbeat, he adopted a faster tempo. His hand sliced through the air. After a few bars, he stabbed the circled finger and thumb of his left hand at the brass section. His hands dropped to his side and he shook his head. "Late again," he said. "Just not good enough."

Otherwise he risked jeopardising everything. And this was personal. Nothing to do with business. Tomorrow was soon enough to decide what to do. He would deal with Carol first and then he would deal with Eddie.

The bag lay under a pile of dirty clothes. He dug it out and slung the strap over his shoulder. If Eddie knew what he was about to do now, he'd have a heart attack. Robin chuckled at the thought.

Outside, the temperature was only a notch above freezing. But it was dry and he didn't have far to walk. Just as well, since he couldn't risk taking the car. He stepped under the canopy of poles and planks erected after the accident about a month ago when a window lintel had fallen from the third floor and struck a pedestrian on the neck. Workmen had arrived days later and covered half the block in scaffolding. They hadn't been back since.

He passed Mrs Henderson, an old lady who lived in one of the ground floor flats in his building. She was wheeling a tartan shopping trolley behind her. He said, "Good morning," as he overtook her. She peered at him through her thick-lensed glasses, and nodded her tangle of white hair at him.

He turned the corner and crossed the road, the heel of his hand tingling. He wondered how the PI's nose felt.

† † †

Hogging the centre of the congested post office, two freestanding display racks forced the queue along the side of the walls. More racks, stuffed full of leaflets, spanned the length of the near wall. Opposite, protected by a clear anti-bandit screen (that's what they're called, so Eddie said), two cashiers served with an unremitting lack of urgency. Robin observed the fat one, who looked about sixty. As she chatted to her colleague the flab under her chin wobbled.

When he reached the front of the queue he said, "A first class stamp, please." Her hairspray caught in his throat and he coughed before he had time to cover his mouth.

She said, "And then, well, I shouldn't say," and tore a single stamp out of a book. He pushed a fifty pence piece through the gap at the bottom of the grill. "But there could be some trouble," she carried on, counting his change from neat piles stacked in a velvet-lined box. Her podgy white fingers pushed the money towards him.

"I'll see you later," he said. Only then did he get her full attention.

"What did you say?"

He smiled at her and scooped up his change.

"Do I know you?"

He said, "Not yet," and left. She'd know him soon enough, though.

10:59 AM

Ailsa Lillie buzzed Pearce into the building without a word. When he knocked on her door it opened a crack. She kept the chain on.

"Who is it?" Her voice was deep and came from the back of her throat. She wasn't from Edinburgh. Her accent carried a north-east lilt.

"Can I come in?" He smiled at the slice of face that had appeared between door and doorframe. It looked as if someone had dunked her head in a sack of flour. Her hair was grey, her face pale except for the purple bruise over her eye.

"Why?" Her head shook. She looked about forty.

He lowered his voice. "You owe a friend of mine some money."

"Who?"

"You know who, Ailsa. Let me in."

"You seem nice," she said. "But I'm a poor judge of character. You could be a serial killer for all I know."

"You owe Mr Cooper three hundred quid. You think a serial killer would know that?" He hesitated, then continued, "All I want is for us to agree on some kind of mutually acceptable repayment terms."

Her eyes dropped. Without looking up she said, "Mutually acceptable?"

He nodded slowly. The door clicked shut. Seconds later it opened fully and she stood in front of him.

"Close the door behind you." She turned away from him, feet

silent on the carpeted floor. "The bedroom's this way."

"Wait." He stepped into the hallway and eased the door shut. She ignored him. He watched her disappear into the bedroom. She moved like somebody much younger. He slipped the chain back on. "Ailsa," he said. "Ms Lillie," he said. After a moment he followed her.

She was lying on her stomach on the unmade bed, her right leg dangling over the side. Repetitively, she dragged her toes over the surface of a faded red rug that was threadbare along the edge.

"Ailsa."

"You keep saying my name."

"I'm trying to tell you—"

"What's yours?"

"My name's not important."

"I'd like to know." She swivelled her hips and faced him, arms stretched over her head. "Oh please, at least grant me that. After all…"

"Pearce," he said.

"You *are* nice." Her green eyes shone. "Sit down next to me, Pearce."

He strolled towards the bed and sat down.

"How do you want to do it?" she said.

"What happened to you?" He reached towards her. When his fingertips were an inch from her face she turned her head away.

She laughed, but there was no humour in the sound that rasped from her throat. "What happened your face?"

She mumbled into the pillow.

"I didn't hear you." He leaned closer.

"What do you care?" Suddenly she sat up, pointing a pistol at him, holding it as if it was scalding her palm. She was shaking violently.

"If you shoot me Cooper will just send someone else." He held out his hand. "Someone who might not be as nice as me."

"Are you a bit thick, Pearce?" She clamped her other hand around the one that was clutching the gun and tried to steady her aim. "If I shoot you," she explained, "I'll go to prison. Cooper will be the least of my worries. I'll be safe."

"I might not be as thick as you think. Why don't you tell me about it?" he said. "You borrowed the money from Cooper to buy that gun, didn't you?" Her gaze flickered and he continued, "I would guess that the weapon was purchased with a certain person in mind. Am I right? Maybe that special person is the same one that knocks you about. How am I doing so far?"

Her lips twitched. "Not bad," she said.

"And might that be him?" He pointed to the framed photograph on the wall above her head. She didn't look, but she nodded. "Husband?" he asked her, then noticed that the fingers gripping her gun were free of jewellery. They had stopped shaking, but her knuckles were white as young bone. "Just a boyfriend?" he said. "Why don't you leave him?"

When she laughed again it was as if someone had wrapped her larynx in sandpaper. She said, "I tried that."

He lifted his eyebrows. "And you came back?"

"He didn't like it."

"Who cares what he likes or doesn't like?"

"If only it were that easy, Pearce." She gulped and lowered her hands. "As long as it involved me alone. As long as he didn't touch anyone else, I was prepared to take his best shot."

Gently, Pearce prised one of her fingers off the gun.

"This is nothing." Her hands fell apart and the gun slid onto the bed. She touched her bruised eye. "Compared to what he did to Becky."

"Your sister?" He picked up the gun. It was heavier than he'd anticipated.

Ailsa Lillie shook her head. Her eyes blazed. "Rebecca's my daughter."

He examined the weapon. Nickel, he guessed. CCCP engraved on the butt. "How old?"

"Eighteen." She paused, then added, "Old enough."

"For what?"

"A fractured cheekbone and a broken jaw."

"She doesn't live here?"

"You kidding? Becky left home when she was sixteen." She smiled and said, "She's a hairdresser."

"She his daughter?"

"No, thank God."

"This isn't loaded." He showed her the empty magazine.

"Christ, don't I know it."

He shoved the clip back in.

"After I'd paid for the gun," she said, "I didn't have enough money left to buy bullets. I didn't realise a box of ammo cost half as much as the gun."

"That's a hell of a mark-up." He looked at her and started laughing. She joined him and sounded as if she meant it. He said, "What's your boyfriend's name?"

"Why do you want to know?"

"You're in a mess, Ailsa. If you want out of it, here's what you do. Tell me his name and where I can find him."

She told him. "He's dangerous," she added.

"I'll be very careful." He handed her the gun. "Take that to whoever you bought it from and demand your money back. You won't get it all, so hold out for half. That's reasonable. Enough to be useful to you, but not too much for him to lose face. He'll see the sense in it if you point out that he can sell the gun again. Will you do that?"

She nodded.

He stood. "I'll be round tomorrow to pick up the money."

She grabbed his hand. "What are you going to do?"

He shrugged. "Have a word with your boyfriend. Tell him it's over. That you don't want to see him again." He slipped his fingers out of hers and rubbed his chin.

"He'll kill her." She clutched his hand again. "He'll kill Becky."

"She has nothing to worry about."

She didn't believe him. Creases lined her forehead and wrinkles erupted at both sides of her mouth.

"I promise you," he said, "neither you nor Becky will ever see him again."

Her forehead smoothed out once again and she looked almost pretty. "I owe your boss money. Why are you doing this? Why are you helping me? You some kind of vigilante or something?"

"Remember what I said?" He gazed down at her. "That I wanted to negotiate mutually acceptable repayment terms? Well, that's what we've been doing. I never meant to imply that I wanted to..." He made a circular motion with his hand. "All that, anyway. It's just business, Ailsa. You're an investment and I'm protecting you like I would any other investment."

She levelled the gun at him, closed her puffy eye and said, "I should shoot you for being such a crap liar."

He turned his back on her. "I'll see myself out."

"Hey," she said. "There's a big guy who works with Pete. His name's Tony. He's nice too. Like you. Say hi to him for me."

11:15 AM

"*N*ot now, Mum." Pearce hung up and turned off his mobile.

"Mothers, eh?"

The male voice registered as an anomaly, although he wasn't sure why. He couldn't think of a compelling reason why a sauna had to have a female receptionist, but that's what he'd expected. Maybe this guy doubled as a security guard. Pearce looked up. So much for that theory. You didn't see many security guards less than five feet tall. Behind the semi-circular counter Shortarse's face was a bag of tension. "Where's Pete?" Pearce asked him.

"Pete?" Shortarse's mouth stretched and slackened and stretched again. You couldn't tell if he'd just stubbed his toe, or if he was about to burst into hysterical laughter.

"How many Petes you got working here?"

Shortarse shrugged.

"Any of the girls called Pete, are they?"

Shortarse's lips twitched.

"Thompson," Pearce said with his eyes closed. "Thompson," he said again. He opened his eyes and stared. "I'd like to see Pete Thompson."

"Ah." Shortarse's head bobbed up and down. "Mr Thompson." His lips pulled tight and his jaws clenched and he said, "Got an appointment?" Pearce said nothing and the little man continued nodding his head. "You need an appointment to see Mr Thompson."

Pearce clipped his mobile onto his belt. A muscle tugged at his cheek.

"An appointment." Shortarse nodded hard and fast.

"Mind your head," Pearce told him. "All that shaking, it's liable to snap off."

Shortarse's face paled and his eyebrows lifted. His head was motionless as he picked up the phone on the desk, pressed a couple of numbers and said, "Tony, we got a funny boy out here." He dropped the receiver. It bounced out of the cradle and clattered onto the desk. Shortarse muttered as the dialling tone moaned at him from the upturned phone and he was picking it up again as a door at the rear of the corridor sprang open and a man burst out, stiff-armed and heavy.

The big man glowered at Pearce, twisting the knuckles of one hand against the palm of the other as he plodded along the short corridor. "Can I help you?" He was much taller than Pearce. Much wider, too. His jacket strangled his swaying arms. He stopped a couple of feet away and straightened his tie. Flat nose. Cauliflower ears. He looked nothing like the photograph of Ailsa's boyfriend.

"You must be Tony," Pearce said. "Nice to meet you."

"Never mind who I am. Who are you?"

"I'm looking for Pete."

"I didn't ask who you were looking for. I asked who you were."

"Five minutes. That's all."

Tony changed hands, twisting his knuckles as if he was sharpening them against the grindstone of his flattened palm. "*Pete* doesn't want to see you."

Pearce flexed his fingers. "I might have to insist."

Tony chuckled. "Okay," he said. "Insist."

Pearce said, "You're a bodybuilder, right?"

"Yeah."

"Which means if I stood still, you could probably pick me up."

Tony gave him an appraising look. "With one hand."

"Good," Pearce said. "Now, here's your problem."

Tony moved his weight from one foot to the other. After a while he said, "Go on."

"I don't intend standing still."

Tony sighed. "So why don't you walk right on past me, if you're such a hard man."

"I will," Pearce said. "But there's something I have to ask you first. I'm puzzled, you see." He gripped the lip of the reception desk with both hands. "Pete doesn't know who I am, right?" He let go of the desk and turned. "So how the fuck does he know he doesn't want to see me?"

"Not my place to ask."

"Five minutes." Pearce slapped his hand on the desk.

"Don't hit the furniture."

"Five minutes," Pearce said, smacking the desk again.

"You hard of hearing?" Tony eyeballed Pearce. "Or are you just dim?"

"Everybody thinks I'm thick today. That's what Ailsa Lillie said."

"You know Ailsa?" Tony's eyes narrowed.

"She's why I'm here."

"Why didn't you say so?"

"I was having fun," Pearce said. "Actually, I have a message from Ailsa for Pete."

"I'll pass it on."

"I have to deliver it in person."

Tony shook his head and stopped rubbing his hands together. He turned and retraced his steps. The office door closed behind him with a bang.

Pearce looked at Shortarse. "Something amusing you?"

The little man cocked his head. His mouth was stretched into a definite grin. "What if it is?" he said.

The door opened again. Tony said, "You got your five minutes."

Pearce walked down the red-carpeted corridor and entered Thompson's office. Ailsa's boyfriend sat behind a huge desk fingering his moustache. He didn't get up to greet Pearce. Didn't even look at him.

Pearce followed Thompson's gaze. Opposite his desk a bank of monitors silently relayed the events taking place in some of the sauna's private rooms. Four of the screens were blank, but, despite the early hour, two others showed signs of activity. Bottom left, a topless masseuse churned the fleshy lower back of an anonymous customer stretched out on a towel beside a Jacuzzi. On the next screen, the one Thompson couldn't take his eyes off, the masseuse was naked and on her knees, the customer's dick sliding in and out of her mouth. Somehow, she managed to look bored.

Pearce said, "Surprised you have punters already."

Thompson didn't look at him. "Been open half-an-hour."

Pearce looked at Tony, back at Thompson, back at the screen. He said, "Want me to wait till they're finished?"

Thompson swivelled in his chair. "Who the fuck are you?"

"I have a message." Pearce turned to face him. "From Ailsa."

"Yeah?" Thompson glanced at Tony and his lip curled. "Yeah?" he repeated.

"She never wants to see you again."

"Yeah?" Thompson's eyes were wide. They grew wider. "Yeah? She doesn't, eh?"

"If you go anywhere near her or her daughter I'll do much worse than I'm going to do now."

"Yeah?" Thompson started to laugh. Suddenly he stopped. "What do you mean by that?"

Pearce turned to Tony and said, "You can leave if you want."

Tony said, "Why would I want to do that?"

"You asked if Ailsa was okay. She's worried about her daughter." Pearce waited a moment. "Becky walked into a wall. Big solid motherfucker. Broke her jaw."

"Pete?" Tony said. "You promised, you prick."

Sweat was beading on Thompson's forehead.

"Ailsa got scared," Pearce continued. "Bought herself a gun. She thinks Pete's somehow responsible for Becky's little accident."

Thompson opened his mouth, closed it again. He shook his

head. "Wasn't me, Shithead. Tell him, Tony, you useless fuck. And, by the way, don't call me a prick again. Well? Tell him."

"Incredible," Tony said. "Fucking incredible. Somebody ought to teach you some manners."

Behind him, Pearce heard Tony shuffling towards the door. "She was all set to put a bullet in you, Pete. Until I persuaded her that killing you might be a bit excessive." Pearce pulled out a chair. "I thought we could talk. Man to man." He sat down, aware that Thompson was looking over his shoulder, still hoping that Tony would intervene. "Be reasonable about this."

"Tony? Where are you going?" Thompson's Adam's apple bounced up and down as if he'd swallowed something that was still alive. "You're fired." The door clicked shut. "Tony?" Ailsa's boyfriend said in a strangled voice. "Fucking faggot."

"Stop it," Pearce said. "That's not nice, Pete." He rubbed the back of his fingers over his chin.

Thompson said, "What do you want?"

"What Tony said," Pearce answered. "Teach you some manners."

11:27 AM

*B*ecause the car was running smoothly, Eddie had time to think.

A right pair of lunatics, both thinking the other was crazy.

First impressions of Robin were that he was, well, a bit neurotic. Messed up, no doubt, by his brother dying so young and all. According to Carol, he pissed the bed until he was in his teens. And there was that business with the water pistol. A big joke, maybe, but you could see how it happened with a father like that and the medical problems with his hands and the disappointment with his musical career. You could see how it led to him going schizo.

Carol, of course, was hardly Miss Sanity herself. The result of what she called her "quirky" childhood. She grew up on a farm in the Borders, a solitary child with elderly parents and no near neighbours. She wrapped dead animals in kitchen foil and buried them in her private graveyard at the bottom of an untilled field. Apart from weasels. They were in the privileged position of having their desiccated bones and tiny sharp teeth collected and stored in jam jars under her bed. What disturbed Eddie was that she had started with animals her dogs or other wild creatures had killed and then moved on to doing her own hunting. Setting traps. Snaring rabbits and things. Nothing too big.

The question was, did that make her crazy? Who was to say that, in similar circumstances, Eddie wouldn't have amused himself in the same way? He'd known her for a long time now and if she was crazy he'd have noticed. Obviously she wasn't completely stable or she wouldn't have had that spell in the psychiatric unit where she met Robin. But everyone gets depressed, don't they? More than just a letter's difference between sad and mad. Well, that was his opinion.

Until last night. He had little doubt now that Carol was as crazy as a lobotomised bug. He wished he could talk to Robin about it. Perversely, her husband was the very person who could shed some light on the question of her sanity. But if he knew that Eddie and Carol were....well, Eddie didn't want to go there.

"Don't do that."

"What?"

"Chew your lip."

Eddie stopped chewing his lip and started thinking about the night they'd spent together.

She had woken him up, screaming. He rolled over and wrapped an arm around her waist.

She shrugged his arm off and scrambled out of bed. She wouldn't shut up. He pulled the quilt over his head, but it was no good. He could still hear her. He pulled back the quilt and yawned and swore and switched on the bedside lamp. The bedroom was cold and his mouth tasted of rotten eggs. He rubbed his eyes. The bookcase swam into focus, the umbrella plant leaning against it. Discarded clothes lay jumbled on the rug. Carol was standing in the corner with her face in her hands rocking backwards and forwards like something, well, like something let loose from a lunatic asylum. Her nightdress was wet and clung to her left leg.

He swung his feet out of bed and stumbled towards her. He stepped on a hairbrush and swore. When he reached her he grabbed her wrists and yanked her hands away from her face. Her slender hands wriggled out of his grip and went straight back to her face. "What's the matter?"

She stamped her feet like a toddler having a tantrum. He clamped both her wrists in one hand and squeezed until she yelled. He slapped her. He didn't want to, but he couldn't think what else to do to calm her down. When he let go of her hands she immediately shielded her face with them again. He reached out and grabbed her. Her hands were slippery.

It took about ten minutes and the same number of slaps to calm her down.

He asked again, "What's the matter?"

"It was touching me." Her breathing was jerky. The words came out as five distinct syllables punctuated by sharply drawn breaths. She said it again. "*It was touch-ing me.*" She looked at him with her smoky grey eyes. "It woke me up. Scared me."

"What was touching you?"

Her face looked like invisible fingers were clawing at it, scratching holes in it from which tears streamed out.

It was 02:31, according to the alarm clock.

By 02:54 he had an answer.

What had happened was this. He had been snuggling up against her in his sleep. He slept naked. At some point during the night he got an erection. She had woken up, felt his penis pressing against her and proceeded to wet herself.

No big deal. His cock touching her had scared her so much she'd pissed herself. Now why was that? He couldn't begin to understand. And she wouldn't discuss it. Still, no big fucking deal, eh?

Carol's public persona, the one he thought he'd fallen in love with, was as false as the blue varnished fingernails of the hand now gripping the stolen car's steering wheel. As false as the two blue varnished fingernails that clamped the cigarette she raised to her lips. The real Carol was a crazy woman with a penis phobia. God, but Eddie wanted her. Blood rushed to his cock. If only he could unbutton his trousers and whip it out, yeah, whip out his cock and invite her to wrap her lips around it. The thought made him giddy. Oh, sweet Mother of Christ. But his cock was repulsive, remember? Instantly, his penis shrank. He lowered the window and let the wind bite into his cheek. Before long the whole side of his face was numb. He closed the window and the car soon filled with smoke.

"How's it handling?" he asked her.

"Good."

"Thought you'd like it," he said. "You got on well with the Sierra we used last time." Eddie had put false plates on the car and he'd stick the taxi sign on the roof later. They were heading west. He looked at his watch. Less than an hour and a half to go.

"Think we should head back to town?"

Eddie leaned back in his seat and closed his eyes. "Took the words out of my mouth," he said. "Wake me up when we get there."

11:42 AM

Pearce walked over to the window. Thompson turned in his chair. Pearce put his hand into a gap in the blinds and spread his fingers.

Thompson's office looked out onto an abandoned church. Behind a low wall ribbed with black spiked railings, thistles flanked a cement path leading to an oak door. Above the door, a stained glass window had been smashed and subsequently boarded up. All that remained of the original design was a single pane depicting a circular object, possibly a halo. Two drunks sat on a stone step beneath the window, shivering as they took alternate swigs out of a can of Special Brew.

Thompson coughed.

Pearce continued observing the winos. One of them got up and pissed where he was standing. Heels planted solidly on the ground, he moved his toes from side to side, spraying urine this way and that, until his bladder had emptied. He shook himself dry, sat down and reached for his beer. His shoulders rocked when his friend pointed to his groin and he realised his dick was still hanging out. He got to his feet again and sorted himself out.

Apart from the drunks in the churchyard the neighbourhood was deserted.

Pearce said, "Quiet around here."

"Yeah," Thompson said, a wobble in his voice. "It is."

"You in a hurry?" Pearce stepped away from the window.

Thompson shook his head and wiped his nose with the back of his hand.

Pearce unclipped his mobile and selected number two in the phone's memory. Number one was his mum's home number. Number two was her work number. Her boss, Denise, answered and went to fetch her.

A short time later, sounding breathless, his mum said, "We're busy."

"Don't let them work you too hard."

"What did you want?"

"Just returning your call."

"Oh." She paused. "I'd forgotten. It was nothing really," she said. "Just a feeling. Oh, I don't know." She paused again. "Seems silly now. Probably nothing. You didn't hurt Willie Cant, did you?"

He could see her expression. Frowning, tight-lipped. The look she wore when he'd been bad. Like when he strangled that girl at school. Isla somebody. Even though it was an accident. They were playing a game. Kiss, Cuddle or Torture. He caught her, pinned her to the ground and tried to kiss her. She struggled. In preventing her escaping he'd managed to choke her half to death. Looking back on it now, that was probably when he became aware of his own strength.

An accident. Nobody believed him. Not even Mum.

Thompson's chair squeaked.

Pearce looked at him and the poor fuck flinched. Pearce said to his mum, "Can I meet you for lunch?"

"That would be nice. I'm on an early shift. Get off around one. Where do you want to meet?"

"I'll come and get you."

"Listen, I've got to go. Denise is covering for me and she won't like it." She made a kissing noise and hung up.

Pearce dug into his back pocket and pulled out the piece of paper Cooper had given him. Of the four names listed, there was only one left. Corrigan, Domenic hadn't been at home. Cant, Willie he'd seen. Ditto Lillie, Ailsa. Which left Muirton, Jack. Address in Sighthill. No phone number.

Thompson was gnawing at his thumb.

"You got a phone book?" Pearce asked him.

The sauna manager almost fell off his chair in his eagerness to oblige. One by one he hauled out each of the four desk drawers. "Sure there's one somewhere," he said, after determining that the last drawer was empty. He slammed it shut, opened the top drawer and started searching again.

"Doesn't matter." Pearce dialled directory enquiries.

"But it's here." Thompson pulled out the drawer and tipped the contents onto the floor. A Gideon's bible landed with a thud. A box of matches spilled open. A packet of chewing gum rolled under his chair. Various other items bounced out of sight under the desk.

"Muirton," Pearce said into the phone. He spoke to Thompson: "Can I have that pen?"

Thompson stooped to pick up the biro that had come to a halt against Pearce's steel toe-capped boot and handed it over.

"42 Sighthill Drive West." With the pen, Pearce tapped the second drawer down. "Paper, please Pete."

Thompson slid out the drawer and tore off a sheet from the notepad he found inside.Pearce took it from him and wrote down Jack Muirton's phone number. He wasn't home. Pearce left a message on his answering machine, warning Jack what would happen if he didn't pay up tomorrow. When the tape ran out he hung up.

Thompson was scratching the back of his hand.

Pearce placed his phone on the desk. "Take your trousers off," he said.

"Wait a minute." Thompson swallowed. "Can't we sort this out?"

"I don't know. Can we?"

"You want money? I'll give you money." Thompson fumbled in his pocket, located his wallet and brandished it with a look of triumph. He snapped it open and held out a wad of bills. "Here." He waved the money at Pearce. "Take it."

"I don't want your money."

"Take it," Thompson pleaded. "All of it. There's a grand there."

"That's a lot of money."

"Never know when it might come in handy."

Pearce said, "Thanks," and stuffed the money in his back pocket. A grand. Exactly the amount he'd borrowed from Cooper. Enough, now, to pay off only half the debt. "Remove your trousers."

"Come on," Thompson said. "Let's be civilised."

"Please," Pearce said. "How's that? *Please* take your trousers off."

Thompson threw his empty wallet onto the floor. His voice was quiet. "What you going to do?" His fingers moved towards his belt and rested on the buckle.

"Get a move on," Pearce said. "And you'll find out."

"Can I have my money back?"

"What do you think?"

Slowly Thompson unfastened his belt, slipped it out of his trousers and folded it in half. He stroked the leather strap with his thumb, then held both ends and pulled it tight. Spinning, he lashed out. The strap hit Pearce high on his left bicep. Thompson roared and swung the belt again. Pearce caught it, held it firmly and dragged Thompson towards him. Thompson stopped yelling and let go of the belt. Pearce looked at the pink mark on his arm, then switched his gaze to Thompson.

Without a word Thompson unbuttoned his trousers, pulled down his zip and dropped his trousers.

"Off," Pearce said.

Thompson untied his shoelaces, removed his shoes and stepped out of his trousers. Although his shirt hung over his groin, he cupped both hands in front of his boxer shorts. "What now?"

"Take your pants off."

"You're joking."

"Do we have to go through this again?"

"Fuck you. You want to see my cock, you faggot? Well, fuck you."

The belt buckle caught Thompson just above the eyebrow. He staggered sideways, a look of shock on his face. He started to moan. One hand left his groin to cradle the side of his head.

After a while he said, "I'll leave Ailsa alone."

Pearce watched him for a moment, and lowered the belt. "I know you will."

"And Becky. I'll stay away from both of them."

"I know you will."

"I promise." He looked up. "I'll do whatever you want." He wiped his nose. Snot lodged in his moustache.

"That's good," Pearce said. "I want you to take off your pants."

11:50 AM

*J*ust over an hour to go.

Robin sat at a window table for four. At each place setting a plastic stand held a piece of white card with the word RESERVED printed on both sides in a bold red typeface. Outside, saplings in wire cages dotted the wide pavement in a parody of a Parisian boulevard. Fake cannonballs—sculptures alluding to the traditional one o'clock firing of the cannon from the Castle—pitted Leith Walk's paved, elongated traffic islands.

In the café, music blared. Jazz, heavy on drums and sax, percussive piano muted in the mix. He spread his fingers and stabbed a few chords on the tabletop.

When he was thirteen Robin had auditioned for three of Britain's top music schools: St Mary's in Edinburgh, Douglas Academy in Glasgow and Chetham's in Manchester. All three offered him a place. He chose Chetham's because, at the time, it had the best reputation.

Shortly after his fourteenth birthday his dad drove him south to his new school. Robin sat in the front seat telling his dad how much he was looking forward to improving his technique so that he could have a shot at the Liszt B minor Sonata, one of the hardest pieces in the piano repertoire. In those days the only trouble he experienced with his hands was an occasional stiffness, easily remedied by submerging them in a bowl of hot water for a few minutes.

Dad reached into the glove compartment and took out a half bottle of whisky. He took a long pull. "I don't care about your arsing *technique*."

Robin cringed. He waited for it. It came.

"You're a leech."

His dad's favourite insult. It had become a nickname, almost. Leech. My son, the leech. "Sorry, Dad."

"Don't cheek me, you little shit." He took another sip. "Leech." A muscle tugged at his upper lip. "Bloodsucker." His lips were pulled back from his teeth. "Parasite."

"I wish you wouldn't be like this, Dad."

His father's face was twisted with rage. He got like this when he drank, which was so often it seemed normal these days. So normal that it never occurred to Robin that his dad shouldn't be driving.

Robin hummed quietly to himself. Chopin's C-sharp minor Nocturne. He tapped out the notes on his thighs.

Dad said, "This money the council have given you."

Robin broke off mid-bar. "The bursary?" The fees were five grand per annum, a sum well beyond his parents' means.

"You'll be there for four years. That's twenty grand. Bleeding us tax payers of twenty grand, right?"

Robin didn't want another hiding. He said nothing and started playing the Chopin again.

"On top of the money we've already spent on bloody piano lessons. See, you've been sucking the life out of me most of your life. And for what? For all this arty-farty crap you and your mother like." He slapped the steering wheel. "Waste of fucking money. *My* fucking money."

"Dad, I need you to—"

The slap stung his cheek. The second slap made his lip bleed. He shielded his face with his hands, tasting warm, salty blood.

"Pathetic," his dad said. "Fourteen years old and look at you, crying like a wee girl."

"I'm not." He lowered his hands to let his dad see his defiantly dry eyes.

Dad mumbled, "Can't even kick a football straight."

They didn't talk for the rest of the journey, Dad sipping his whisky and Robin trying not to cry. When they arrived at his new school, his dad helped carry Robin's few personal items to his dormitory on the upper level of a two-storey prefab. Across the courtyard Palatine House still bore an external resemblance to the Victorian railway hotel it once was. Inside, as Robin recalled from his post-audition guided tour, cacophony erupted from four floors of practice rooms, each identically furnished with a music stand and a Daneman upright piano. To the right, cloisters led to the Baronial Hall, location of public lunchtime recitals. Above the spiked railings that fenced in a croquet lawn, Manchester Cathedral dominated the skyline.

He turned to his dad and said, "I really thought you'd be proud of me."

"I'd be bloody proud of you if you stopped pissing the bed. That would be something to be proud of. But I don't suppose you could do that *legato* in three four time, eh?" His dad left without saying goodbye.

All Robin wanted to do was play the piano. He didn't care what his father thought. The man was a philistine and a drunk and he wasn't worth crying over. While Robin was still in his mother's womb, parasitically clinging to her body, he had managed to suck the life out of his father. At least, that's how Dad saw it.

Once upon a time, Dad had fancied himself as a jazz drummer. Robin had heard him play only once, on a kit in a music shop when they were looking for a new piano for Robin. And the truth was, much as Robin hated to admit it, his dad had been quite talented. But, when Mum became pregnant with Donald, Dad had given up his musical aspirations in favour of a regular income in the bakery department of a meat-processing factory. When Robin followed his brother into the world two years later, Dad saw no way out of his mind-numbing job. According to Mum, that's when the drinking started, and after the accident, it accelerated rapidly.

Funny thing was, once he'd arrived at his new school, and despite the growing frequency of his nightmares, Robin never wet the bed again.

Four years later, music school was over. Since starting college he had been practising eight hours a day. One day, about a month into first term, bolts of fire started shooting down both arms. His fingers hurt when they moved and his wrists burned when they bent. The doctor diagnosed tendonitis and prescribed physiotherapy. Three months later, three months without being able to practice, he was no better, so the doctor prescribed anti-inflammatories, which, after a few days, enabled Robin to play for a couple of hours without pain. This joyous state lasted for all of a week, when he woke up one day to discover his arms were numb, he had difficulty moving his fingers even slightly and his wrists were grossly swollen. He spent the next year and a half seeing all sorts of specialists who could only agree on one thing: he had one of the most severe cases of ulnar neuropathy any of them had ever seen. On good days he tried to play. Most days, something as physically undemanding as brushing his teeth brought tears to his eyes. He left college after fifteen different treatments, including two operations to relocate the ulnar nerve, had failed to help. Mum was heartbroken when it became clear that he wasn't going to be the great concert pianist she'd always dreamed he'd become. His dad said it was all psychosomatic attention-seeking bollocks and the boy ought to get a bloody honest job and stop moaning like a fairy. But by then his leech of a son didn't care what Daddy thought.

"Sir."

Robin heard the waitress clearly enough over the keening of the soprano saxophone, but for no good reason he pretended he hadn't.

"Sir."

One more time? No. He turned his head.

"Would you mind sitting over here, sir?" Her arms were bare, the skin pale and lightly freckled. Her left hand held a notepad and, with her right, she tapped a pencil against her teeth. She was in her late teens.

"What colour's your hair?" he asked her.

"Excuse me, what—"

He smiled at her. "You mind me asking? You look like a red-head. But I can't tell." His eyes rolled upwards. "Because of your hat."

"Have to wear hairnets and these stupid things." She pushed the stupid thing, a hat, back with her pencil, exposing an extra millimetre of damp forehead. "Can't have hair in the food."

"Rules, eh?"

"Tell me about it."

"You know what?" he said. "The hat sort of suits you."

"Yeah?" She laughed. "Right."

"Your eyebrows are fair. But I'm banking on you being a red-head." He nodded. "You going to put me out of my misery?"

She clamped the pencil between her teeth.

"My wife has red hair," he continued. She'd have shot him if she heard him say that. Carol didn't have red hair, or even reddish brown hair, or, God forbid, ginger hair. "Auburn, she calls it."

The waitress frowned, chewed her pencil, slid it out of her mouth and waved it around as she spoke. "I just sort of think of my hair as brown, you know. Light brown. But it's got traces of red in it. In a certain light, sometimes, it can look auburn." She nodded. Pointed her pencil at him. "Definitely."

"Sheila." The voice belonged to a fat waiter balancing a tray of assorted drinks above his head while he struggled to squeeze through a narrow gap between two chairs. A patch of sweat stained the armpit of his purple shirt. "Can you get table seven when you're finished with the gentleman?" He lowered the tray and began distributing drinks to a large family group seated at an adjacent table.

Sheila made a clicking sound with her tongue.

"Boss?" Robin asked.

"Yeah," she said. "Better take your order."

"You need me to move?" Robin started to stand up. He bent his knees and rested one hand on the edge of the table. "Thing is, my wife's meeting me in a couple of minutes and I told her I'd get a window table. She's bringing a friend, too, and I don't want to disappoint them. I don't suppose I could—"

"Stay where you are." She tucked her notepad and pencil into the pocket of her apron, reached over and picked up two of the "reserved" signs. Robin handed her the other two, which she clutched to her chest. "You want a drink while you're waiting?"

"Double espresso," he said, sitting down again. "Thanks." He watched her shuffle into the centre of the room and drop the signs on one of the two empty tables. She hastily positioned them, turned and smiled at him. He gave her a little wave.

"New girlfriend?" Carol waggled her blue fingernails at him in imitation of his gesture to the waitress. He didn't look up. He couldn't look at her face. Something about it made him feel like bursting into tears. The face of infidelity. The face of a liar. "Nervous?" She sat opposite him, lit a cigarette and slid the packet across to him. He ignored her silent offer. She shrugged. "Talking about it helps, Robin."

"Not in public," he said.

He turned his head and looked out the window. *Talking about it helps. Talk. Don't talk.* Her eyes mocked him. Her mouth sneered at him. When she spoke, her tone was laced with irony. She was sleeping with Eddie. Eddie's hands had been all over her breasts. He'd tasted her, been inside her. Robin glanced at her. She was sucking a cigarette, lips twisted as she blew smoke out the side of her mouth. He'd never seen anything so ugly. He hated her. He hated her so much it made his fucking teeth hurt.

She caught his eye and he managed a flicker of a smile. She might as well have scraped out all his fillings with her fingernails. Her face was pale and cold as porcelain. Her and Eddie. Robin had photographic evidence. Jesus, he wanted to reach out and stroke her cheek, touch her lips, trace the straight line of the one part of her body she liked. But he couldn't. Instead he imagined ramming his knuckles into the slender bridge of her oh-so-cherished nose. Wham. The surprise in her eyes. Wham. Blood spurting out of those pinched slits of nostrils. Wham. Blood running down her face, wham, through her fingers, wham, on her lips, wham, in her mouth, wham, wham, fucking wham. Fucking wham. Fucking wham. Wham. Wham.

Like the PI. Oh, shit. He groaned aloud and disguised the sound with a cough. His shirt clung to his back. The music was suddenly too loud, the urgent *glissandi* of the sax like the wailing of a tortured animal. He felt cold. He looked at Carol and she smiled, her nose as perfect as always.

Someone punched him lightly on the shoulder and said, "Robin."

Carol moved over and Eddie sat next to her. Eddie had too many teeth, otherwise he might have been considered handsome. His cornflower blue eyes and blonde curls made him look at least five years younger than his thirty years. Without asking, he removed a cigarette from Carol's packet on the table and said, "What's been happening?"

Carol started to talk. Let her, Robin thought. This was for his benefit. *As if they haven't been fucking each other's brains out.* She was telling Eddie what she'd been doing since the last time they'd met. Right. Eddie was pretending to listen, interjecting her monologue with an occasional grunt or two, straw-coloured eyebrows raised in mock surprise, sucking his teeth now, lips retracted, slowly shaking his head.

Clouds of smoke drifted between them.

A waitress—not Sheila—came over to their table and Robin ordered another coffee. A single, this time. Carol asked for a cheese and tomato toastie and an iced mineral water. Eddie wasn't hungry, but he agreed when Carol suggested he might like something light, like an almond croissant, for example. "And a latte," he added.

Robin could see her fingers itching to touch her boyfriend's coat sleeve. Were they playing a game? Did they want him to guess, was that it? That fuck-me smile she gave him? Robin looked away. Outside, people were wrapped up tight as parcels against the cold. Traffic pulsed up and down Leith Walk. The heavy sky was the same dirt grey as Carol's eyes. He turned and, controlling his voice, said, "You ready for this one, Eddie?"

"Always." Eddie patted his coat pocket.

12:07 PM

*N*othing like seeing a naked man to remind you of prison. Ten years of communal showers. Ten years of sex-starved cons leering at you. When he was released two months ago, Pearce had found immense pleasure in the simplest things. Like getting out of bed when he felt like it, putting the light out when he wanted to, choosing what he wanted for dinner, and shitting in private.

He realised he was staring at Thompson's dick. It was very pale, fat, and equipped with an enormously long foreskin. "Turn around," Pearce said. "Put your hands behind your back."

Thompson turned, the front of his thighs pressing against the edge of his desk. His hands moved slowly towards his side and stopped, hovering there. Pearce snatched the bastard's wrists and jerked them together. Thompson yelped. Pearce held both wrists in one hand and fumbled on the floor for the naked man's shirt with the other. When he found it he stuffed one of the sleeves in his mouth and ripped it off at the armpit. He bound Thompson's wrists together with the strip of material.

Thompson howled. "That's cutting me."

Enough. Pearce spun him around and head-butted him. Thompson swayed, jaw gaping, and as his legs buckled, Pearce shoved him backwards. He thumped onto the desk, head striking its polished surface with a crack. His eyes rolled upwards and his eyelids fluttered and closed. He lay still, head tilted to the side, mouth hanging open, tongue blanketing his teeth. Slowly, his chest rose and fell. When he exhaled he emitted a sound somewhere between a wheeze and a low whistle. Tied behind his back, his hands forced his hips in the air. His prick nestled in the crease between his balls.

Pearce grabbed his mobile and dialled Julie's number, even though he was sure she'd chucked her phone. *You want to get engaged, Pearce?* Hope was a killer, wasn't it? A bland English voice told him to leave a message. In the same strangled falsetto he'd used a dozen times before, he said, "You want to get engaged?" His chest felt tight and he was breathing heavily. Maybe she'd kept her phone, after all. He didn't know for certain. His voice whined. "Want to get engaged, Pearce? Want to get engaged?" The phone cracked in his hand, the casing split at the bottom. The hairline curve looked as if somebody had pasted an eyelash onto the plastic. He stopped squeezing it.

He flicked the switch in his head and his anger instantly disappeared. If he closed his eyes now he'd see his dog, Angus, cowering under the school bus, bright pink front leg stripped of fur and skin all the way to the shoulder. Pearce kept his eyes open and said in a normal voice, "Why is the world full of scum?" Thompson moaned. Pearce clipped the phone back on his belt. His forehead had struck Thompson between the eyes and they'd puffed up already. He moaned again. His eyes were open and he was dribbling out the side of his mouth. He looked drunk.

"Can you hear me?" Pearce asked him. Thompson tried to push himself up, but fell back immediately. Tied behind his back, his arms couldn't support him. Pearce leaned over the prostate figure. "This is going to hurt," he said.

Thompson struggled to lift his head off the table. "I won't touch her again."

"Correct." Pearce stepped away from the desk to pick up the drawer Thompson had emptied in his search for the phone book.

"You don't need to hit me any more. I'll leave Ailsa alone. And Becky." Thompson's voice was shrill. "I won't touch either of them." Again he tried to raise himself. "Christ, I'm dizzy." He managed to hold a semi-upright position for a handful of seconds before falling backwards.

"Nearly ready." Pearce aligned the drawer and slid it back in a couple of inches.

"What are you doing?" Thompson rolled onto his side and lashed out with his left foot.

Pearce grabbed his ankle and crushed it between his fingers. Thompson let out a cry and stopped kicking. His whole body went limp. Pearce didn't let up. He could feel his nails digging into the skin. "Why do you do it, Pete?" Pearce grabbed hold of the other ankle and started pulling Thompson towards him. Thompson's naked arse squeaked against the desk's polished surface. "Why do you hit women?" Thompson's buttocks were at the edge of the desk, balls dangling above the empty drawer. He screamed when he realised Pearce's intention. Pearce had to shout over the racket. "You really think you can get away with it?" Thompson's legs flailed ineffectually in Pearce's grip. He stopped yelling to take a breath. Pearce said, "I don't like it."

"What's it to you, anyway?" Thompson tried to sit up. "You fancy her? You can have her."

"Nothing like that." Pearce let go of an ankle to push him back down.

"What, then? Your dad beat up your mum or something?"

Pearce grabbed Thompson's ankle again and started to laugh. "He was never close enough to be within punching distance."

"Don't do it." Thompson tried to sit up again.

"Just what is it you think I'm going to do?"

"Slam my fucking balls in the drawer."

"Okay." Pearce switched his grip from Thompson's ankles to his knees.

"What?"

"You've suffered enough." Pearce helped tilt him forward until his feet were planted either side of the desk drawer.

"I promise," Thompson said. "I won't touch either of them."

Pearce grinned and jumped forward. His heels pinned Thompson's bare toes to the ground.

Thompson yelled and tried to move. His head brushed against

Pearce's t-shirt. His hands were immobilised and Pearce's boots were crushing his feet. Thompson rocked from side to side. After a moment he sat still and shuddered and looked down between his legs.

Pearce heard the splash of water on wood. He placed the flat of his hand against the front of the drawer and said, "One. Two..."

12:32 PM

"It's the bloke in the photos." Kennedy pressed his phone hard against his ear, straining to hear the decidedly nasal tone of his boss's voice above the rattle of traffic along Leith Walk. Kennedy sidestepped a couple of men carrying a cooker from the back of an illegally parked van into a second hand white goods shop. "Yeah, the one shagging Greaves's missus." He shivered. The smell of hot pastry wafted out of Greggs, making him wish he could dash in and grab a cheese and onion pastie. But he couldn't. Not when he was busy tailing them. "Edward Francis Soutar? That his name?" He paused before saying, "She's here too."

Robin Greaves, a blue sports bag slung over his shoulder, was tucked in behind his wife and her boyfriend. Kennedy lurked twenty feet behind, the hand holding his phone stiff with cold. He switched the phone to his left hand, which, for the moment at least, still had some feeling in it. The traffic lights on the near side of the road turned red. "You can stop shouting," he told his boss. His boss insisted he wasn't shouting, then asked in precisely the same tone and at the same volume where Greaves's party was headed. *Party.* "How should I know?" Kennedy held the phone away from his ear and stared at it. After a minute he repositioned it and said, quietly, "He didn't take his car. He walked."

His boss's voice continued blaring in his ear. Kennedy stuck his numb hand inside his coat. Up ahead the trio turned down a side street. He quickened his pace as the cold seeped through his boots. Each step felt like someone was slapping the soles of his feet with a plank of wood. "Gonna have to go," he said into the phone. He hung up, dropped the phone in his coat pocket and turned the corner.

It took a couple of seconds to locate them. A line of cars huddled in the shelter of a long block of tenement flats. Water dribbled from a first floor overflow pipe. A puddle had formed on the pavement and was now trickling down from the kerb onto the road, licking the front wheel of a two-year-old, white Ford Sierra with a taxi sign fixed to the roof. The woman sat behind the wheel. Edward Francis Soutar was snuggling into the seat beside her. Crouched in the back, Robin Greaves looked up as Soutar slammed the door shut.

Kennedy fumbled for his phone and dialled the office. The line was busy. He tried his boss's mobile.

After four rings his boss said, "Hang on. I'm on the land line."

"That's why I phoned your mobile." But nobody was listening. Kennedy lit a cigarette and waited.

As he stubbed it out his boss came back on the line. "What is it?"

"Can you check your report and find out if Greaves's wife is a taxi driver?"

"She isn't."

"You sure?"

"She's a temp."

"You absolutely positive?"

"I got my nose fucked up. My brain's fine."

"This is important. Would you mind double-checking?"

"Double-checking?" Kennedy heard chair legs scraping the floor as his boss stood. "Double-checking?" The clank of the filing cabinet's drawer opening. "If it keeps you happy, I'll double fucking check."

"Thanks."

"Don't mention it." He sighed. "Okay. Here it is. Ready?" Kennedy said nothing. His boss cleared his throat and continued, "Carol Wren is registered with—"

"That her own name?"

"She uses her maiden name, yes. Some women do. May I

continue?" His boss confirmed Carol Wren's recruitment agency. It specialised in office personnel. There was no indication that she owned, drove or had ever driven a taxi. "What's the significance?"

"Tell you later." Kennedy disconnected the call. He stood at the corner, leaning against the wall. He lit another cigarette. Inside the car there was very little movement. A few minutes later he stubbed out his cigarette and lit another one. Both hands were freezing now. He stamped his feet and winced as a hundred tiny knives stabbed his heels. Still nothing happening in the car. What were the bastards doing? They were sitting in the damned car, that's what they were doing. That's all they were doing. Not moving. Not speaking. Just sitting there. Listening to the radio or something. Soutar even had his eyes closed. Maybe he'd fallen asleep. Carol was staring straight ahead. Greaves had slumped forward and was resting his chin on his chest, eyeing the knuckles of his interlocked fingers.

Kennedy looked at his watch and wondered once again why he was doing this, choosing to stand here in the cold while his extremities turned to ice. He'd become a PI for the excitement, the adventure, the danger. He blamed Hammett. Chandler, you could forgive. But Hammett? What a bastard.

PI novels had saturated Alex Kennedy's teenage years. From the moment he read his first Chandler he was hooked. He read all of Chandler, then Hammett, then Ross Macdonald. All the while he was amassing a stack of out-of-print fifties and early sixties PI pulp novels from charity shops and flea markets. His favourite PIs were Max Thursday and Johnny Killain. Men who thrived on danger and excitement. Men who thought two-to-one was pretty fair odds. Men who could take on a brick wall and before long have it begging for mercy. Kennedy blew into his cupped hands. Hammett had been an investigator himself and should have known better. He had no excuse for making this shitty job seem exciting. Nothing happened. Nothing. Zero. Zilch. In the office you made phone calls and surfed the net. You filed a report, made more calls and did a bit more surfing. Out of the office you sat in a car for hours on end watching zip. Occasionally, like today, you didn't even have the luxury of a car to sit in. You had to stand in the cold and watch very little turn into fuck-all. If you were really bored you could always capture the precise moment nothing happened by snapping a photograph, which is what Kennedy would have done if he hadn't left his bloody camera in the car. He eased another cigarette out of the pack. As he lit up he noticed a movement in the Sierra. Something happening at last? He dropped the lighter in his pocket and watched as Soutar turned round and passed something to Greaves. Greaves weighed it in his palm and, with a flick of his wrist, held it to Soutar's head.

Kennedy grabbed his mobile and dialled the office. This time the line was free.

"What?"

Kennedy's throat was dry. He swallowed. "How quickly can you get here?"

"Can't you handle it?"

He swallowed again. "This could be more serious than just your nose."

"What the fuck you on about?"

"They could leave any minute. Phone me on your mobile once you're on your way."

In the white Ford Sierra, a grinning Robin Greaves handed the gun back to Edward Francis Soutar.

Kennedy's boss said, "I can't leave the office."

"You'll want to be here," Kennedy said. "Believe me."

12:40 PM

"I spent the morning sharpening the point of a long screwdriver with a file," Pearce told Thompson.

Thompson was crying like a little boy whose lollipop has been stamped on by the school bully.

"Think you can be quiet a minute?" Pearce knelt down and untied Thompson's hands. "I knew where my sister's dealer, Priestley, lived."

Thompson's shoulders bounced with each breath that leaked out of him.

"I paid him a visit." Pearce remembered a sign on the wall. Blacket Neighbourhood Watch. He'd laughed at that as he walked along the row of semi-detached villas. Some of them had stone balconies. They all had private gardens and burglar alarms stuck on the front of the building, a sure sign that there was something worth nicking inside.

Thompson started to crawl under his desk, moaning, teeth vibrating against his lower lip.

Pearce had opened a wrought iron gate and walked up a path that curved towards a white wooden porch with a slate roof. Very pretty. He'd rung the bell and admired the lawn while he waited. When Priestley answered, Pearce stepped inside and closed the door. No fuss.

Thompson blinked rapidly.

"I stuck him with the screwdriver," Pearce said. "Twenty-six times. Once for each year of her life."

A peculiar noise came out of Thompson. It sounded as if he was about to break into song.

Pearce ignored him. Justice wasn't cheap. It was true that Pearce had paid the bill with ten years of his life, but he had no regrets. The scumbag had deserved it. Still, Pearce didn't know if he could do it again, knowing how far into the future ten years can stretch.

He tossed what was left of Thompson's shirt at his naked body. "Get dressed if you want. I'm leaving."

Wedged under the desk, Thompson's body spasmed as if jolts of electricity were shooting through his chest. His hands were jammed between his legs, protecting the balls Pearce had threatened to crush in the desk drawer. His creased cotton shirt stayed where Pearce had thrown it, draped over his left knee. A soft moan slipped out of his oddly grinning mouth and the bubble joining his parted lips popped as Pearce leaned over and gently shut the desk drawer.

"You've had your warning." Pearce prodded Thompson with his boot. "Unless you have a burning desire to join a girls' choir, keep away from Ailsa. If you don't, I promise you'll be hitting the high notes. Unless I'm in a bad mood. In which case I'll make a pincushion out of you. You paying attention, Pete?"

Thompson nodded vigorously and cried out when the back of his head bumped against the edge of the desk.

"I'll be checking. Can I trust you?"

Thompson sniffed. "I'll stay away."

"Okay." Pearce held out his hand.

"Don't." Thompson crossed his arms in front of his face. "Please."

Pearce touched Thompson's elbow with the back of his hand, lightly. "Shake."

Slowly Thompson lowered his arms, red eyes dripping, face shining with tears. His lips quivered as he held out his hand.

Pearce grabbed it and squeezed. Quickly, he turned and left. He was finished here and he didn't want to keep his mum waiting.

12:51 PM

*G*reaves, Soutar and Wren were still in the Sierra. So far so good.

Kennedy spoke into his phone: "There's a parking space over here."

"Where's here?"

"Leith Walk end, on the corner." Kennedy stood on tiptoe. "Want me to wave?"

"Don't bother. I see you."

Kennedy put his phone away as he saw his boss's red Saab rolling towards him. Cold hands tucked under his armpits, he sauntered towards the vacant parking spot opposite the Sierra. The Saab arrived first, gliding to a stop. Kennedy opened the passenger door and folded himself into the seat. The engine was still running. He made a show of rubbing his hands together and looked across at his boss. Half-a-dozen strips of Micropore crisscrossed his bandaged nose. "Who fixed you up?" Kennedy asked him.

"What the hell are they up to?"

"Okay. Just ignore me."

"Did you notice any other weapons?"

"Apart from the gun?" Kennedy was thinking that maybe this job wasn't so bad after all. At last something big was happening and he was stuck in the middle of it. "Nothing much. Couple of hand grenades, flame thrower, missile launcher."

"I don't need that kind of crap right now."

"Did you do it yourself? I wasn't aware we had a first aid box."

"It's the law."

"Where's it kept?"

"Filing cabinet. Third drawer down. At the back."

Kennedy said, "Greaves was cleaning his fingernails with a knife."

"What kind?"

"Sharp."

"What kind?"

"I don't know." Kennedy held his hands about a foot apart. "Big."

"A bread knife?"

"Smaller." His hands drifted a couple of inches towards each other. "Serrated edges."

"Hunting knife, maybe."

"Don't you want to know about the gun?"

"I don't know anything about guns. Do you?"

"Not really. Wouldn't mind one, though."

"What would you do with a gun?"

Shoot fuckers like you. "Dunno."

"Well, that's fascinating."

"Greaves gave it back to Soutar." Kennedy paused. "Soutar has it now. I know that much." He paused again. "It's black," he said.

"Black. Soutar has a black gun. Now that's a lot scarier than a pink one, don't you think?"

12:57 PM

*R*obin's stomach lurched as Carol drove too fast over a speed bump. When Eddie handed him the gun earlier he'd asked if it was loaded. Eddie had nodded and the temptation to pull the trigger and watch Eddie's head leave his neck was enormous. But he'd resisted. Had a bit of fun pointing the gun at Eddie before handing it back like a good boy.

"Oops," Carol said.

"You want to get us arrested?" Eddie said.

"Up yours, Soutar."

As for Carol. Robin squeezed the leather sheath of the hunting knife in his pocket as he glanced out the window. *Lean forward. Grab her jaw. Tilt her head back. Slit her throat. All over in seconds.* Behind a fence, a bunch of kids played football on a gravel pitch. Outside a church advertising a coffee morning, a kilted piper braved the cold. Robin caught a snatch of the pipe's muted drone, the chanter's not-quite-in-tune skirl, rapid grace notes ornamenting the melody.

Carol slowed to a virtual standstill as the car approached another speed bump. "Is this better?" Eddie shook his head. "Well?"

"You want to swap? Want me to drive?" Eddie's eyes bulged and for a moment Robin thought his wife's lover was going to hit her. Maybe Eddie did too. Maybe that's why he folded his arms. "You want to go inside with Robin? I can wait outside, you know. I can sit in the car with the engine running without *too* much difficulty."

They sounded like a married couple. Robin unzipped the sports bag and tapped Eddie on the shoulder, the sound of bagpipes distant now.

Eddie ignored him and carried on, "You want the gun, Carol? Huh? Think you've got the balls?" He stuffed his hand in his jacket.

"Eddie, take this," Robin said. Eddie was getting excited and not for the first time. Last time he ended up on the verge of losing control, forcing Robin to take over and clean up his mess. Sometimes he reminded Robin of his brother. *Remember Mrs Strang?*

"Easy." Carol took a right onto Easter Road. "Nothing to it," she said. "Point. Squeeze. Bang."

Remember spying on her?

"You think that's all there is to shooting someone?" Eddie angled his head to see what Robin was offering him. "Point, squeeze, bang? Like you're following a fucking recipe or something?" His hand came out of his pocket empty.

Robin said, "Or a dance step."

Eddie snatched the balaclava from Robin. "Of course, you'd know all about pistols. Skoosh, skoosh."

Ignore that. Where was he? Yeah, Mrs Strang. Spying. Before he went to music school, he used to play this game with Don. Their old neighbour went to bed early. Husband dead, both sons left home, she lived alone in a boxy two-storey house at the end of the road. At nine thirty they would creep up her garden path, sidle round the house, peek through the gap in the curtains of the downstairs bedroom and scarper when she got into bed. They never saw her naked, although they did once catch her in her underwear. One night, sheltered in the high-fenced back garden, Don noticed Mrs Strang's back door was ajar. *So what did we do?* Once inside, they sneaked through the old lady's kitchen and into her brightly lit hallway. The sitting room walls muffled the sound of a television. There was a staircase on the left with a walk-in cupboard underneath. Don opened the door, revealing a vacuum cleaner, a mop in a bucket, a sewing machine, jars arranged on a long shelf, and a line of kid's books—each with an orange bookmark sticking out the top—on a smaller shelf underneath.

The stairs creaked. Don dived inside the cupboard, closing the door behind him. Robin heard the sound of a key turning in the lock. By locking himself in the cupboard, Don had shut Robin out. Robin stayed still as Mrs Strang's footsteps moved slowly down the stairs towards him. She was old, hard of hearing. Did he have time? Yes, if he didn't stop to think about it. He ran back through the hall, through the dark kitchen, out the back door, round the path along the side of the house, up the path to the front door and rattled the letterbox. His only thought, to protect his brother. When Mrs Strang came to the door he addressed her in an exaggeratedly loud voice. Several times she told him she wasn't deaf, but he kept shouting, wanting to make sure Don heard him, that he knew it was safe to come out. He thought Don would never get the message, but after a while the cupboard door behind Mrs Strang opened and his brother tiptoed along the hall. By the time Don had disappeared into the kitchen Robin had listed all the chores he could think of and Mrs Strang, mean old cow that she was, wasn't prepared to let him do any of them. "You should be in your bed. What's your game, huh?" She almost spat her teeth out. "Wash the car? At quarter to ten at night? Go home or I'll have words with your father."

"Either you pull the trigger," Carol was saying, her narrow shoulders lifting. Robin caught her eyes in the rear-view mirror. "Or you don't," she said, still looking at him as she spoke to Eddie. Her shoulders dropped. "What's the problem?"

"I don't have a problem."

"I didn't say you did."

Robin cleared his throat. His mouth was dry. "We're nearly there."

"I can see that."

"You want me to do it, then?" Carol said. "Give me the gun."

"I'm not going in there with you, Carol," Robin said. "Forget it."

"She's bluffing," Eddie said. "That right, Carol?"

Carol turned left, slowed, indicated again. She stopped no more than ten feet from the post office entrance and slumped over the wheel. Over the engine's purr she said, "Get out before I strangle the pair of you." Eddie opened his mouth to say something and Carol said, "Out." Still draped over the wheel she repeated, "Out. Out. Get out."

"Aren't you going to wish us luck?" Eddie flung the door open and climbed out.Robin joined him on the pavement. "Ready?"

Eddie slammed the door shut. "One second." He took a deep breath and exhaled loudly. The boom of the Castle's One O'Clock Gun launched a startled crow skywards. Squawking, it floated back down and perched on a window ledge two floors above the post office doorway. Eddie said, "Time."

"After you," Robin said, tucking his thumbs inside his balaclava.

1:00 PM

*R*obin counted them quickly. Six men and eight women, lined up against the off-white walls of the post office. Sixteen hostages including the cashiers, which ought to be plenty. One of the male patrons was built like a concrete slab. He'd have to be watched. Still, that wasn't for Robin to worry about. Crowd control was Eddie's job. Eddie had the gun and, as he liked to point out at every opportunity, it wasn't a fucking water pistol.

That particular jibe was a reference to the fact that five years ago Robin had held up a petrol station with a plastic water pistol. He didn't remember much about the hold-up. It all happened so quickly. But he remembered crying a lot and at one point having to squirt the attendant to try to get him to move. Didn't work, though. The idiot had just stood there with his jaw hanging open. The judge seemed to find it all mildly amusing, although he never said so.

After his release a year later from the psychiatric hospital's secure unit, Robin had had no place to stay. Carol persuaded Eddie, who'd just lost his job, to take him in and when she got out six weeks later, she joined them. For a while, it was a workable arrangement. Courtesy of their housing benefit cheques they helped pay Eddie's mortgage until he got back on his feet.

But there's more to life than just paying the rent.

Shortly after Carol's release Robin stole a cash register drawer from a Princes Street bookshop. He yanked it out from under the counter and fled with it under his arm, trailing dozens of wires. Carol was waiting in a car parked round the corner on Castle Street. It had been her idea, her dare. She dropped her cigarette out the window as Robin flung open the back door. He threw the drawer inside and climbed in after it. "Drive," he shouted.

When they got home they found Eddie waiting for them. He

helped prise the drawer open. It contained forty-six pounds and seventeen pence.

That's when Eddie made his proposal.

"There are two types of thieves," he maintained (and he should know, Robin remembered thinking. A year in the police force must have taught him something about criminals). "Those who get rich and those who get caught." He paused for dramatic effect. "Planners get rich," he continued. "Opportunists and risk-takers, like you pair of useless fucks, get caught. And they won't send you to a loony bin this time. If you don't start using your heads you'll be in jail before you know it. Look at this." He picked up a handful of coins and dropped them back in the cash drawer. His head moved from side to side. "Look at it."

"You're right," Carol said. "Did you have something in mind?"

He opened his mouth and showed her his crooked teeth. "Do you know the two ingredients present in most successful robberies?" They didn't.

"Hostage-taking," Eddie told them. "That's number two. You have any problems with that?"

Robin looked at Carol. She shook her head and looked at Eddie. She said, "What's number one?"

Leaning over, he stared into Carol's eyes. In a quiet voice he said, "Violence."

And he was right. The first post office robbery had been a long time in the planning, but it was worth it. Nine months later, Robin hoped the second would run as smoothly.

Stooping to fish in his bag, he located the wedge and slid it under the door. Next he found the card, flipped it over and pressed the Blu-tacked edges against the small, solitary window-pane. From the outside the sign read: "Closed for lunch due to ill health. Back at 1.30." He stuck his hand in his pocket, fumbled for the sheath and popped the button.

When he turned to face the starkly lit post office interior, Eddie, balaclava stretched over his face, was striding towards the head of the queue, hand dipping into his pocket. The woman at the front, staring at her feet, didn't notice the man wearing the dull yellow balaclava. She didn't notice when he pulled his hand out of his pocket and pointed a doctored Brocock Orion 6 pistol at her. Behind her, some of the other customers were beginning to back away. Somebody said, "Jesus." Somebody else moaned.

Robin grimaced. He hated this part. He picked up his bag and moved away from the door.

The woman was in her early thirties, smallish, a muddy river of long brown hair streaming over the sides of her face and down her light blue padded coat. A long scarf was wrapped several times around her neck and she was wearing jeans and sturdy white boots. Eyes downcast, she was deep in thought. Trouble with her boyfriend, trouble with her kids, health problems, money problems—whatever her worries, they were about to be put in perspective. Her ungloved right hand clutched a paperback book-sized parcel and her gloved left hand held her other glove, which she was slapping lightly against her hip. Her gaze was still fixed on the floor when Eddie stepped in front of her and pointed the gun at her leg.

Originally an air cartridge pistol, his weapon had been adapted. Special steel sleeves had been fitted inside the chamber, thereby enabling the gun to fire live rounds. Eddie had paid two hundred pounds for it.

He shot her in the left thigh with a .22 calibre bullet.

She collapsed as if her bones had liquefied.

The other customers moved like a single mute organism. In stunned silence they retreated to the far wall. Eddie faced the two cashiers, who had remained frozen from the moment they heard the gunshot. "You know who we are?" he said. He waited a moment, then said, "Evelyn Fitzpatrick." He was referring to the woman who'd made them famous, the sixty-five year old he'd shot three times in each knee. The local press had loved it. Would she live, would she die? For the next few days they printed four editions instead of the usual three. Sales soared. Until she pulled through. "Be cool," Eddie said. "Don't go pressing any alarms or I'll empty my gun into this lovely lady here."

Robin moved forward and examined the woman on the floor. A purple stain blossomed on her left leg. Her head lay about a foot from the counter. Her eyes were screwed shut and her mouth hung open. Robin leaned over and touched her cheek. Her eyes snapped open and she blinked several times. Her face was whiter than Evelyn Fitzpatrick's.

"You'll be okay," he said. "Just stay quiet. Understand?"

"Please don't—"

"Shhh."

She nodded.

The roar of Eddie's gun was still ringing in Robin's ears as he picked up the injured woman's parcel and set it on the counter. Robin spoke to the fat woman, the one whose hairspray had choked him when he spoke to her before lunch. "What's your name?"

Her voice was a whisper. "Hilda."

"Well, Hilda." He smiled, although the balaclava probably spoiled the intended friendly effect. "I'd like you to unlock the door, and take this"—he showed her the sports bag in his right hand—"and fill it with lots of money. Think you can do that for me?"

She mumbled a reply.

"I didn't catch that, Hilda."

"The hatch. You can pass it through the hatch."

"If we wanted to pass it through the fucking hatch we would have said so," Eddie said. "You want her to get another bullet?" He indicated the sprawled figure by aiming his gun at her. "You want that on your conscience? I don't think so. Open the door, Hilda. And do it now. We don't have all fucking day."

On the other side of the partition, Hilda waddled across the room. Robin shifted his gaze to the female customers huddled together in the corner. One or two had their arms around each other and a few were crying. All had their heads turned away, instinct telling them to avoid eye contact. Of the six men cowering against the wall, one was trying to outstare Eddie. Not the concrete slab he'd noticed earlier, but a frail elderly man who looked like someone had pissed in his mouth and he couldn't get rid of the taste. He smacked his lips, ran his tongue over his false teeth.

Eddie noticed him too. His arm swung away from the woman on the floor and pointed at the old man. "Fuck you looking at?"

The old man stared at the gun. He raised his hands. Both palms were deeply lined. His gnarled fingers trembled.

The woman on the floor screamed.

Eddie's arm jerked. He yelled, "Shut up." He waved the gun at her.

"She's been shot in the leg," Robin said. "She can't help it."

"I didn't ask your opinion. Just make her shut up."

From the huddle in the corner came another scream.

"Shut the fuck up."

"How am I supposed to make her shut up?"

"I can't hear you."

More screams from the corner. One setting off the next, like dogs barking. Robin approached Eddie and shouted in his ear. Eddie nodded, aimed at the wall and blew a hole in it.

Silence.

A chunk of plaster swung from side to side, a thin strip of wallpaper all that held it to the wall. Robin watched as the paper tore and the plaster dropped, landing on the shoulder of the woman cowering beneath it. She cried out, startled, instantly on her feet, brushing dust and chalk off her coat.

Eddie strolled over to her.

"I'm sorry." She crouched down again. "I'm sorry, I'm sorry." She crossed her hands over her bowed head.

Eddie stared at her. He said, "Any more fucking racket and I'll put a bullet in your eye." He looked around. "That goes for all of you." He walked towards the prone figure near the counter, scuffing his heels on the floor. "Including you." Placing one foot either side of the wounded woman, he said, "I don't care how much your leg hurts."

The partition door opened and Hilda said, "Give me the bag."

Robin squeezed past Eddie and handed the cashier his sports bag. "Be quick," he told her. "And Hilda? Just money, please. No fancy dyes, okay?"

1:03 PM

*F*rom the first he heard of the post office robbery nine months ago Pearce had been concerned for his mother's safety. While he was in jail he'd repeatedly suggested she might look for another job. Of course she'd brushed his concern aside. Danger? What danger? When he got out, he tried again. It wasn't as if it was her money, now, she'd argued. Play along with the robbers, she'd said, and you didn't get hurt. So that's what she would do if it happened. Which it wouldn't. Not in *her* post office.

He pointed out that someone *had* got hurt. And because it had worked, next time the gang would follow the same routine. Walk straight in and shoot some poor bastard before anybody had time to react. But not a cashier, she replied. Cashiers, she claimed, were perfectly safe behind the anti-bandit screen.

When he saw the notice on the door of the post office where his mum worked, he knew something was wrong. The smaller post offices were often inadequately staffed, those earmarked for closure, like this one, particularly so. After a couple of gins last week she'd ranted about increased workloads, ridiculous productivity expectations and training handouts on topics like "Queue Reduction Management" or "Understanding ERNIE: Inside Premium Bonds" which you had to read in your own time because there wasn't anyone to fill in for you while you read them at work. He didn't believe the sign on the door. A couple of ill-nesses and, yes, the post office might have been forced to close for half an hour, but if they'd had to close unexpectedly she'd have called him.

He couldn't afford to hang about. She was all he had.

A taxi idled by the kerb. He ran over to it and tapped his fingers on the window. The redhead behind the wheel looked annoyed by the interruption. When he didn't go away she finally stopped brushing her hair and rolled down the window.

"Sorry to bother you," he said. "You been here a while?"

"Waiting on a fare. From forty-two." She looked at her watch. "He's late."

"Seen anything unusual?"

"Like what?"

Pearce shrugged. "Obviously not." He patted the bonnet. "Do me a favour?"

"I don't know you. Why would I do you a favour?"

"Phone the police." That got her attention.

She banged the flat of her hairbrush against her palm. Her pale face got paler. "Why would I want to do that?"

"I think a robbery might be taking place."

She laughed. "In there?" She indicated the post office with a casual flick of her blue fingernails. "It's empty."

"Call the police anyway," he said.

"You call them, if you're so concerned."

"I would," he said. "But I don't have time. Got to get started on breaking down that door."

1:04 PM

*E*ddie's mobile still played *Für Elise* despite repeated promises to Robin that he would change the tune. He held the gun in one hand, phone in the other. The music stopped. He frowned. "Thanks. We'll be out in a minute."

"What is it?"

"Tell Fatso to hurry up," Eddie said.

"What's happening?" Robin stood in the partition doorway, watching Hilda shovelling wads of notes into the bag. "Can you speed up, Hilda?" He turned to Eddie. "Well?"

"We're getting a visitor."

Robin slid his knife out of its sheath. "Armed Response Unit?"

"Not yet," Eddie said. "Just a concerned citizen."

"Done," Hilda said. "It's all there." She showed Robin the open bag, smiling. He nodded and she zipped it up.

"Bring it here," he said.

Her smile dissolved when she saw the knife. She moved slowly towards him, one chubby hand holding the bag, the other clutching her throat.

"Give it to me," he said.

Her eyelids fluttered as if she was about to faint, but she stayed upright and handed over the bag. She wiped her hand on her thigh.

Banging. Robin glanced at Eddie. More banging. Regular. Insistent. Someone pounding on the front door. Their visitor, the concerned citizen. Robin couldn't tell how Eddie was reacting behind the balaclava. More banging. It stopped and a muffled voice said, "I'm coming in." Silence. A shout accompanied by a screech as the wedge under the door was driven back a couple of inches. Robin set down the bag as a hand reached round the gap at the side of the door and sent the wedge tumbling across the floor. As the door swung open, Hilda dashed forward. He caught her by the wrist and dragged her in an arc straight into his arms. She wriggled until he rested the blade of the knife against her lips. She was panting heavily and her hairspray tickled the back of his throat.

"Let her go." The man who spoke was inappropriately dressed for the cold weather in a white t-shirt and black jeans. He stood in the doorway, chill air gusting in from behind him.

"Who the fuck are you?" Eddie said.

"Get the money," Robin said to Eddie.

"It's at your feet. You get it."

"I don't have enough hands, okay?"

The man in the doorway stepped forward.

Eddie said, "Back off or I'll shoot the fat cow."

"I wouldn't advise it," the man said. "The fat cow's my mother."

Robin said to Eddie, "Pick up the money and go."

"I want to take this fucker out."

"Just do it, for Christ's sake." Robin felt his mouth dry up. Hilda was shaking in his arms, wafting hairspray up his nostrils.

Eddie reached over and picked up the bag. Hilda's son stood against the wall with his arms folded. "You going to try to stop us?" Eddie asked him.

"Not my money," he said. "I don't care what you do with it as long as you leave my mother alone."

Eddie shrugged and moved slowly towards the door. Hilda's son ignored him as he walked past. Eddie opened the door. "Take Mummy with you," he said to Robin and disappeared, the door banging shut behind him.

Hilda's son unfolded his arms and his hands squeezed into fists. Big fists. His arms were ugly with muscles. He dropped his gaze and examined his knuckles. "If your friend had stayed," he looked up again and Robin stared into his cool blue eyes, "you might have had a chance. He had a gun." He glanced at the woman Eddie had shot. "And it looks like he was prepared to use it. You, on the other hand, only have a knife." He took a step forward. "And I don't believe you're prepared to use it."

"You don't think so?" Robin pressed the serrated edge of the blade lightly against Hilda's throat. She tilted her head back and made weird gulping sounds. Dragging her with him, he started shuffling backwards towards the door, trying to keep his hands steady. His left nostril itched. He sniffed. His eyes began to water. He sneezed. Fuck. He shook his head. Blinked. Hilda trembled against him. He sneezed again.

"You fucking cut her you fucking piece of fucking shit." Hilda's son lunged towards him.

Robin shoved Hilda in the back. He grabbed the door handle and was almost out in the fresh air when he felt a tug at his coat. His foot slipped and he was dragged back.

He heard something tear. He stumbled forward, holding onto the doorframe. He couldn't get away no matter how much he pushed with his legs. Shit, it was like running in thigh-deep water. Hilda's son wasn't going to let go easily. Robin tried once more to pull away and again the fierce grip held him back. Panic seized him. He had to get out of here, out of this room, escape from these people who were yelling now, away from Hilda and her son, whatever the cost. It was him or them. Survival was all that mattered. Turning, he swung the knife upwards from his hip. Hilda's son wasn't where Robin expected him to be. He was behind his mother, arms wrapped around her waist, trying to drag her away from Robin. Robin watched with horror as his knife plunged into the side of Hilda's neck. She sank to her knees, eyes wide, staring straight ahead. Only when Robin pulled the knife out of her flesh did she let go of his coat.

Her son slapped his hand over the wound. Blood spurted through his fingers. His face was expressionless. "Mum," he said. He said it again. Then he shouted it: "*Mum.*"

Robin turned and ran.

1:05 PM

*R*obin tossed his scrunched up balaclava on the seat beside him.

"I *almost* killed Evelyn Fitzpatrick," Eddie said. "It was easy."

"Point, squeeze, bang," Carol said.

"Yeah." Eddie turned round in the front seat and stared at Robin. "Six fucking times."

"Not the same as stabbing somebody, I'll grant you." Carol crossed her hands on the wheel as she turned off London Road. A police car passed them going the other way. "Not as personal."

"Why don't you shut up and drive?" Eddie said.

Robin didn't know why Eddie was so pissed off. "She was bleeding pretty heavily," Robin said, ruffling his hair. The balaclava had flattened it. "Maybe the ambulance will get there in time."

"Who gives a shit," Eddie said. "We got the money."

Carol had the gall to say, "No thanks to Robin."

"Fuck you." He couldn't believe the bitch. A surge of anger immediately brought sweat to his brow. If he smashed her skull with a brick would there be a satisfying crunch? Fuck, he'd kill her now and take the consequences. He still had the knife in his hand. He could—no, what was he thinking? Jesus, he couldn't trust himself. He needed something to occupy his mind. The sports bag, containing an indeterminate amount of cash, was tucked on the floor behind the passenger seat. He said, "I'll count the money."

"Clean up, first," Eddie said. "You've got blood all over your sleeve."

Robin raised his arm and touched the dark stain. It was still wet. "Oh, shit," he said, looking to his right. "It's all over the door." He grabbed his balaclava, rolled it into a ball and started wiping the door with it.

"I wouldn't do that," Eddie said.

He stopped. "Why not?"

"It isn't yours."

"It is." Robin scrutinised the balaclava. "I just picked it up off the seat. Anyway, what difference does it make whether I use mine or yours?"

"Not the balaclava. The blood isn't yours, Fuckwit."

"I know, Eddie. Fucking joke, okay?"

"You want to hear something funny?" Eddie faced Robin, lips pulled back in an exaggerated smile. He didn't wait for an answer. "Several strands of your hair will be attached to that balaclava. The act of rubbing it will dislodge some of those aforementioned hairs, which will then attach themselves to the viscous liquid being rubbed." His smile disappeared. "You with me?"

Robin threw the balaclava aside. "Just trying to clean up."

"Well, all you're doing is spreading your DNA around like a fucking reckless arsehole."

"Something on your mind, Eddie? Go on. Spit it out."

"Spit it out, eh?" Eddie said. He took a deep breath. "Okay, okay." He turned to face the front. "I just wondered why? I mean, I asked you to take her hostage, not fucking kill her? Why the fuck couldn't you do as I asked?"

"I didn't mean to."

"Oh, you didn't fucking mean to. That's all right then. Excuse me if I think it was fucking unnecessary."

Robin grinned. "The man who shoots people in the legs *for effect*, thinks that I might have been unnecessarily violent?"

"Not quite," Eddie said. "I think you might have been unnecessarily stupid. Either that or you're a prime fucking headcase."

"It was an accident." The car trundled under the bridge at Abbeyhill, Carol keeping well within the speed limit. An advertising hoarding at the Scottish Parliament construction site displayed a telephone number for Crimestoppers.

"You stabbed her, let me get this right, in the neck. *Accidentally*?" Eddie forced a laugh. "Try telling that to the police. Eh, Carol?"

She ignored him. "Lose the knife, Robin."

He'd kept the knife in his hand even while he was trying to wipe Hilda's blood off the door. Blood was beginning to congeal on the blade and the handle felt sticky. "I might need it again."

"What for?" Eddie said. "Another accident?"

"At least put it away, Robin."

He dug the sheath out of his pocket. His hands shook as he slid the knife inside its leather cover. His hands shook as he leaned over and lifted the outside flap of the sports bag. His hands shook as he dropped the knife in the bag and clipped it shut. His hands shook as Carol turned into Holyrood Park.

Salisbury Crags swelled on the right. Couples strolled along the footpath that twisted up the volcanic ridge. Arm in arm. Hand in hand. Arms around one another. Further along, towards Arthur's Seat, couples and kids. Couples and dogs. Couples and kids and dogs. No one walked in Holyrood Park alone. He wondered if Carol and Eddie went walking in Holyrood Park. His hands kept shaking as Carol nosed the car into one of the few available spaces in the car park.

"Take your coat off, for God's sake," Eddie said. "You can't go home with that shit all over your sleeve."

"She tore the coat. I heard the lining rip."

"Stick it in the bag with the money."

Robin started to unbutton his coat. "I'm going to freeze."

Carol said "Diddums," and turned off the engine.

Maybe he would beat her to death with his bare hands.

Eddie lit a cigarette, offered Carol one, and then Robin.

Robin shook his head. "Truth is," he said, wrestling with his coat sleeves, "I feel a bit sick."

"Oh, Petal." Carol pulled a sad face.

Robin freed his arms, unzipped the bag and stuffed his coat on top of the stacks of banded notes. Closing his eyes, he visualised Hilda with blood gushing out of the puncture wound in her neck. Slowly, her face changed to Carol's. He opened his eyes and smiled. "So," he said, "what time are we meeting tomorrow?"

Eddie frowned while he sucked on his cigarette. Holding the smoke in, he said, "Make it ten o'clock, if that's okay." After a moment he exhaled, a single wisp of smoke trickling out of his open mouth. "I wouldn't mind a bit of a lie-in."

1:07 PM

*K*ennedy's boss said, "Fuck me."

About a dozen people had come running out and now they were milling around the post office entrance as the emergency services started to arrive. Some of them seemed distraught, whilst others were sitting on the pavement, shocked into an appearance of utter calm. Kennedy squinted through the open doorway. Inside, a man in a bloodstained t-shirt supported a woman's head in his lap, his hand pressed against her neck. Blood ran down his elbow and dripped onto the floor. Next to the counter a woman lay on the floor. Half-a-dozen men carrying fierce-looking weapons and wearing body armour advanced into the post office in a kind of choreographed pattern. He couldn't see past them without getting out of the car and it was too cold for that. "What are we going to do?"

"About what?"

"Them. Greaves and co. His *party*."

"I'll need to think about that."

"What's there to think about? We know who they are, what they've done, their names, addresses." Kennedy paused. "We have to tell the police."

"There are other factors to consider. Let me think about it."

"Mind if I smoke while you're thinking?"

"Not in the car."

Kennedy thought about stepping outside and shivered. "Why don't we follow them?"

His boss shook his head. "Other plans. Anyway, as you said, we know where they live."

The armed police had moved away from the entrance. Kennedy

could see the man again, the front of his t-shirt almost completely red. The woman in his lap didn't move.

1:09 PM

$\mathcal{S}$he looked dead.

Pearce squeezed her hand. Cold and clammy. No response. Not so much as a feeble twitch. His voice cracked when he asked, "When will you know?"

The medic shook his head. "Can't say. She's lost a hell of a lot of blood."

Pearce stared at the medic's hands. Disposable gloves. Fingers dipped in the spillage from his mother's neck. "What are her chances?"

"Given the circumstances, she's doing as well as can be expected."

"That's not an answer." Her eyelids fluttered and Pearce squeezed her hand again. "Please tell me."

The medic sighed. "She's very weak."

"Is there anything I can do?"

"I'm doing all I can. Just hold her hand."

"'Scuse me, son."

Pearce felt a hand on his shoulder. He turned his head to see an old man grinning madly at him, bad teeth bared in a face like a weathered skull.

"Just wanted to thank you," the old man said. "I was caught inside when…" He ran his tongue over his teeth. "Anyway. Just wanted to say thanks for rescuing us from those pair of cunts. No telling what they might have done." He paused, grinning again. "Sorry about your mum. How is she?"

Pearce turned away from the old man. His mother's eyes were still closed. He wondered if they'd stay that way. *No, it can't happen again. It's not an option. I can't lose her.* "I don't feel like talking." *She'll be okay.*

"No bother, son," the old man said. "Best of luck, eh?"

1:12 PM

*A*t least the police had the decency to leave him alone for a while. He guessed they'd spoken to several witnesses who'd confirmed he wasn't a suspect in either the robbery, the shooting or his mum's stabbing. He was a still a major witness, though, and they'd want to speak to him at some point. It was no surprise when a detective sergeant said he'd follow the ambulance and ask Pearce a few questions at the hospital, if that was okay.

Pearce asked if he had a choice.

1:13 PM

*D*ry air scraped his throat.

A crowd had gathered. Dressed for winter in hats, scarves, gloves. Breathing hard. Breath gathering in clouds above them. Near the front, Pearce spotted a man in a Santa costume. A butcher stood in his shop doorway with his arms folded across his dirty blue and white striped apron.

Traffic had come to a standstill.

Nothing moved. Silence pounded in his ears.

Pearce followed the stretcher towards the nearer of the two ambulances. He felt guilty when he let go of her hand.

"Wait." A man with a heavily strapped nose was threading a path through the crowd. A uniformed policeman exchanged a few words with him and let him past.

When the man smiled, Pearce felt hollowed out.

The man handed him a business card. "Call me."

Pearce didn't look at the card. Lawyer, doctor, journalist. Who cared? He slotted the card beside Pete Thompson's cash in the back pocket of his jeans and climbed into the waiting ambulance.

PART TWO

TRANSCRIPT FROM 999 CALL RECORDED ON
JANUARY 12TH AT 11:14 AM

Caller: I need you to listen. Someone might have been hurt. I heard loud bangs and crashes and a woman screaming, you know, like several piercing screams and then a man yelled, "I'm going to fucking murder you, you crazy bitch."
Operator: Do you have an address, sir?
Caller: Where the attack took place? Sure. 2F2, 1138 Polwarth Gardens.
Operator: Can I take your name, please?
Caller's reply is muffled.
Operator: Could you repeat that, sir?
Caller hangs up.

12TH JANUARY
8:20 AM

*P*earce turned on the cold tap. Water bounced off the sink's green enamel and splashed his stomach. He twisted the tap anticlockwise, then reached for the towel that hung from a hoop under the sink, bottom edge dangling less than an inch above the cork-tiled bathroom floor.

Blue with a white border, the towel was a present from Mum. "What are you supposed to give someone who's just out of prison?" she had asked. "I didn't know, so I made you this." In the top corner she had embroidered a dove in flight. She'd drawn it freehand and he only knew it was a dove because she'd told him. One day, while she was at work, he had taken the measuring tape out of the toolbox under the sink and measured the bird's wingspan. Those were big wings. Eleven point two times the length of its body, to be exact. The creature's head was tilted skywards, neck stretched like a chick demanding food.

Pearce crumpled the towel in his fist and rubbed the damp hair on his belly until the skin between his stomach and groin turned pink. It helped that the towel was rough. He folded it in half and draped it over his shoulders.

When he turned the tap back on, it coughed a couple of feeble jets of water into the sink before the flow steadied. He held his hand under the tap, fingers curled like talons. Gradually the back of his hand began to ache as the cold seeped through his skin and wrapped around his bones. When he could bear it no longer, he withdrew his hand and replaced it with the other one. He left it there till it throbbed.

It seemed a long time since he'd left the hospital.

At ten past four in the morning the air was still, the sky cloudless as he trudged down Forrest Road. Puddles of yellow light spread on the pavement and the layer of ice on the road looked like chalk. Traffic lights signalled to no one but him.

The palms of his hands hurt.

A plane passed low overhead. He looked up and saw five white lights, one of which was flashing, and a single flashing red light. The engine created two distinct sounds, a low thrum and a quieter high-pitched whine. In a little while, silence returned.

Interruptions were few during the long walk home. Approaching Chambers Street, he heard a shout and the sound of hurried footsteps, but when he turned the corner there was no one in sight. Later, on South Bridge, a car drove by, horn blaring and kids cheering out of an open window. Further on, a flattened cardboard box served as a bedroom wall for the pile of clothing quietly grunting in a disused shop doorway. Outside a corner shop a taxi disgorged its drunken occupant onto the pavement. The driver swore and the drunk swore back. Much later, now in a residential area, a woman crossed to the other side of the street as she passed Pearce, swaying, muttering, her coat wrapped around her as tightly as a shroud.

As he neared home, the occasional light shone from kitchens and bathrooms of early risers. A white cat jumped off a windowsill, hissing at him as it ran under a parked car. He'd never met a cat that could tolerate him. For all he knew, his armpits gave off an unpleasant odour that only those little fuckers could smell.

The outside door of his mum's tenement flat was unlocked. Someone had kicked it open a couple of weeks ago and broken the lock. The stairwell lights revealed four half-moons engraved in the skin of each hand where his fingernails had been digging into his palms. He splayed his fingers, stretching the skin.

On the first floor landing a dog started to bark. Pearce had probably set it off by dragging the smell of cat in with him. The barking didn't relent until he was standing in front of his door, rummaging in his pocket for his keys. A ten pence piece poked out of his pocket, clattered onto the stone landing and started to roll towards the stairwell. He slammed his boot on top of the coin and the sound was like a thunderclap. Downstairs the dog started barking again.

The flat was dark and cold.

His mum's bedroom door was open, a shaft of moonlight draped across the empty bed. He walked over to the window and pulled the curtains.

In the kitchen he grabbed a can of Stella out of the fridge and took it into the sitting room. He removed his boots and stretched out on the sofa, knees bent, head resting against a pile of cushions. The beer tasted sour.

After a second sip, he went back to the kitchen and poured the beer down the sink. The smell made him nauseous. He drank some water from the tap, splashed some on his face and drank some more.

Back in the sitting room he selected a CD from his mum's collection. Her twelve CDs were heaped on the floor next to the CD player. In the dark he couldn't make out which album he'd chosen, but it made no difference. Mum never put her CDs back in the right box. He opened the case and prised out the disk.

Power. Flick to CD. Play.

Seconds later he eased the volume down, smiling. Burt Bacharach. "Close To You."

He lay down on the settee and drifted in and out of sleep until dawn began to burn the morning sky.

8:21 AM

*P*earce turned off the tap and looked at himself in the mirror. He brushed his chin with the back of his freezing hand. He needed a shave.

Later.

He checked his mobile. Cracked, but still working. No messages. He looked at his watch and called Ailsa Lillie.

She slurred her hello.

"You okay?" he asked.

"Who's that? Pearce? Christ. Give me a minute. Let me wake up. Christ."

"Want me to phone you back?"

"It's okay." She yawned. "Christ. What time is it?"

He told her. "Shouldn't have phoned so early," he added.

"It's not early. I'm just a lazy bitch." She yawned again. "So, did you see him?"

"Yeah. I told him not to come near you or your daughter again."

"And?"

"He said he wouldn't."

"That's it?"

"That's it."

"Christ. That easy. You believe him?"

"I think so. I gave him something to think about."

"It's nice of you to phone, Pearce. Even if it is the middle of the night."

"How about you? Did you take the gun back?"

The tone of her voice changed. "No, I fucking didn't." She made an angry noise in her throat. "If you must know, I tried. But Ben wasn't around and apparently nobody knew where he'd gone."

"Good."

"I'll get your money—what?"

"It's not a problem."

"I thought—"

Thompson's cash bulged in Pearce's back pocket. "Your ex is paying off your debt. In full."

"No way." Ailsa's voice rose. "How did you get him to do that? Only time he ever gave me anything was in return for sexual favours."

His throat felt dry. "This time you're getting something for nothing. No blowjob required."

"I don't want anything from him."

"Take it. It's yours."

"I don't want his money."

"He gave it to me. I'll pay it for you."

"I've got my pride, Pearce."

"Okay, you can owe me instead of Cooper. How's that sound?"

"Better."

"Ailsa, I—" He closed his eyes. Mistake. He was back in the post office, his mum standing in front of him, knife against her throat. His knees buckled. He took a step forward to steady himself. *Stop it.* He tried to open his eyes. He didn't want to see this again. His eyelids were heavy and wouldn't budge. His mum's sweet scent wafted across to him. His tongue felt thick when he said to Ailsa, "Something happened yesterday."

"With Pete?"

"Something else." He heard his mum's breathing, saw the fear in her eyes. As he watched, her attacker dropped the knife and ran. Mum strode forward, slung her arms around Pearce's waist and told him she was fine, just fine. *Lies. Nothing but lies.*

"You going to tell me or do I have to guess?" Another pause. Finally Ailsa said, "I'm awake, now, Pearce, but I might as well go back to sleep if you won't talk to me."

The moment his mum died, a firework had started flying around inside his skull. A young nurse tried to console him. She called security when he threw a chair at the wall. He apologised. Didn't point out that he *could* have thrown the fucking chair out the window. And could have thrown the nurse and the fucking security boys out the window after it. They let him sit for a while and, gradually, the anger seeped out of him as it became clear what he had to do. He'd never really had a choice. He saw the years stretch out forever. His life was over. God knows how long he'd get this time. His mum shook her head and accused him of having failed to learn anything.

His eyes snapped open. The illusion vanished. She was wrong. He had learned something. The last ten years may not have taught him much, but one thing he knew. This time he wasn't prepared to spend all morning sharpening a screwdriver.

He said to Ailsa, "I need your help."

9:15 AM

*T*he cash was bundled in hundreds.

Robin flicked through a stack of tenners. The notes were limp and faded, well-used. He pressed the wad against his nose and inhaled. Sour beer, fag-ends in loaded ashtrays, the lingering trace of cheap perfume, two in the morning, the barman who looked like his father saying, "You're a leech, son," a woman whose name he didn't know leaning against his shoulder, lifting her head, breathing against his cheek, hair tickling his chin, lifting her head, whispering in his ear, whispering her name, whispering her name again and again, as her eyebrows darkened and fattened and wriggled and fell on his neck.

He sat up with a start, frantically rubbing his neck. Fucking leeches. He'd dreamed of leeches for sixteen fucking years. Ever since his father... Breathing too fast. Ah, fuck you, Daddy. Why couldn't he dream about something else for once? Deep breath. Should he write down the dream while he remembered? No, his current therapist wasn't interested in dreams. Some were, some weren't. This one seemed more interested in his early sexual experiences. Slow. Deep. Breath.

First orgasm? Ten years old, standing up in the bath. Makes my knees buckle. Think I've damaged myself. Think I'm going to tell you?

Picking the money off the floor where he'd dropped it, he lobbed it onto the table. He stretched, reached for a smoke. Fuck sex. It wasn't worth getting excited about. Boom fucking boom. His lighter was low on fuel, but after three attempts it finally sparked. He eyed his money through the flame. Fourteen stacks of tens, six stacks of twenties, a single stack of fifties. Not bad for a nutter. Above the table, smoke coiled and drifted. He snapped off the lighter and exhaled through his nose while thirty-one thousand tax-free pounds flaunted itself on the table in front of him.

With Carol and Eddie out of the way, the money was all his.

He had a plan, one that might even work. If he got caught, what the fuck, he'd plead insanity. He wouldn't be short of witnesses.

He'd sat up all night drinking coffee, chain-smoking, watching television with the sound off, listening to news reports on the radio. Time after time he counted the money, flicking through the notes with hands that wouldn't stop trembling. Several times he got up to wash his face. He cleaned his nostrils with both ends of a twist of toilet roll and when that failed to remove the stench he shoved a couple of cotton buds up his nose. Finally he smeared toothpaste around the inside of his nostrils. It stung all right, but it didn't get rid of the stink of the post office cashier's hairspray.

He checked on Carol. She was sleeping like a baby, dreaming sweet dreams about Eddie, no doubt.

When the news report came at five thirty he was slouching on the settee. He wasn't tired. He was thinking, trying to concentrate, locked in the process of making a difficult decision. Weighing up the pros and cons for what was easily the tenth time that night, he concluded once again that it was all over for Carol. It had to be. After all, what did he have to lose now? The newsreader answered him, speaking with utter detachment: "The woman stabbed by a robber in an Edinburgh post office last night has died of a wound to the throat. Mrs Hilda Pearce—"

Two words repeated in his head. *Has died.*

Scores of scented leeches clung to his face. He stumbled to his feet, stomach muscles contracting. Leeches crawled down his throat, squirmed in his oesophagus, lodged in his lungs, choking him with the scent of Hilda Pearce. He couldn't breathe. His heart thumped. He was dizzy, sick, scared. Was he scared? Really? Yes, he was fucking terrified.

Hilda Pearce had really fucked him up. There was no turning back now.

No more doubt, then. No more denial. Who cared that it wasn't his fault? Accident or not, he was a killer.

The newsreader confirmed it: "—is now a murder investigation."

A killer. Fat black perfumed slugs bloated his belly.

He scurried to the bathroom and vomited into the toilet bowl for minutes on end. His stomach cramped with each spasm, pain causing his eyes to water. When his stomach was empty he puked bile, shivering from head to foot. Afterwards he leaned his sweating forehead against the wall and hugged himself. His gut felt like it had been tied in a knot.

Bile coated his tongue and each time he swallowed, tiny balls of fire scorched his throat. And those words pounded in his head like a second heartbeat.

Has died.

Suddenly he realised his head was hurting where it rested against the wall. He jolted upright. Maybe he'd fallen asleep for a few minutes. But, no, he couldn't have. Not with this much adrenalin shooting through his bloodstream. He wasn't tired. Definitely not. His watch read twenty past seven. An hour and fifty minutes had passed since the news report.

He got to his feet and turned on the shower. If he wasn't asleep, then where had the time gone? Oh, God. Maybe it was happening again. He must have been asleep, if only because there was no other explanation. Clumsily, he started to undress. Naked, he stepped into the shower cubicle and closed the door, standing under the spray, head bowed, hands clasped in front of his chest, while hot needles jabbed the back of his neck. The smell was stronger now. He squirted liquid soap into his palm and lathered his body. He shampooed his hair. Rinsed it.

After he stepped out of the shower he brushed his teeth. He shaved. He lined his nostrils with aftershave. It stung like a bitch.

9:16 AM

"*W*hat is it?" Ailsa Lillie held the door open with one hand. With the other she shielded her bruised eye.

Pearce ignored her question. "You dyed your hair." Today, her hair was dark brown with a reddish tinge. Yesterday, he seemed to recall, it was uniformly grey.

"Gold star for observation." Her mouth tensed.

"What I meant to say," he said, "is that I like it. You look ten years younger."

"Christ, I must have looked old before." She was dressed in faded blue jeans and a burgundy halter-top. Her feet were bare. Not exactly a winter costume, he thought. He glanced at his bare arms. Who was he to speak? "You going to tell me what's going on?" she asked him.

As he stepped inside, his arm brushed against hers. He said nothing.

Her eyes widened, asking the question again. She rubbed her arm where he'd touched it.

He couldn't look into her eyes for long. His gaze dropped. Shit. Straight to her tits. And guess what? She wasn't wearing a bra. He looked up and discovered two cracks running along the ceiling, forming a jagged X where they crossed. He felt her hand warming his bicep.

When he lowered his head she jerked her hand away. "How's your daughter?"

"Becky's doing okay," she said, moving quickly down the hall. She turned. "She still sounds like shit and she can't talk for long, but she's improving. I told her about you. She said to say thanks."

"She still in hospital?"

"She's in Glasgow, staying with my sister. Thought she'd be safer there."

"I didn't realise. I assumed she was still—"

"She's been out a couple of days. They only kept her in overnight. Hospital beds are precious commodities."

"Right. Maybe I'll get to meet her sometime."

"Maybe," Ailsa said.

He stole a last glance at the ceiling and strode towards her. She turned again and he followed her into the sitting room. He felt clumsy in his boots, thinking he was going to tread on her toes.

She sat on the settee and he sat next to her. She faced him, feet angled towards each other, big toes touching, toenails flashing red.

Something hard was growing in his chest. He coughed into his balled fist. *Just ask if you can borrow the gun. She doesn't need to know anything else.* "It's my mum," he said. He coughed again. "She was in an accident."

Her face froze. Her hand sprang from her lap and her fingers wrapped around his wrist. "Is she—was it serious?"

He leaned back and stared at the opposite wall. Above the boarded-up fireplace hung a painting. Dozens of ovals, some stretched fat in shades of red, others thin in shades of green, dominated the canvas. Randomly placed black curved lines looked like someone other than the artist had added an assortment of eyebrows. While she stroked the back of his hand with her fingertips, he told her what had happened.

She didn't interrupt once. When he'd finished she said, "I'm really sorry, Pearce. Christ, that's awful. I don't suppose they know who…"

He continued to stare at the painting. His mouth was so dry his tongue was beginning to crack. Something was about to burst out of him. He swallowed.

"Look at me," she said. She shook his hand up and down as she squeezed it. "If there's anything I can do…"

He swallowed again, gently removing his hand from her grasp. Slowly he turned to look at her.

"It's okay," she said, eyes shining like polished jade.

He shook his head. "It's very far from okay." His voice quietened. "I thought I'd feel sad, you know." He paused. "We were close." He locked his fingers together in his lap. "But I don't."

"You will."

"Yeah?"

"Promise," she said. "It might take a while, but it'll come."

"I've waited ten years. I haven't…" He clenched his fist. "I mean, my mother—I ought to be grief-stricken, but I'm not. I'm angry, all right. And a bit tired and incredibly hungry. But," he unclenched his fist, "that's nothing out of the ordinary."

"You're describing a normal reaction."

"I am?"

When she smiled at him he noticed how white her teeth were. "What do you want to eat?"

"Don't go to any trouble."

"I haven't had breakfast yet. It's no trouble."

He got to his feet. "I'll take you out somewhere. Anywhere you like. Pete Thompson's paying."

"Sit down," she said. He flopped back onto the settee. "I'm taking nothing from Pete. Now, what do you want? Eggs, bacon, sausages?" He nodded. "Baked beans?" He nodded again.

"Can I do anything?" he asked, as she bounced across the carpet on the balls of her bare feet.

"Come into the kitchen with me if you want." She stood in the doorway with one knee bent. "Keep me company."

9:29 AM

*H*ilda Pearce's smell was still there, tinged, now, with a sickly sweet putrescence, as if the smell from the mound of black bin bags littering the pavement below had seeped through the narrow gaps in the planks the scaffolders had laid.

Calmer now, Robin turned away from the window. The sound of six-shooters penetrated the wall as his deaf neighbour sat down to watch his first cowboy movie of the day. Robin looked at the clock. Almost, darling. Almost time to go.

Carol had left early, saying she wanted some fresh air, that she'd walk. Fuck her. She'd be straight into a taxi, round to Eddie's, shedding her clothes before she was in the door. Did she think he didn't know?

Stubbing out his cigarette, Robin began to place the cash in a leather holdall. He had to take the money with him. If the opportunity didn't arise, it was important that everything carried on as normal. *The money's right here. Nothing to get your neck in a twist about. Knickers. Knickers in a twist.* He fastened the bag and carried it into the hall. The peg where his favourite jacket usually hung was empty. He'd thrown it out with the rubbish last night, along with the sports bag.

The black, knee-length overcoat he'd worn only a couple of times still smelled new. He pulled it tight over his chest and fastened the buttons. Returning to the bathroom, he pulled the plug in the sink and the crimson water drained away. He studied the knife. Water droplets gleamed on the blade. It looked clean. At least, it looked as if somebody had tried to clean it. It was unlikely to pass a forensic examination, but who cared? He wiped the knife with a hand towel, then soaked up the residual moisture with a couple of tissues.

In the sitting room, he slotted the knife in its sheath. Before opening the front door he dropped the sheath in his overcoat pocket. His hands were shaking less now, but his legs still felt weak as he ran down the stairs.

He stepped outside. Dirty cotton wool clouds filled the sky. He slung the holdall in the back seat of the car and tilted the rearview mirror. Why did he do that? There was no need, since the mirror was exactly as he'd left it. Carol hadn't been anywhere near the car, so he didn't need to adjust the fucking mirror. *Neck in a twist?* He had to keep it together. He took a deep breath. *Keep him at bay.*

Six feet in front of the car, four pigeons were pecking at the ground. When he turned on the ignition, three flew off. He revved the engine and the remaining pigeon's head bobbed up and down. Briefly, its wings fluttered. For a moment, it looked as though it was about to hop forward, but it stayed where it was, unwilling to relinquish its roadside snack.

Robin stepped out of the car and walked towards the bird. "I need you to get out of the way," he said. "What's the matter? You got a death wish?"

The pigeon shook its head and took off, hardly flapping its wings. Effortlessly, it hovered into place on a nearby lamppost and cocked its head.

Robin returned to the Clio and squeezed himself into the seat. His new coat was heavy. His arms felt clumsy, like weights were pressing down on them. The fabric was making his wrists itch. *Do it.* He bounced his palms off the steering wheel. *Do it, do it, do it.* He pulled out from the kerb. *Neck in a twist?* That would be a bit of a bloomer.

He remembered nothing of the drive to Eddie's flat. Suddenly he was there, crawling along Polwarth Gardens, searching for a place to park. As usual there was little choice and the fact that he didn't want to park too close to the flat further reduced his options. He found a space big enough for the Clio at the end of the road. He reverse parked and cut the engine. Slumped in his seat, he had an angled view of Eddie's second floor flat. If he leaned forward he could see the tenement block's bright red entrance door. Carol was up there right now. Fucking Eddie.

Robin clutched the knife in his pocket. Could he do this?

On the pavement opposite, a young woman turned and shouted at a toddler lagging several feet behind, splashing in a puddle. The toddler bent his head and shuffled forward. She waited. When he was close enough, she grabbed his arm and shook him. He didn't react. She smacked him. Still he didn't react. She yelled at him and smacked him harder. He started to bawl.

A bus trundled past and stopped at the end of the street. Nobody got out. A skinny teenage girl in flared trousers got on.

A light drizzle began to dot the windscreen. Cars buzzed past in swarms. Mother and toddler vanished into a newsagents on the corner of the street. Robin took the knife out of its sheath and scraped the blade over the fine hairs on the back of his hand.

Yes, he could do this.

When he looked up again, Carol was standing in Eddie's doorway. Very clever. They both knew how punctual Robin was. She'd timed it well. If he hadn't known better, he'd have sworn she'd just arrived.

9:47 AM

*T*he kitchen was hot and smelled of fried sausages.

Ask her for the gun. Pearce finished his fourth piece of toast and marmalade and said, "No more. I couldn't."

Ailsa poured a fresh cup of coffee. When she leaned forward, he saw down her front. *Oh, Jesus. Stop staring at her tits.* He moved his plate to the side, adding it to the small pile already assembled, shuffling the knives and forks around until she sat down again. *Ask her.* Her chair was at the side of the little table. She crossed her legs and her foot dangled inches from his shin.

He added some milk from the carton and took a sip of coffee. "I need your gun," he said.

"Don't be stupid."

"Give me the gun, Ailsa."

"Look, Pearce, I know—"

"If you don't give me your gun, I'll pick one up somewhere else."

"It's not that easy."

"You found one no problem."

"I've got a dark past. I used to know some bad people."

"What am I? A saint?"

"I don't know who you are." She brushed her newly dyed hair out of her eyes. "What are you going to do with it?"

He took another sip of coffee. He stared at her, holding her gaze. She really did look much younger. "Kill somebody."

"For Christ's sake." She looked away, tongue sticking through slightly parted lips. Her eyelashes fluttered, then her tongue slid back in her mouth. "That's fucking stupid. Why?"

"You need to ask that?" He cradled his mug in both hands. He pressed his palms together, imagining the mug breaking like a skull in a vice.

"Let the police handle it."

"Let's say Thompson had gone too far." He eased the pressure on the mug, picked it up and drank the rest of his coffee. "Let's say he had killed Rebecca. What would you have done?"

"I can't think about that, Pearce."

"Twiddled your fingers while Thompson laughed at you? Sat around doing nothing while the police went through the motions of looking for your daughter's murderer? You think they give a shit?" He paused. "You already have the gun. You're halfway there. You're only missing the ammo. If Thompson had killed Rebecca you'd have found a way to get some fucking bullets, wouldn't you?" When she didn't reply he asked her again, "Wouldn't you?"

Slowly she nodded her head.

"Help me, Ailsa."

"Oh, God, Pearce."

"I'm taking the gun," he said. "If you want to give me a name or a phone number for the ammo, I'd be grateful."

She slumped forward as if her neck was broken. "Ben doesn't give out his phone number."

"That his name? Ben? Ben what?"

"That's all I know. Anyway, I doubt it's his real name."

"Where can I find him?"

She raised her head. Her eyes were closed. "I'll tell him what you need."

He said, "When?"

She opened her eyes. "Pass me your mobile."

He handed it to her.

"This is a bad idea." She started to dial. "You'll end up in prison. Or worse." She punched in the last number and held the phone to her ear. "Alice?" Her voice carried a false gaiety. "Yeah, fine. Joe-Bob around?"

Pearce carried the dishes over to the sink.

"Aha. I'll try again in twenty minutes."

He turned on the tap and tested the temperature with his thumb. "You seriously expect me to believe that there's someone living in Edinburgh called Joe-Bob?"

"How do you know I dialled an Edinburgh number?" She laid the phone on the table.

"Of course," he said. "I was forgetting. Glasgow's famous for its Joe-Bobs."

"Joe-Bob lives in Haddington, if you must know. And it's a nickname. He hates country music." She moved towards him. "And, no, I've no idea what his real name is."

He fitted the plug in the sink. "Joe-Bob?" He squirted a generous coating of washing-up liquid over the dishes.

"Honest to God." She was standing next to him, resting her buttocks against what was probably the cutlery drawer.

"So where does he fit in?"

"Friend of Ben's. He'll set things up for us."

"Why can't we set things up ourselves?" He turned off the tap.

"Ben doesn't work that way."

"What, he only talks through an interpreter?" He grabbed a plate and wiped a streak of baked bean sauce off it.

"Ben sells weapons." She folded her arms. "He's careful who he talks to."

He rinsed the plate and slotted it in the drying rack. "How come you know this guy?" She looked down at the floor. "Sorry," he said, plunging his hands back into the soapy water. "None of my business."

Her hand moved across her face. Her fingertips traced the curve of her eyebrow. "Joe-Bob used to be my dealer."

Water splashed onto the linoleum as Pearce grabbed her wrist. His fingers were slippery. Soapsuds popped on the back of his hand. His forearm itched as water trickled towards his elbow. She yelled and wrenched her hand out of his grip.

"What's wrong with you?" She balled her fists. "Huh? You want to see my track marks, is that it?" She spread her fingers and brought her arms together, exposing their white undersides. She clenched her fists again. "Well?"

He examined her veins. They looked normal. "I don't see anything."

"You don't get track marks from smack, Shithead. You smoke it."

He nodded. "You ever mainlined?"

She shook her head.

"Ever tempted?"

"Of course." She looked at the floor. "Despite seeing what it did to my friends." She raised her head. "Christ, what is this?"

"You clean, now?"

"What do you think?"

"You said Joe-Bob used to be your dealer. That could mean you've stopped taking drugs. But it could also mean you've found a new dealer."

"I don't want to talk about this any more."

Pearce tipped the water out of the basin.

"You asked how I knew Joe-Bob," she said. "Now you know and I hope you're happy."

He looked for a towel to dry his hands.

She watched him for a minute, then reached under the counter, pulled a dishtowel off a hook and tossed it to him. "I thought you were nice."

He dried his hands, folded the towel in half, folded it again and placed it on the counter next to the sink. "You saying you'd prefer it if I didn't care what you stick in your veins?"

"It's none of your business."

"Right."

"Anyway, I told you, I've never injected." She padded towards the table and sat down. "I never did much smack, even. Joe-Bob ran a sideline in Temgesic. That was my poison."

Pearce's knowledge of Temgesic came from two sources. In a random drug test during his time at Barlinnie two percent of the prison population had tested positive for Temgesic. That was an impressive one point five percent more than cocaine. Also, his sister had used Temgesic more than once to tide her over to her next fix. In both cases the explanation for his source of information was too personal to reveal to a woman he'd only just met. No, that wasn't it. Ailsa would find out about his past one way or the other. Either he could tell her or she'd read it second hand, splattered all over the papers. No way the press would miss the opportunity to cash in on an ex-jailbird headline. Well, in her own sweet words, it was none of her business. He forced himself to frown.

"Pills," she explained. "Buprenorphine. Synthetic morphine. Heroin substitute, basically. With an intensely euphoric side effect. Joe-Bob used to get a steady supply from addicts who got them on prescription to help wean them off heroin. Never worked, of course. Temgesic just became a kind of currency. Part exchange for a fix."

"And you bought these pills from Joe-Bob?"

"For a while, yeah."

"But you don't any more."

"Do I look like a junkie? Anyway, he doesn't deal these days."

"Gone up in the world?"

She nodded. "Ben's lieutenant."

Pearce picked up his mobile and handed it to her. "Want to try him again?"

9:56 AM

*E*ddie closed the toilet door with his foot. He fastened his belt as he walked along the short corridor and opened the sitting room door. Sinatra was singing "L.A. Is My Lady." Eddie joined in briefly, breaking off when he saw the gun. He swiped it off the table, knocking Carol's handbag spinning. It toppled, dropped to the floor, and he said, "What's my gun doing here?"

The sitting room was long and high-ceilinged. An empty settee hugged the opposite wall and matching blue director's chairs sat at each end of an oriental rug. Towards the window, dark-stained floorboards shone under the glare of a pair of tasselled Art Deco table lamps. Flames from the gas fire flickered in the draught he created as he walked past.

Carol had her back to him. She opened the heavy, green curtains and stared out the window, dragging for an insanely long time on her cigarette.

His voice rose. "Hey, I'm talking to you."

She turned slightly and raised her eyebrows. "It's going to rain." She picked a glass ashtray off the floor and placed it on the window ledge.

"Carol, why's my gun here?"

The hand holding the cigarette brushed at something on her skirt. When he moved towards her she blew an endless stream of blue-grey smoke at him. He said her name again and repeated the question.

Her breasts swelled and lifted as she inhaled again. She tapped ash into the ashtray, exhaling curls of smoke through her nose.

He strode up to her, grabbed her upper arm and aimed the gun at her head. "Why," he said, "was this lying on the table?"

Her eyes were cold as pebbles. "Let go of my arm, Eddie."

"You think I won't use it?" He flicked off the safety. "Answer the question."

"Have I been a naughty girl?" She tilted her head and gave him a wide-eyed innocent look.

He dug his fingers further into her bicep. "Just tell me what you were doing with the gun."

"Sticking it down my knickers," she said. "Isn't that what you'd like? Rubbing my crotch with it. Getting all hot and wet and turned on." She ran her tongue over her upper lip. "Feel," she said, prising his fingers from her arm and guiding his hand downwards.

"We don't have time," he said. "Robin'll be here any minute."

She kissed his throat as she slid his hand over her skirt. "He's not here now." "Hang on." He turned the weapon's safety back on. She kept a tight hold of his left hand, now high on her thigh under the skirt, while he reached over to place the gun next to the ashtray on the window ledge.

At the outset she had said, "I'd be happy if I never had sex again." Eddie had dared presume that Robin was an inconsiderate lover. Later, she'd quashed that particular theory when she said, "When I orgasm, all I feel is rage."

He looked at her now and wondered what had caused this change in her feelings. Was it when he squeezed her arm? Or when he pointed the gun at her? Was this her response to physical danger? To become aroused? It certainly looked that way. This was new to him. New and not altogether unpleasant.

He hadn't imagined it would be like this. In fact, most of the time he believed it was never going to happen, and now that it was, he was having trouble accepting the evidence of his own senses. But yes, he was going to, they were going to…

At first, he was aware of a prickling sensation. Then, a vague sense of heat, a burning pain which very quickly became intense. He cried out. The back of his hand was on fire. He tried to move it and her grip increased. He looked down between her legs. She'd hiked up her skirt. He watched in astonishment as she ground her cigarette out on his hand. She threw her head back and laughed. Yelling in her face, he wrenched his hand away and the dead cigarette butt fell on the floor. She reeled back a few steps.

"Jesus." He was too puzzled to do anything but stare at her. His hand throbbed and shaking it didn't help. "Jesus." He turned and headed for the kitchen. In front of the door he turned round and walked back to her. "I don't get it," he said.

She had her back to him again, forehead pressed against the windowpane.

"What was that for?"

She started swaying her hips, stretched her arms over her head and pressed her palms against the glass. Sinatra crooned along to an early-eighties guitar and synthesizer funk backing track.

Eddie reached past her gyrating buttocks and snatched the gun off the ledge. He noticed her eyes were closed. Only Carol could look out of a window with her eyes shut. Not that there was anything to see. Directly opposite, empty flats. Below, empty yellow washing lines strung across four poles in an empty shared garden surrounded by tenements. In this flat, if you wanted a view, you looked out the bedroom window. He gave Carol a final glance, tucked the gun under his belt and went to the kitchen.

The cold water eased the pain, but when he moved his hand away from the flow, the stinging heat returned almost immediately. He put his hand back under the tap and left it there while he decided what to do about Carol.

She was unpredictable, hostile, violent. Which might be tolerable if he was getting a fuck every now and then. But she wasn't giving out so much as a sniff. In bed, on that solitary occasion, she'd slept on her own side, not touching him, as if she was another bloke forced through circumstances to share his bed.

He ought to tell her it was over. Soon. Come to think of it, why hang about? He'd tell her right now, right this minute, before he changed his mind. *I'm not interested, Carol. You're fucking crazy.*

He turned off the tap and tried to dry his hand with the dishtowel. His scorched skin complained when he put pressure on it.

He threw the towel on the counter and flexed his fingers. *It's over. I've taken all the shit I can take from you. Look what you've done to my hand. Look at it. It's over. No, don't argue. It's over.*

"How's your hand?" She had crept up behind him. She wrapped her arms around his waist and her interlocked blue-nailed fingers hovered millimetres above his groin.

"Hurts like a mother."

"Let me put some cream on it."

"There's something—"

"The way I feel about you..." She unlocked her fingers and pulled on his arm. When he faced her he saw her eyes had misted over. "Sometimes it scares me." She held his wounded hand in hers. "Sometimes I lash out without thinking." She raised his hand to her lips and kissed the place where she'd burned him. "Forgive me?"

Eddie blinked. The heat of her lips had intensified the ache in his hand. It was exquisite. He wrapped her in his arms and held her against his chest.

She snuggled into his neck, lips brushing his throat. She said, "I think Robin knows about us."

10:06 AM

*P*earce said, "Well?"

"Joe-Bob says it'll be no problem getting the ammo. Unless he phones back to say otherwise, we're meeting him at lunchtime."

"We?"

"He knows me. He wants me to go along."

"Fair enough. But why does it have to be Joe-Bob?" Pearce said. "What about Ben?"

"You got a problem with Joe-Bob?"

"I've always had a problem with drug dealers."

"Tough. Ben can't make it." Ailsa studied the back of her hand. "He's not feeling so good. Last night somebody decided to bounce his head off a metal pipe." She turned her hand over and examined the lines on her palm. "So it's Joe-Bob or nobody."

10:18 AM

*P*earce was about to head for Cooper's flat when his mobile rang. Instinctively he thought, *Mum*. Then he remembered she was gone, stabbed by the fuck in the balaclava. He squeezed his fist, felt her blood running through his fingers and propped his elbows on the kitchen table, trying to stop shaking inside.

Ailsa passed the phone to him.

He clutched it too hard. "Hello."

Silence.

"Hello". No answer. He didn't play this game. He hung up. Ailsa was looking at him. He shrugged. The phone rang again. "Speak," he said.

"Don't hang up."

Something sharp and thin and white-hot stabbed his gut.

"It's me. Julie."

The bitch who had set him up. The bitch who had walked away with an engagement ring worth a grand. More than that, though. She'd walked away with his pride. He said nothing. The searing pain in his stomach was incredible.

"Pearce? You there?" She sighed. "Look, I just wanted to, um... Look, I heard on the radio, you know, about your mum. I just kind of, well, in the circumstances—"

Ailsa mouthed, "Who?"

He breathed through pursed lips. "Little bitch who robbed me," he said.

"Why did she do that?"

He breathed in. "She's a worthless piece of shit."

"Pearce, you arsehole, I'm trying to—"

"Shut your mouth."

"Who are you talking to?"

"Not you, Ailsa, sorry."

"Who's Ailsa?"

"A friend. You want to speak to her?"

He handed Ailsa the phone, then paced up and down the kitchen while Ailsa and Julie introduced themselves to each other. Gradually his stomach settled. Ailsa wasn't saying much, just listening, occasionally frowning, nodding, shaking her head. He stopped at the table and held his hand out for the phone. Without a word, Ailsa handed the phone back to him.

Julie was saying, "—'cos, as I said, I doubt if the dumb bastard could get it up anyway."

"Stop it," he said. "Don't you ever—"

"Oh, you again. Limp dick."

"Fuck you."

"You wish."

"Where's my money?"

"For God's sake, Pearce, give it a rest. You'll never see your money again. I've got it. Well, actually, I've spent most of it already. You gave me the receipt, Dickhead. You want to know what I've bought?"

"You didn't have to do that."

"Do you? Huh? Want to know what pressies I've bought myself?"

The pain lanced his gut once again. He screamed into the phone, "My mother is dead and you're still alive, you fucking bitch, you fucking crap fucking piece of shit. It can't be like this. It can *not* be like this."

"I didn't fucking kill her. Don't blame me."

Ailsa plucked the phone out of his hand and spoke into the mouthpiece. "Leave him alone." She turned the phone off and laid it on the table. "Pearce?"

"Shit." He rubbed his forehead with the back of his hand.

She waited a moment before asking, "Who was that fucking piece of bitch-piss-fuck-crap-shit, or whatever it was you called her?"

He shook his head. "A mistake."

"There been many of them?"

He said, "Not recently," and sank into the nearest chair. He let his head drop. A slow throb had replaced the jabbing pain in his stomach. "Mum was fond of reminding me I was a useless great pillock." His eyes stung and his head pounded and he needed some rest. He massaged his temples. "Where Julie was concerned, Mum was absolutely right."

He felt Ailsa's warm hand on his arm, just below his wrist. "You want to go to bed?" she asked him.

His throat was dry and his voice cracked when he said, "There's no time."

She stared at him. After a while she moved her hand from his wrist. She crossed her arms, resting her hands on her biceps. "I meant—"

"I know what you meant." He pushed the base of his mobile with his finger. It swivelled. He pushed harder and the phone turned full circle. He rotated it the other way. When he looked up she was still staring at him. He glanced back at the phone and traced the crack in the case with his fingernail. "There's a lot to do," he added.

"Sure."

"I've got to get Cooper's money to him."

"Yeah."

"Before our lunch appointment with Joe-Bob."

"Aha." She placed her elbows on the table and leaned forward, supporting her chin in her cupped hands. "You should have a nap. You look exhausted."

"I don't nap."

She sat up. "Sleep, then."

"When I'm asleep," he said, "I stay asleep. Nothing wakes me."

"I'll wake you."

He looked at his watch. "I've got to get moving." He made for the door.

"You want to take the gun?"

He turned. "No point. Got no bullets until this afternoon. You keep it safe for me." He took another couple of steps towards the door.

"Pearce?"

He stopped. This time he stayed facing the doorway, one hand resting on the handle. "What?"

"Do you think Pete Thompson's really gone for good?"

He took his hand off the handle. "You still worried?"

"When you're here I feel okay. But I know the minute you walk out the door I'll begin to have doubts."

"I'm pretty sure he got the message," Pearce said. "But I'll go see him again if you want. Just to make sure."

10:36 AM

*H*e ambled down the path towards the red door, hands thrust in his coat pockets, looking, to any casual observer, perfectly relaxed.

The entry buzzers were arranged in two rows of six. Taking his right hand out of his pocket, he pressed the buzzer that said SOUTAR.

"Is that you?" The voice sounded familiar, but it was badly distorted by the phone speaker. He waited. After a while the buzzer sounded and he pushed the door open. He stepped inside and watched the door swing shut behind him.

The walls in the communal staircase were shit-brown in the dim light. An overpowering smell of ammonia hung in the air. He started up the stone steps. They were damp. A mop in a bucket rested against the wall on the first floor landing. A bike was chained to the railing. On the second floor the light was a little better. Looking at the roof he could just make out a small oval skylight. The smell didn't seem so strong now. Or maybe he'd just grown used to it.

He stopped outside E. Soutar's door. The brass nameplate gleamed in a rare shaft of sunlight. Anticipation made him bite his lip. He slipped off his gloves and crammed them in his pocket. He rang the bell.

Seconds later the door opened.

"Where's the money?" The man who asked the question was blonde, in his late twenties. The collar of his white shirt was open and his sleeves were rolled up. His left hand was bandaged. His mouth stayed open after he'd finished speaking.

"Mr Soutar?" There was something familiar about him. "Is— I've come about—is, is Robin here?"

"Robin?" She appeared behind Soutar.

"I'm looking for Robin Greaves."

"Don't fuck about. Where's the money?"

He looked at Soutar. He looked five or six years older when he narrowed his pale blue eyes. "What money?"

"Oh, shit," the girl said. "Oh, shit. Oh, fucking shit. What's your name?"

"Don," he said and smiled.

"Oh, Jesus fucking Christ! This is just what we need."

"Shut up, Eddie."

"What the fuck are we going to do now?"

"Shut up, Eddie. I'm trying to think."

"He's fucking flipped again, Carol, hasn't he?"

"Shut the fuck up, will you? You're not helping."

"You want me to go?" Don asked. "If now isn't a convenient time…"

Carol shook her head. "Where's the money, Don?"

He shrugged. This persistent questioning was becoming irritating. "I don't want to answer any more questions. I'll leave now."

"Stay."

"Maybe another time."

She said, "Don't let him go, Eddie."

It happened so quickly Don didn't have time to react. Somehow Eddie was behind him, arm around his throat, and Don's wrist was locked behind his back. The door slammed shut. Carol ran ahead into the sitting room. Don flapped his free hand at the forearm slowly choking him. Eddie pushed Don's arm further up his back. The bandaged hand didn't seem to be much of an impediment to him. Eddie's hot breath tickled the back of Don's neck.

"This is very fucking bad timing," Eddie said, leaning against him.

Through the open door Don could see that Carol was now posing by the window, hands on hips, face expressionless as Eddie escorted him towards her. Casually she tapped a cigarette out of a packet on the window ledge. She lit it and sucked in the escaping cloud of smoke as it was about to drift out of her mouth.

She was small and pale-skinned and the way she smoked excited him. He knew just by looking at her that she was someone he could fall in love with.

Eddie shoved him. He fell, landing at her feet.

"What are we going to do with you?" she said.

"You know how to handle this?" Eddie said. "I certainly fucking don't."

Don raised himself into a seating position. "I don't know anything about any money."

"Shut up."

"Yeah, shut up."

Don rubbed his wrist. "Whatever you say, guys."

She took a step away from him into the centre of the room. She bent down, picked up a dark blue handbag off the floor and set it on the coffee table. "You're Donald, huh?"

"You can call me Don if you like."

Eddie stuck his hands behind his back and wriggled like a man with a terrible itch. His face contorted. His teeth were crooked and he had a slight overbite. When his hands reappeared one of them was holding a gun. He pointed it at Don. "Your name's Robin, you fucking lunatic." The gun shook dangerously.

Sweat trickled down Don's back, irritating his skin. This Eddie character had problems.

Carol said, "You can put your hands down."

Don put his hands palms down on the floor on either side of him.

"Ask him about the money, Eddie?"

"Why me?"

"Give you something to focus on. Keep your finger off the trigger."

"Don't tempt me," Eddie said. "Where's the money, Don?"

"I don't know anything about any money. How many times do I have to tell you?"

Carol said, "Of course you know where the money is. Think. Where did Robin put the money?"

Don said, "For heaven's sake—"

Eddie waved the gun at him and yelled, "Where is it?"

"I don't know." And suddenly he remembered why he was here.

"I came to ask Ms Wren here about her experiences with certain prescribed pharmaceuticals."

"Is that right?" Eddie said. "I thought you were looking for Robin."

"I was. They're married, aren't they?"

"Don't get fucking smart. Can't you do anything, Carol?"

"It's hopeless," she told Eddie.

"Try. Maybe you can find a crack."

She asked Don, "Why me? Why Robin?"

"You're on our company's list."

"How did you get our names?"

"Royal Midlothian Hospital. From the time you were admitted for treatment. Don't worry. The information's confidential."

"How did you find me?"

"I spoke to Robin yesterday. He said you'd both be here."

Eddie was chewing his lower lip. He stopped for a moment to ask, "What pharmaceuticals?"

Don tried to remember their names. He saw the bottles in his hand, clearly enough to read the labels. "Sulpiride. Mellaril. We're studying what we call paradoxical side effects."

Eddie said, "What's that?"

"It's what we call it when a drug does the opposite of what it's designed for."

Carol said, "I don't think this is leading anywhere."

Eddie lowered his gun-arm. "Fear might snap him out of it." He raised the gun again and said, "Talk."

"I don't know what you want me to say," Don said. "I've already explained."

Carol said, "Please tell us."

Don looked at her. "I know nothing about any bloody money." He started to hunt for his wallet. "Let me show you my business card."

Eddie rolled his head back and said, "Fuck. You'd swear he was genuine, Carol."

"He is," Carol said. "Absolutely."

Eddie tried again. "Is the money in your car?"

The persistent bastard wasn't going to give up. "You think I'm stupid, Eddie?" Don was fed up with this. He decided to give Eddie something to think about. "I left the money at home."

"I told you you should have brought it, Carol." Eddie took a step towards Don and offered him the gun. "You shouldn't have let it out of your sight."

"He was fine earlier."

Don stopped fiddling in his pockets. Was the gun some kind of peace offering? Maybe Eddie was letting Don see that the gun wasn't loaded, his way of indicating that Don was never in any real danger. It was all a game. Eddie rotated the weapon one hundred and eighty degrees and held it by the barrel. Eddie raised his arm. Don shivered as a more realistic interpretation of his plight flashed into his mind. Eddie wasn't offering him the gun after all. He groped for the gun with his outstretched hand, but he was too late. The butt struck his skull half-an-inch to the left of his crown. His vision turned red, then purple. His ears roared and he grunted. The second blow hit him further forward. The front of his head exploded with white light. He fell forward and the last thing he remembered was the salt taste of the floor.

10:40 AM

*R*ows of elegant Georgian town houses, or tenements masquerading as town houses, built to a gridiron plan, the New Town lay in the shade of the Old Town to the north of Princes Street Gardens. You'd think you couldn't get lost, but the first time Pearce had tried to find South Broughton Place he ended up having to phone Cooper for directions. The street was missing from his city centre map.

"It's kind of an extension of Union Street," he remembered Cooper saying. "Should rename it Cooper Street, really. I own three-fifths of it. Not a big street, I suppose. But still. Sixty per cent of even a small street, property prices in the New Town being what they are, that's a fair wee whack of dosh." He paused, waiting for Pearce to request specifics. Since Pearce had no interest in the loan shark's personal fortune, he said nothing. Undaunted,

Cooper said, "Millions, if you must know, son. Millions."

Pearce came to the bottom of the hill. It levelled out and the road widened. South Broughton Place was on the left. The doors were numbered one to five.

An elderly man, armed with a pair of shears, stood at the end of his garden and nodded as Pearce walked by. Two doors along, Pearce opened the gate, strolled past a weed-choked flowerbed and approached a silver-grey sandstone building. He checked Thompson's cash was still in his pocket before pressing the buzzer.

The money was an excuse. What he'd really come for was information.

Cooper's voice said, "What?"

"Pearce."

A pause. "Can't say I expected to see you. But come on up."

The door buzzed. Pearce shoved it open and walked inside.

Cooper lived at the rear of the ground floor. The silver nameplate on his door was the size of a laptop computer. Pearce was about to knock when he noticed the door was slightly ajar. He pushed it fully open, poked his head inside and said, "Hello." When nobody answered, he stepped inside and closed the door behind him. He looked along the corridor. Somewhere in the flat someone was singing. A kid's song. Tuneful enough, if a bit throaty. He said, "Mr Cooper." No reply. He headed towards the singing and found the loan shark in a child's bedroom. Pearce tapped on the door.

Cooper looked up and his mouth snapped shut.

"The door was open," Pearce said.

"Left it for you." Cooper's hair was tousled and stubble peppered his chin. A baby nestled in the crook of his arm, its eyes closed. He saw Pearce looking at the baby and said, "Sally's out."

Pearce had never heard of Sally. "Sorry I missed her."

"You know her?"

"Never had the pleasure."

"Probably the only bloke who hasn't." Cooper muttered something that Pearce didn't catch.

"What was that?"

"Sixteen." Cooper dragged his slippered feet across the carpet. "Wee slag." He sat down on the end of the bed. "Thinks she knows it all." His eyes lit up. "Suppose we all do at that age, eh?"

Pearce leaned his shoulder against a mahogany wardrobe. "I never realised you had a daughter."

"I don't." Cooper scowled. "Sally is this little bastard's mother." He inclined the baby slightly towards Pearce. "My son." He rocked his son in his arms. "Gary."

"I kind of put my foot in it there."

Cooper screwed his face up and made a dismissive gesture with one of his hands. "Who gives a shit? You ever feel old, Pearce?"

Pearce rubbed the back of his hand over his cheek. "Sometimes."

"You ever fucked a sixteen year old?"

"Not since I was fifteen."

"Skin's tight as a drum. Amazing. And that's not all that's tight. Different now she's had him, though."

"Is that right?"

"You want my advice? It isn't worth it. Makes you feel ancient."

"Thanks for the tip."

"Skin's like—"

"How old's Gary?"

"Huh?" Cooper's forehead creased. "Nearly four months."

"He's quiet." Pearce shifted his weight from one foot to the other, moved his shoulder away from the wardrobe and leaned back against the wall.

"He's asleep now." Cooper shuffled towards the crib snuggled in the corner of the room. He pulled the blanket over his son and tucked in the baby's arms. "I want the best for him. That's why I gave him a famous name." He kissed Gary's forehead. "Gary Cooper. Give him a head start, eh?"

Pearce said, "You never mentioned him before."

"Don't like to publicise it." Cooper moved towards the door. "Fatherhood's for pansies, isn't it?"

Pearce didn't comment. You couldn't argue with that kind of reasoning. He followed Cooper down the corridor and into the sitting room.

Cooper said, "Drink?"

Pearce shook his head.

"What can I do for you?" Cooper pointed to a huge settee wrapped in several lurid throws.

Pearce assumed the extended finger was an invitation to sit down. He took the roll of notes out of his back pocket and sat down. "Got some money for you."

"You astonish me."

Pearce fanned the money. "Why?"

"Your mother passed away last night and yet here you are with my money," Cooper said. "That's professionalism. I admire that."

"You heard, then?"

"I hear everything. You know that." The olive-green leather chair hissed when he sat down. "Get much?"

"It's not all for you."

"Never is. Sad fact of life, that."

Pearce counted three hundred and laid the bills on the glass coffee table in front of him. "Ailsa Lillie. Paid in full." He thought of the old man with the socks. The old man his mum had once fancied. "Cant," he said. He counted out Cant's debt. "Paid in full." He still had plenty left to pay Joe-Bob for the ammo. Cooper hadn't moved. Pearce said, "You want to count it?"

"You think I don't trust you?" Cooper arched his leg over the arm of the chair. His slipper dangled from his foot. "You did a good day's work."

"Don't forget my commission."

"What's that? A hundred and sixty? You've still got a way to go."

"I'll pay it all back." Pearce slid what was left of the money back in his pocket.

"I don't doubt it."

"Mr Cooper." Pearce made a fist with his right hand and squeezed. "I need to ask a favour."

Cooper grinned. "You want to borrow some more?"

"Nothing like that."

"Well, what?"

"I know you keep your ear to the ground." Pearce swallowed. "Nothing much happens that you don't know about." He squeezed his fist tighter. "Have you heard anything, anything at all, about who might have killed my mum?"

"I wish." Cooper looked at the ceiling. "I really wish I could help. But you might as well ask me for the Queen's bra size." Cooper grabbed Pearce's eyes with his own. "Tell you what I think?"

Pearce didn't trust himself to speak. He nodded.

"It's a new outfit. This gang hasn't worked in Edinburgh before. At least, not before the current pair of robberies." His foot made circling motions, then started bobbing up and down. "It hasn't worked in Glasgow, Liverpool, Manchester or Newcastle either. If it had, I'd know. None of the gang socialises with any of my acquaintances." His foot stopped moving. "Even the police don't have a clue where to start looking."

Pearce plucked some red fluff off one of the throws. "What are you saying?"

"You won't find him."

Pearce rolled the fluff between his fingers. "Will you at least let me know if you hear anything?"

"Of course," Cooper said. "Tell you what, why don't you take a few days off, eh?" He moved his leg from the arm of the chair and planted it on the carpet. "You're probably a bit upset. And there'll be the funeral and all that." He stood. "What do you say, son?"

For a moment Pearce studied the ball of fluff balanced on his index finger. He flicked it into the air with his thumb. It landed on the other side of the table. "That's kind of you." He got to his feet.

"Sure you won't stay for a quick drink?"

Pearce said, "I have an appointment at a massage parlour."

10:42 AM

"*H*e's inside." From his car, Kennedy had watched Robin Greaves cross the road and walk up the path to the red door.

Edward Soutar had left through the same door a couple of minutes ago. "Want me to wait?"

"Yeah. Phone me again when he—"

"Hang on. We need to talk."

Kennedy could hear his boss clearing his throat. "What about?"

"You know."

"If I knew I wouldn't ask."

"Pish." Kennedy made a smacking sound with his lips. "Right. I'll start. Why haven't we contacted the police?"

Kennedy's boss said nothing for a while. "Should we be having this conversation over the phone?"

Kennedy tapped the fingers of his left hand on the steering wheel. "Want me to return to the office?"

"Stay where you are."

"Answer my question."

"Look, it's none of your business."

"You've made it yours, though."

"What's that supposed to mean?"

"You gave that bloke—what's his name?—the one whose mother got knifed?"

"How would I know?"

"It was in the paper. Pears? Preece?"

"Pearce."

"That's right. Gordon Pearce. Coming back to you now?"

"I'm busy, Kennedy. Where are you going with this?"

"You gave him your card."

"So what?"

"What reason could you possibly have for giving him your card?"

"I don't have to answer this."

"So it's okay with you if I call the police and tell them that we have some excellent information on the post office robbery gang?"

"They won't thank you. Anyway, it has nothing to do with you."

"Then what am I doing tailing Robin Greaves? Why am

I watching Soutar's flat? And why did you give Pearce your card?"

"I don't pay you to ask questions."

"You don't pay me at all. When was the last time? Let's see. Two months ago."

"I pay you to follow orders."

"You can take your orders, wrap them in shiny reindeer Christmas paper and shove them up your hairy—"

"You're so close to getting fired. You don't know how close, Kennedy, but if you were any closer you'd be—"

"Fine." Kennedy's heart was thumping. He hung up. He let out a long breath and waited. When the phone rang a few seconds later, he said, "I find what you're proposing morally repugnant and I feel it's my civic duty to inform the authorities of your intentions."

"You wouldn't."

"Try me."

"Tell them. You don't know what I'm proposing."

Kennedy said, "Pearce is going to get in touch with you. If he doesn't, I guess you'll get in touch with him. Shouldn't be too hard for someone in our line of work." His boss was silent at the other end of the phone. "Either way, you're going to let Pearce know that you have the name of his mother's killer. How am I doing so far?"

"You can't prove anything."

"I don't need to. Just by telling the police, I'll ruin your plan."

"Go on. What's my plan?"

"To sell Pearce the information."

"The man's fresh out of prison. It says so in today's *Scotsman*, even if it doesn't mention what he was in for. He doesn't have a job. He doesn't have any money."

"Interesting you remembered that snippet of useless information but you couldn't remember his name."

"Some things stick."

"They do, don't they?"

"Don't say it."

"Will I carry on, then?"

"This is ridiculous. Okay, I'll play. How's Pearce going to pay?"

"Setting aside the fact that Mr Pearce might have come into an inheritance, there's also the issue of the stolen money."

"Are you suggesting—"

"Absolutely." Kennedy's throat tightened but he managed to keep his tone level. "In return for Greaves's name and address Mr Pearce is going to locate the loot and hand it over to you."

His boss laughed. It sounded forced. "Supposing—for argument's sake—supposing he agreed. Why would I do this? I don't need the money."

"On the contrary. You desperately need the money."

"The business is doing well."

"The business is fucked and you know it. If the business is doing well, why didn't you pay me last month?"

"A temporary cash flow problem. I told you."

"Temporary, my arse. What about the drinks machine? Why's that gone? Suppose that's temporary, too?"

"You wouldn't go to the police, would you?"

Kennedy didn't reply.

"Okay. Shit. How deep is your moral repugnance?"

"Make me an offer."

"Twenty percent."

"Deeper than that."

"Thirty."

"Still wracked with guilt."

"Forty?"

"Keep going."

"Forty-five?"

"Come on, you can do it."

"Fifty, you bastard."

"Now I feel a wave of peace washing over me. Fifty percent, I can live with."

"You bastard."

"You told me that already. One more thing."

"You bastard."

"I want to be there when you meet him."

"What the fuck for?"

"We've agreed on a fifty-fifty split, yeah?"

"Yeah."

"Well, I'd like to know how much I'm getting fifty percent of."

10:44 AM

"*Y*ou're back." Carol moved away from the window. Faint birdsong drifted up from the garden below.

Robin was disorientated. He had fallen asleep and woken up with a terrible headache. "Where's Eddie?"

She described the sequence of events from the moment Don had arrived to the point where Eddie struck Don with his gun butt.

Robin put his hand to his head and wished he hadn't.

"Eddie took your keys. Went to see if you'd left the money at home." She sat down on the couch and took out her cigarettes. She offered one to Robin and he accepted. She lit it, then lit her own.

Robin said, "So Eddie just left you here on your own?"

"Technically, he left me here with Don."

"You felt safe with Don?"

"Don was out cold."

"Not for too long."

"Eddie left me the gun."

"Where is it?"

"Secret." She formed a gun with her fingers and aimed it at Robin. "I promised Eddie I wouldn't play with it. Unless I had to. Bang, bang." She blew on her fingertips. "'Bye, 'bye, Don."

Robin muttered, "I can't believe Eddie left you on your own. Does he know how dangerous Don is?"

"He didn't want to." She put her hand on Robin's leg. "I had to persuade him."

"Excuse me," Robin said, tapping his fingers on the back of her hand. "I need you to let me go to the loo."

"Robin." She fetched an ashtray and sat down again, putting her hand back on his leg. "Do you have any idea what's happening to you?"

His resolve almost disappeared. His thigh glowed under the warmth of her hand. *She is on top of him, lust contorting her flushed face. Sweat trickles between her naked breasts. She moans as he slides inside her. Her mouth twists in a sneer and she cries, "Eddie."*

"Got to go," he said, getting to his feet. She didn't stop him.

He closed the sitting room door, walked to the bathroom, opened the door, gently closed it again and crept to the bedroom. He eased the door open. Some of Eddie's clothes hung over the back of a chair. A pair of black trousers, a white shirt, a sock. He tiptoed over to the bed. A nightdress lay on top of the quilt. Robin picked it up. He didn't recognize it. It smelled freshly laundered, but it didn't smell of Carol at all. He pulled back the quilt and looked for stains. White sheets. It was hard to tell. He let the quilt fall back. Only one pillow was indented. Over by the little sink a glass propped up two toothbrushes. One blue, one purple.

He bent over and sniffed each pillow in turn. He folded the nightdress and placed it on top of the pillow on the left. He thought he detected the slightest trace of White Musk. His face was wet. He moved to the dresser. On top of it, in a bowl cluttered with feminine paraphernalia, was a photo of Carol in her late teens, wearing a low-cut black dress, black sunglasses, large gold hoops in her ears, short unpainted fingernails, unsmiling. He wondered who had taken the picture. He turned it face down on the dresser. An adjustable oval mirror on a wooden base reflected part of the bed, a night table, Eddie's trousers, Eddie's jacket, Eddie's sock, a chair with the sleeve of Eddie's shirt dangling over its back.

The short scissor blades cut slowly through the cotton. The repetitive opening and closing action of fingers and thumb caused a dull ache in his fingers. By the time he'd finished, his hand was throbbing and the pain was making him angry. He placed the scissors back in the bowl. With stiff fingers, he tied a knot in the severed shirtsleeve. When he pulled the ends tight, the fabric felt strong. He relaxed, snapped his wrists, relaxed, snapped his wrists. He imagined standing behind her, the shirtsleeve wrapped around her neck, the knot crushing her windpipe. He imagined hearing her cough and splutter, stumbling backwards as she gasped for air. He wiped his face on the cuff of Eddie's sleeve, rolled it up and stuffed it in his pocket.

He needn't have bothered.

When he returned to the sitting room, she was standing in the alcove gazing out of the bay window at the tenement block opposite. She had put on a CD. She behaved as if she lived here. Her head was lowered and her hips were rolling with the music. Louis Jordan was singing "There Ain't Nobody Here But Us Chickens."

Robin fumbled for the strip of cloth in his pocket. Sweat on his forehead gathered and cooled and began to itch as he edged past the bookcase, past the spot where Don's unconscious body must have fallen, beyond the part of the floor covered by the rug and onto bare floorboards that creaked the moment he set foot on them.

Still she didn't hear him. Her head stayed down, slowly moving from side to side as she listened to the music.

He shifted his weight and shuffled a step forward, wrapping an end of the sleeve around the knuckles of each hand. Another step. The cotton was stretched tight enough to trampoline a bullet. He couldn't do this. He couldn't bring himself to kill her. She was no more than four feet away now, the hem of her skirt rising on the right as her left knee bent. He inched closer, the ringing in his ears drowning out the song on the stereo. Closer. Still closer. He could feel the heat of her body.

His heart hammered in his chest. He heard this morning's newsreader saying, "...has died." *Has died.*

Robin looped the makeshift ligature around her neck. The instant Eddie's sleeve touched her, she yelled. Instinct launched her forward, away from her attacker. A waft of White Musk haemorrhaged from her skin.

She croaked, "Robin." She lurched forward, one foot dangling in midair as he held her back. "Help. *Robin.*"

He slid the cuff end of the sleeve over the shoulder and pulled it through the gap underneath, as if he was tying a shoelace. She cried out. He pulled both ends until the muscles in his arms burned. He dragged her back towards him, fingers whitening as they gripped the fabric. The pain in his right wrist flared and he struggled to hold on.

"I know about you and Eddie," he said in her ear. For a moment she was still. Then a quiet growl came from her throat and she lunged forward. Quickly, he changed his grip. The pain eased momentarily. "Please be still," he said as he crushed her throat. The pain flooded back and his vision blurred as tears welled in his eyes.

She struggled for a while longer, silent now, her cries choked off. Eventually she sank to her knees.

He pulled harder, crying out as pain tore at his fingers. Her hands clutched feebly at her throat and he jerked his wrists sideways, again and again, until her hands fell away. He yelled as he made one final effort to force her to be still. Her arms jiggled puppet-like by her sides. He held on. In his right arm every muscle, every sinew, every tendon was on fire. Still he held on. Her arms stopped moving. He waited. Longer. Finally he let go. Her head cracked off the floor when she fell forward.

At last she was still. It was over.

He stumbled towards the CD player, his legs barely supporting him, and turned it off. In the silence he said, "What have I done?"

Nobody answered.

Robin sat on the floor, massaging his fingers. He stared at the body. There was something he had to do now, but for the moment he'd forgotten what it was. After a while, he stopped rubbing his fingers. It was doing no good. He dragged himself towards her, stretched out his hand and touched the back of her knee. His hand slid up her leg and his fingers stroked the bare flesh of her thigh. She was cold. Her skin felt like wet clay. Standing up, he placed one foot either side of her and wriggled his hands underneath her stomach. My God, she was heavy. It was as if somebody had filled her tiny frame with cement. Because of his sore hand, he had to bear most of the weight with just his left. Breathing hard, using his right hand as a guide, he rolled her onto her back.

Her forehead had hit the floor hard. Around the left temple and under the eyebrow a swelling had already begun. A canopy over her closed eye. Blood had congealed in her left nostril and the tip of her tongue protruded through pale blue lips.

Strangling her was the easy part.

He tugged the blouse out of her skirt and started to undo the buttons. His fingertips tingled, as if his hand had been immersed wrist deep in snow and was now warming up. He tore at her blouse. Buttons leaped onto the rug and spun on the floorboards. Auburn down coated her pale stomach. He brushed the fine hairs, fingertips prickling, then reached into his pocket and dug out his knife.

He made a tiny incision above her naval, blanking out the pain in his fingers as he forced the blade into her skin. He cut her again. A trickle of blood. No more than a scratch. Once more. Not deep. A thin dark wavy line.

His hand was shaking uncontrollably. The knife fell from his grasp. Bending over her stomach he pressed his lips to the first of the three cuts. His tears dripped onto her belly. It was vital that he finish what he'd begun. He stared at his hands, scrutinising his long, thin pianist's fingers. He couldn't do it. These useless hands that strangled her were not prepared to mutilate her body.

He pulled the blouse over her stomach. The police could work this one out any way they liked. *She's dead. Carol is dead. Do you hear me?* The voice screamed at him: *Your wife is dead. What have you done?* When he looked across at her, he thought he saw her stomach rise under the loose blouse. It was happening again. Fear grabbed hold of him. He started to choke on the smell of Hilda Pearce's perfume. Leeches clung to the insides of his lungs. He ran towards the door. He had to get out. Now.

He didn't quite make it.

10:53 AM

So Cooper wasn't likely to be much help. At any rate, if he knew anything he wasn't admitting it. Still, Pearce wasn't too concerned. Not yet. You didn't spend ten years in Barlinnie without making a few useful contacts. After he'd checked on Pete Thompson he'd get in touch with J-Laing or Big Dunc McNeil. If there was anything those two didn't know about Edinburgh's underworld, it very likely hadn't happened yet.

Shortarse looked as out of place behind the reception desk in the massage parlour as he had the first time round. The little man gave Pearce his best sneer and said, "You again."

Pearce walked straight past him.

"Hey!" Shortarse scrabbled out of his seat. "Hey! Where you going?" Dumpy hands reached for the telephone.

Pearce strode down the corridor and opened the door to Thompson's office.

"Stop." Shortarse sprinted towards him and grabbed his arm. Pearce swung round, fist clenched. The little man let go of his arm and took a step back. "Hey," he said, the muscles in his cheek twitching.

Wearing the same suit as yesterday, Tony was sitting behind Thompson's desk. Ankles crossed, the heel of one polished shoe scuffed the surface of the desk as his leg bent slightly. A bunch of papers sat next to the phone. He spoke into the receiver: "Yeah, I've got to go." He raised his left hand and beckoned Pearce over. "Speak to you later," he said, placing the handset in its cradle.

Pearce approached the desk. Shortarse trailed behind, complaining to Tony. "He barged right past me. I told him to stop."

Pearce glanced at the bank of monitors. Their blank screens indicated that somebody had forgotten to switch them on. Or that somebody had decided to switch them off. He wondered if the girls knew they were no longer under surveillance. Swapping sexual favours for money had to be hard enough without knowing you were being watched. Then again, maybe they found some comfort in the fact that their every move was being monitored. Maybe they'd feel insecure if they knew no one was keeping an eye on them. Or maybe their lives were so sad they didn't give a shit either way.

Reflected in one of the light grey screens, Pearce saw Tony fold his arms.

"It's okay," Tony said to Shortarse. Tony's jacket looked a couple of sizes too small for him. It would have fitted nicely when he was fourteen.

"He wouldn't listen." The little man nodded like a wind-up toy. "I told him to stop."

"It's okay."

"It's not okay. Look what he did to Mr Thompson." Shortarse looked at Pearce, his finger jabbing the air. "You—" His bloodless lips formed a puckered O.

Pearce faced him and said, "Fuck off."

The little man's hand dropped to his side. He was breathing fast, head still bobbing up and down. He looked at Tony. Tony leaned back in Pete Thompson's chair and looked straight back at Shortarse. Shortarse looked at Pearce. Pearce looked at Tony and grinned. Tony grinned back. Shortarse turned and marched out the door. He slammed it shut behind him.

Pearce said, "Morning."

Tony swung his legs off the desk. "Grab a chair." The palm of his right hand drew circles on his left.

Pearce sat down, saying nothing.

Tony clapped his hands once, held his hands together, then released them. After a moment he formed a fist with his right hand and began rubbing his knuckles against the palm of his left. "What can I do for you?"

"Where's your boss?"

Tony said, "Read about your mother in the paper." He looked up. "I'm sorry."

"Thanks," Pearce said. "Where is he?"

Slowly, Tony stood up. "Mr Thompson decided to quit."

"Leave the business?"

"Yeah." Tony picked a biro off the desk and pulled the top off it.

"You want to elaborate?"

Tony shrugged.

"It just doesn't seem likely."

Tony said, "No?" He put the top back on the pen and dropped it on the desk.

"I wouldn't have said so."

Tony hunched his shoulders and breathed out. "I suppose it's fair to say that he required a little bit of persuasion."

"From you?"

"I did sort of steer him in the right direction. Last night. Helped him see how things stood." Tony kicked his chair out from the desk and sat down again. "You might have done enough. I don't know. I had to be sure."

"You sure now?"

"Yeah." Tony looked at his knuckles, then back at Pearce. "Mr Thompson's grown tired of Edinburgh. He's developed a profound desire to travel. Tonight I'm helping him pack."

"Where's he going?"

Tony picked up the biro again and grabbed a piece of paper from the pile sitting next to the phone. "He hadn't made up his mind when I left. But he knows the score."

Pearce raised his eyebrows.

"He can go anywhere he wants." Tony started doodling on the paper. "As long as it's outside a thirty mile radius of Edinburgh."

Pearce said, "What about his flat?"

"Not a problem. He rents."

"And his job?"

"He resigned due to ill health." Tony tugged the lapel of his jacket. "You're talking to the Acting Manager." He pulled at his sleeve. "Until further notice."

"Congratulations." Pearce stood.

"Thing is," Tony said, balling his fist and coughing into it. "I hate to bring this up. But, the way it is, you see, he doesn't have any money, so I've had to lend him some."

"How come?"

"You nicked it."

"You saying a man like Thompson doesn't have any spare cash?"

"I didn't believe him either. But he insisted. Matter of salvaging some pride, I think. I gave him a hundred just to get him to piss off."

"Fair enough," Pearce said. "Split it, then, if you're okay with fifty."

"Fine with me."

Pearce reached into his back pocket.

Tony changed the subject. "How's Ailsa?"

"Good."

"And Becky?"

"Better." Pearce felt awkward all of a sudden.

"Good kid."

"Haven't met her yet. She's in Glasgow. At her aunt's."

"Oh, right. Well." Tony spread his fingers.

As Pearce pulled the cash out of his jeans, he dislodged something from his pocket. He tried to grab it as it fell to the floor. He missed. He bent down and picked up the business card the man with the bandaged nose had given him yesterday outside the post office. The card had fallen face down. Written on the back in blue ink were four words that sent Pearce's pulse racing. His head felt light and for a moment he thought he might faint. He leaned on the desk. Did the note mean what he thought it meant? He steadied himself and read it again. It couldn't mean anything else. It could only refer to his mother's killer. The man with the bandaged nose had written: *I KNOW HIS NAME.*

10:55 AM

Climbing through blackness. Slipping back down. Slipping...

Where am I? Okay. Think. Heaven's sake. Sore hip. Lying down. Hard surface. Floor. Distant lights. Flickering. Come on. Push. Too heavy. Too dark. Slipping...

Stabbing me. Bright lights piercing me. Stabbing my brain. Losing focus. Slipping...

Music in the dark. Heavy limbs. Voices. Danger. Quiet. Stay quiet. Skull latticed with pain. Need to cry out. Mustn't. Rhythm.

Rhythm to the pain. Breathe with it. Don't move. Don't let them know I'm awake. Listen to the singing. Listen to the voice saying, "Help. Robin."

Eyelids. Camera shutters. Open. Snapshot. Bright, bright, bright. Close. Don't move. NO. Breathe. Again. Open. Click. Close. No Eddie. Robin isn't Eddie. Eddie isn't Robin. Robin is...Yes. A noose. Around Carol Wren's neck. Carol, the wife. Eddie, the lover. Make the connection. Got it. Got their secrets. Thanks, Robin.

He blinked again. His head felt like he'd rammed it into a brick wall, taken a step back and butted the wall again. He let his eyelids drop. Could he believe what he just saw?

More words. Something about Eddie. Pleading. Then, clearly, Robin said, "Please be still." Don opened his eyes a fraction. Robin was strangling her. Something cracked. Floorboard, kneecap, skull? Don couldn't tell. Then, panting. After a while, footsteps trailed away. The music stopped. Don's scrotum tingled. Maybe Robin was going to try to strangle him now.

Robin said, "What have I done?"

Don wanted to answer him. Muffled footsteps slithered across the floor. Back towards Don. Robin fondled Carol Wren's leg. He apologised. But for what? What he was about to do?

Nothing as straightforward as murder, apparently.

Robin stood over Carol and turned her over, grunting under the weight. He ripped her blouse open. Took a hunting knife out of a leather sheath and started cutting her stomach. *Not like that.* He was producing nothing more than scratches. The blade had to penetrate. It had to plunge in so deep that you needed both hands to carve out each stroke of the four letters. Don wanted to tell him. No, show him. Jump out and...

Don's head buzzed. Copycat. His arm twitched. This was exciting.

Robin spoiled it by collapsing on top of Carol Wren in tears.

Disappointing, Robin. Eddie would have done it. Eddie would have done it well. You could see it in his eyes when he hit me with the gun. Desire. Pleasure. He has what it takes.

Don closed his eyes as Robin swung round. Relaxed, he felt

Robin press the knife into his palm. Still relaxed, he felt Robin fold his fingers round the handle and give his hand a friendly pat. Now with the knife firmly in his grip Don considered slashing the pathetic creature's face, but Robin had already scurried away.

Thunder rumbled in Don's ears. A blanket of nausea fell over him and he sank to the floor. Hammers pounded his skull. A vice squeezed his brain. *Fuck.*

After a while, he raised himself onto his hands and knees and scrabbled over to Carol, ignoring the pain pulsing through his body like a surging electrical current. He pulled back her blouse, revealing three shallow cuts. Squiggly red lines that ran down towards her pubic hair. Robin hadn't got far with his spelling. The L was complete, albeit faint and much too small. He had carved a semi-circle of the O. The O should be a rectangle, though. An oval was too difficult to form properly at the necessary depth. Straight lines were much easier. Especially when...

Carol Wren coughed.

At first he thought he'd imagined it, but, as he stared at her, her chest bounced and she coughed again. Her whole body stiffened. She wheezed as she drew breath. Don's head cleared. He shuffled behind her and grabbed both ends of the cord still wrapped around her neck. Her eyes sprang open and she looked at him, confused and terrified, pupils darting from side to side. She opened her mouth to scream. He pulled with all his strength. Amputated her scream. She beat the floor with her heels. Kicked a shoe off. Her eyes begged him to stop.

He stopped only when the ligature had bitten so deeply into her neck that in places the white cloth was hardly visible.

Carol Wren's eyes bulged. Red-flecked. No longer begging him to stop.

Don lifted her head out of his lap. He moved his legs from under her and gently lowered her head to the floor. He stood, slid out of his coat, removed his shoes and socks. She was dead now. It was unlikely there would be much blood, but caution never hurt. He didn't want to end up walking home with blood all over his clothes. Bare feet cold on the floorboards, he stepped back onto the rug and pulled his jumper over his head. He took off his shirt and removed his trousers. Almost free. Nobody here to see his scars. He hooked his thumbs in the waistband of his underpants. Stopped. Ridiculous to think that he could strip naked. He unhooked his thumbs. Ridiculous. It didn't matter that she was dead. She was *here*.

He prised her legs apart, knelt between them and opened her blouse.

At least he could do *this*. He placed the knife over the first of Robin's marks. The blade sank into her stomach as he pressed down on the handle with both hands. He dragged the knife about three inches towards him. When he pulled the blade out, the skin instantly closed around the cut. He shoved the knife in once more and jiggled it from side to side as he slid it along the length of the incision. This time, when he removed the blade, the clean edges of the cut remained a millimetre or so apart. Satisfied, he started on the foot of the L, his mouth hanging open as he concentrated.

10:55 AM

*P*earce dialled the number on the business card as he strode along the pavement.

"Eye Witness Investigations." The voice sounded familiar. "How may I help?"

Pearce joined the queue at the bus stop. "Who is this?"

"Eye Witness Investigations. I already said."

"You the guy with the busted nose?"

There was a slight delay before the man replied, "Who am I speaking to?"

"The card," Pearce said. "You wrote on the card." Instinctively he turned it over. "You said you knew his name."

"Ah."

"Who is it?"

"Ah. Well."

"You going to tell me?"

"Well, maybe not over the phone."

Pearce glanced at the half-a-dozen bodies crowded inside the bus shelter. No one was showing an interest in his conversation and, in any case, the almost constant traffic noise at the nearby crossroads prevented him from being overhead. Still, the PI was probably right. You never knew who might be monitoring your calls.

"I'll come to your office," Pearce said. He flicked the card over and studied the address. Not far. Half an hour's walk, maybe. "Should be with you in ten, fifteen minutes." He hung up without waiting for a reply. If the appointment wasn't convenient, too bad. He'd make it convenient when he got there.

Looking along the long stretch of road leading towards Meadowbank, he saw no sign of an approaching bus. If he had to wait too long, he'd hail a taxi. No sign of a taxi either, mind you. He could always steal a car. Or a bike. He'd have to be careful not to get caught nicking it and landing back in jail, though. Jesus, what was he thinking? He couldn't take risks like that. He was tired and his thoughts were jumbled. He kept thinking of his mum, feeling her in his arms, seeing the blood leech from her body, her face pale, lips dry, her breathing shallow.

Pearce didn't believe in God. He didn't believe in eternal life. He didn't believe in immortal souls. He had nothing to help him deal with this. She was dead, like Muriel. Whatever that meant. He had no idea. Death happened to other people. He couldn't afford to dwell on this, so he flicked the switch in his head and annihilated his thoughts. He closed his eyes and saw his mother in the ambulance, a look on her face he'd never seen before and never wanted to see again, not even in his head. He opened his eyes. He'd learned enough on the inside to know that impatience only led to mistakes and regrets. Impulse criminals were the ones most easily caught and he really didn't want to get caught because if he got caught there would be nobody to avenge his mum's death and then where would he be? Nick a car? Fuck that idea.

Another flash of her face in the ambulance. He felt ice in his bones. *Do something.*

A quick check of the bus timetable told him that the number five was due in four minutes. He could wait that long. *Plan. Think ahead.*

The business card. The fact that it belonged to a private investigator gave the claim on the reverse some kind of credence. You might expect a private detective to know something other people, including the police, might not know. Yeah? Okay, you wouldn't necessarily expect it, but you would concede that it might be possible. Shit. He wanted the PI to give him a name. He wanted the name to be the name of his mother's killer. He wanted it badly. But how could the PI possibly have come across that information? And if he had, where had it come from? How reliable was the source? How was the PI going to convince Pearce that the name he supplied was the right one?

Well, Pearce thought as he stepped onto the bus, he'd find out soon enough.

He sat upstairs, looking out onto the wedge-shaped incline on the left that spanned the length of Royal Terrace. A scattering of wooden benches, one of which had been tipped on its back, helped it pose as a park. A tall man, suit trousers tucked into green rubber boots, weaved around a couple of muddy patches, even though his boots were already filthy. Ahead of him, ears pinned back, tail up, a collie paused for a moment before disappearing into the trees.

As the bus turned onto Leith Walk, Pearce's phone rang. He answered it, thinking it might be the PI. It wasn't.

Ailsa said, "Why didn't you tell me?"

"Tell you what?" She didn't reply, so he repeated the question.

"You know," she said.

"Know what? What are you talking about?"

"Christ." She paused. "That you'd been in prison. Why didn't you tell me?"

He said, "Not something I want to brag about." The bell rang and the "stopping" sign lit up at the front of the bus. A tall, bald man in a shabby brown suit shuffled towards the stairs, arms pinned to his sides as if he was wrapped in tight bandages.

"You think I want to read about it in the papers?"

"What have they said?"

"That you just got out of prison."

"That's it?"

"After ten years."

"They say why?"

"Not a peep. Left me guessing. What did you do, Pearce?"

"Now's not the time."

"Want me to guess? Let's see. Ten years." The tall man's bald head disappeared down the stairs. "That's a long time. So, something serious. From what I know of you I'd say it isn't corporate fraud, so I'll plump for either armed robbery or murder." She waited. He didn't say anything, so she said, "Well?"

"It's not that simple."

"I'm sure it's not."

"Stop it, Ailsa. Don't be sarcastic."

"Don't be—Jesus." She hung up.

He sat for a moment, stroking his chin with his knuckles, noticing that the bus had stopped outside a shop that sold wedding dresses. A fat woman wheezed up the stairs, her conical head poking out of a pink coat, the thick lenses of her glasses magnifying her hazel eyes. As the bus stuttered into life again she reeled forward, the hems of her red trousers brushing the toes of her bright orange trainers, and staggered into an empty seat. She turned, a dusty yellow handbag clutched to her stomach, and looked at Pearce. He stared at her until she muttered and looked away.

He dialled Ailsa's number. She didn't reply. He tried again. Still no reply. He left a short message to say he'd try again later.

The bus was crossing the South Bridge when his phone rang again.

She said, "I'm pissed off. Really pissed off. I can't—"

Pearce said, "I killed somebody."

Her voice changed. "What? How? Who? I mean, why?"

"Can it wait? I'll explain when I see you."

She was silent for a while. Finally she said, "I don't know about that. This kind of changes things a bit." She blew hard into the mouthpiece. "I felt safe with you until I heard about this. Now, I don't know. Was it an accident?"

"You don't get ten years for an accident."

"Didn't think so." Her breath rattled down the phone. "He must have done something terrible for you to have killed him."

Pearce said nothing.

"Well?"

"He was responsible for my sister's death." The garishly clad fat woman turned to stare at him again. "I'm on the bus," he said into the phone. "I can't talk now. Tell you later, okay?"

The silence that followed seemed to last forever. At last Ailsa said, "Just one thing. Are you dangerous?"

He considered the question for a moment and said, "I like to think so."

"I mean, should I be scared of you?"

"Either you're scared or you're not."

"I'm not. But maybe I should be."

"That's for you to decide." It was his turn to hang up.

The fat woman puffed her cheeks. She looked like an overgrown baby. Her cheeks deflated and she said, "You'll catch cold. You should put on a jacket." She turned round and looked out the window.

The bus crossed over the High Street and rolled up the shop-lined South Bridge. As it approached Nicholson Street one of the many constructions to have taken place during Pearce's incarceration appeared on the right. Years ago his mum had sent him a postcard of the new theatre. While he was in prison she took it upon herself to keep him in touch with the outside world (which, to her, meant Edinburgh). The distinctive glazed façade of the Festival Theatre was hard to forget. It looked insubstantial, fragile. Behind the glass small groups sat around tables in the ground floor café. Eating and drinking, chatting and laughing. Untroubled, carefree, contented. Ignorant of the pain of losing a sister, of losing a mother, of having failed to protect either of them. Pearce wanted to jump off the bus and lob bricks through the glass at the smiling fuckers, smash some horror into their cosy lives, shatter the brittle membrane that divided joy and pain.

He gritted his teeth, squeezed his fists. When he closed his eyes, bars of orange flashed behind his lids. Maybe Ailsa was right. Maybe she should be scared of him. Women who were close to him seemed to have a habit of dying.

His eyes opened, slowly adjusting to the harsh winter light. The fat woman had gone and a couple of teenage schoolboys had taken her place. Loudly, they were discussing a classmate called Suzie, who, apparently, had a right-sized pair on her and wasn't half bad-looking. Pearce learned that Suzie was in serious need of a good mining, an expression he'd never heard before but the meaning of which was clear enough. The slightly smaller of the two boys wondered if they might not catch AIDS or something, but agreed when his mate suggested it would be worth it.

Pearce got to his feet and clambered down the steps. A mother and daughter stood in front of the double doors, the daughter kicking the heels of her red boots against the step. Pearce waited behind them with his arms folded. As the bus slowed he swayed to the right and was forced to step forward. He grabbed the support rail above the little girl's head. She looked over her shoulder and grinned at him. She jumped up and down on the spot and clapped her gloved hands. Over the hissing of the brakes he heard her say, "We're going to Daddy's."

Her mother looked across at Pearce. As she turned her head he noticed how thin her hair was. Deep lines scored her forehead. When she smiled her lips sank into her face and her dark blue eyes glistened. She said, "I just hope he remembers, Sweetheart."

The doors opened and mother followed daughter off the bus. Pearce joined them on the pavement and watched them walk away hand in hand, the girl skipping along the pavement, dragging her mother after her. They turned the corner and disappeared from sight.

He strode off in the other direction.

The pink door reminded him of yesterday's visit to Cant. Like the PI, his mum's old school mate also had a pink door. Pearce felt inexplicably sad. Pressure built behind his eyes and for a moment he thought he might burst into tears. He flicked the switch in his head. It took a while, but the sadness gradually passed.

He rang the bell and the door promptly clicked open.

The office was upstairs. On a white door a brass nameplate bore the legend *Eye Witness Investigations*. He knocked once, turned the handle and walked in. A filing cabinet and a desk took up half the floor space. The man he'd met yesterday sat behind the desk, a bandage still protecting his nose. Dark bruises circled his eyes. A much younger man sat on a small window ledge, cushioning his buttocks with his hands.

The man with the bandage stood and held out his hand. "Gray." He smiled, pointed to the floor and said, "Same as the carpet."

"You know who I am." Pearce strolled towards him and took his hand. "I hope your information is better than your banter."

Gray removed his hand, his grin fading.

The other man unstuck himself from the window and introduced himself. "Kennedy."

Pearce said, "Which one of you dicks is going to tell me who killed my mother?"

"It's a little more complicated than that," Gray said. "Why don't you take a seat?"

Pearce remained standing. "You said you knew."

Gray's gaze switched from Pearce to Kennedy, then back to Pearce. "Please sit down."

"Give me the name."

"What's it worth?" A slight smile crept over Gray's face.

Pearce stared at him. "You want to take care somebody doesn't take a proper swipe at that nose of yours."

The smile vanished. Gray said, "We'll sell you the information."

"At a fair price," Kennedy chipped in. During Pearce's exchange with Gray, Kennedy had retreated to the window. His hands were stuffed under his arse again.

Pearce said, "I'm skint."

Gray said, "We can help you get some money."

"I'm not interested in money," Pearce said. "What if I just beat the information out of you?"

Kennedy said, "We'll phone the police and they'll sling you back in the slammer before you have time to sharpen your screwdriver."

"You've done your homework," Pearce said. "I'm impressed.

Still, the police would have to catch me first."

Kennedy said, "We can tell them where you're headed."

"Difficult if you're unconscious."

"We'd wake up at some point."

"Not if you were dead."

"You wouldn't kill us."

"You sound confident."

"Hear me out." Gray leaned back in his chair. "This is stupid." He placed his elbows on the desk and steepled his fingers. "Take a seat."

Without breaking eye contact, Pearce pulled out the chair from under the desk and sat down.

Gray said, "Thank you, Mr Pearce."

"My fucking pleasure, Mr Gray." Pearce grabbed the PI's tie and wrenched him forward. A tray tumbled off the desk and an assortment of documents, some handwritten, some printed, spilled onto the grey carpet. Pearce's peripheral vision picked up Kennedy creeping towards him. Pearce said, "You—stay where you are." Kennedy stopped at the edge of the desk. "I don't have time for games." Pearce yanked Gray closer. If the bandage hadn't been in the way their noses would have been touching. Gray was shaking, his slight double chin quivering. He clutched Pearce's arm.

"Don't call me stupid," Pearce said. "Now, tell me his name before I lose my temper."

Kennedy said, "The man who killed your mother got away with a lot of money."

Still staring at Gray, Pearce said, "So?"

Kennedy said, "He still has it."

"And?"

"We want it."

"Go get it, then."

"Look at it as a favour."

"Look at what?"

"We give you his name. In return, you get the money for us."

"You want me to steal the money he stole from the post office and hand it over to you?"

"Yeah."

"Why should I?"

"Either we give the name to you, or we give it to the police. If we give it to the police..."

"You'll be fucked," Gray said. He coughed. "I'm choking. Let me go."

Pearce snapped his wrist downwards. Gray's face bounced off the surface of the desk. When he sat up again his eyes were wide with shock and a red stain was beginning to blossom on his bandage.

Without letting go of his tie, Pearce said, "Shut up."

Kennedy swallowed. Quietly he said, "What do you say?"

Pearce said, "Give me the name."

Gray said, "No way."

Pearce bounced him off the desk again.

Above Gray's moans, Kennedy said, "Robin Greaves."

Tearing the bandage off his nose, Gray said, "What are you saying, you stupid—"

Pearce said, "I told you to shut up."

Gray cupped his hands over his face.

"The money was in a blue sports bag," Kennedy said. "You would have seen it in the post office. I think he's switched the cash to a brown leather holdall."

Pearce said, "What's his address?"

Kennedy told him.

Gray moaned. He said, "Now we've got nothing to bargain with."

Pearce looked at him. "You never had." He let go of Gray's tie and got to his feet. "How reliable is this information?"

"Hundred percent. On the day of the robbery I tailed him from his flat to the post office." Kennedy stood up too.

"I'm only interested in Greaves," Pearce said. "Not the money."

Gray slurred his words. "What's that mean?" He tried to stand up and fell back in his chair. "You would not believe how much my fucking nose hurts."

Pearce said, "It can always hurt more."

*H*e'd lost a couple of minutes afterwards. A minor victory for Robin, who'd retreated now, gone where Don couldn't touch him. Don padded across the room and stepped into the corridor. The door on the left led to the kitchen. He walked past it and tried the next one along. *Voila.* He slid into the bathroom, head pounding.

Daubs of blood had dried on his fingers. He ran his hands under the tap, then grabbed a bar of soap and lathered his palms. Blood foamed and swirled in the sink. He checked his hands for more spillage after rinsing them thoroughly. They were clean.

Ignoring his scars, he examined his near-naked body. It seemed blood-free. He checked in the mirror, amazed at how the pain in his head had bleached his lips. No blood splatters, though. That was good. Ah, but he was dripping all over the floor. He should dry his hands. A couple of towels hung on a rail. No, using her towel was filthy, like sharing a toothbrush. Saliva flooded his mouth. He swallowed. Better. He wasn't going to choke. He unrolled a pile of toilet roll, bunched it up and dried his hands with it. He threw the soggy paper down the toilet and flushed it. A clear thumbprint remained on the handle.

Look at them. He turned as he passed the mirror. *Look at them.* Hypertrophic scarring. *Look.* Red curls of thickened skin snaked across his chest. *Lower down.* Livid welts burned into his abdomen. An L, an O, a V.

Enough.

He returned to the sitting room. Carol lay on her back with his word carved in her stomach and his knife buried in her naval. He rummaged in his coat pocket and took out his gloves. A bit late. His fingerprints were everywhere. But he could wipe them off before he left.

Unwinding the ligature from round her neck, he noticed the cuff for the first time and it dawned on him that he'd killed her with a shirtsleeve. Who'd have thought a shirtsleeve could be used as a lethal weapon? He spread out the material and was wiping the handle of the knife when the phone rang. He stopped what he was doing and stared at the phone.

Carol spoke, her answering machine broadcasting a short message. Eddie's voice followed. "Pick up, Carol. *Please*. Carol. You there? *Pick the phone up*." There was silence for a few seconds. "Carol, answer the fucking phone."

Don retraced his steps. Wiped the doorknob. Wiped the knob on the other side. Wiped the taps in the bathroom, the flush handle, inside and outside door handles. He tried to think what else he might have touched. Back in the sitting room he started to dress. When he put his trousers on, he felt something missing. He patted his pocket, then shoved his hand inside. His wallet had gone. And his keys. The bastard had nicked them. All he had left was some loose change.

No prizes for guessing where Eddie had phoned from. He sounded distressed, poor chap. Well, what was Don was supposed to do now? Thanks to Eddie, he couldn't go home. He couldn't stay here. He couldn't go to the police. He needed somewhere to hide, somewhere to think. His head ached like a split tooth. He took off his gloves to button his shirt. He put on his shoes, put the gloves back on. He needed to talk to Robin. *Okay*. Robin believed he'd killed Carol. *Okay*. Robin didn't know Don was aware of his visit. Consequently, Robin would assume that when Don woke up he'd think Eddie had killed her and set him up. So, logically, if Don got away he'd accuse Eddie of framing him. That is, if he went to the police. *I woke up and she was already dead. Honest. I don't know how my fingerprints are on the knife.* He needed money. He no longer had his bank or credit cards. Eddie had seen to that. If Don was going to survive, he needed cash and, as far as he could gather, Robin had a pile of it. Another good reason for finding him. They could be of help to one another.

The shock of waking up next to what he'd assumed was a dead woman, the savage headache induced by the pistol-whipping—these events were more than enough to send the average brain into systematic shutdown. He could use that. Robin would sympathise. Perfectly reasonable that Don would be a little confused. Then when Don explained Eddie's role in the set-up, Robin wouldn't be able to refuse assistance without admitting that he was the killer. He would be safe, or at least, he would think he was safe. No reason to suspect Don of anything. Which would mean that Don could monitor Eddie's activities from the safety of Robin's home. Once he'd found out where the money was stashed, he could then decide what to do with the pair of fucking buffoons.

Heavens, it was good to be back in charge.

The door buzzer interrupted his thoughts. He froze. After a short while it sounded again: loud. Again: urgent. Again: insistent. Quiet seconds dragged by. He heard the sound of a buzzer in a neighbouring flat followed by the remote hum of the main door unlocking. He heard footsteps in the stairwell. Voices echoing.

The footsteps stopped outside the door. Someone banged on it. He remained still. More banging. He glanced at Carol. Pale and carved. Looking lovely. Back at the door. Was that Eddie outside? Could he have arrived already? No, he hadn't had time. *Don't move. Stay quiet. Whoever it is, they'll realise no one's home and go away.*

A voice said, "Open up." Paused. Then said, "Police."

Shit.

11:26 AM

*F*ucking traffic. He'd be better off walking.

Eddie wrenched the gear stick and accelerated. His hand still throbbed where the beautiful mad bitch had burned it with her cigarette. *Please let her be okay. Please.* She hadn't answered the phone. He was worried. She'd told him Don was dangerous and he'd left her there with him. *Fucking idiot.* He got out his mobile and tried her again. *Come on.* No answer. He chucked the phone onto the passenger's seat and turned the corner. He hoped nothing had happened to her. After all, he hadn't even found the fucking money.

PART THREE

"Anybody home?"

Don's heartbeat accelerated.

"This is the police."

The sitting room door was wide open. He stared through the doorway at the white door at the end of the corridor. As he watched, a splash of light burst through the vertical slit of the letterbox and hit him between the eyes. Head raging with pain, he flung himself against the wall, a split second before a new voice blasted through the opening: "Hello." Don looked at Carol. The voice came again: "Hello!" Her body was safely out of the policeman's line of sight. The bell rang seemingly endlessly. "Open up." The letterbox clattered shut and a while afterwards the bell stopped ringing.

For a moment Don succeeded in ignoring his headache and tried to figure out how the police had arrived so quickly. It must have been Eddie. Somehow he must have discovered something in the flat. Then he'd phoned the police, informing them of his suspicions (of what, though?) and letting them know that his girlfriend, who, incidentally, wasn't answering her phone, was last seen in Don's presence.

All of which left Don trapped.

What could he do? Well, he could give himself up and confess everything. But, despite the headache, he was having too much fun. What, then? He could hardly toss Carol's body into the garden below. Could he jump out the window? Not without injuring himself. Perhaps he could hide the body, pretend he was a flatmate of Carol's and invite the police into the flat. He didn't like that idea either.

Unfortunately, it was the best plan he had. A number of factors counted against it, though. The flat wasn't designed for hiding dead bodies and even if he found a suitable place to stash it, the police would want to look around and, inevitably, they'd locate Carol stuffed in the linen cupboard or wherever. *Fuck this headache.* The police would want to see some identification. They'd want proof that he lived here. And if, miraculously, he got away with everything up to that point, Eddie would arrive and screw things up.

So. He had to stick with his original plan. Get to Robin and use his money. Don pressed his fingers against his temples and moved the skin in circles. It didn't help. The pain was getting in the way. He had to get rid of it.

Carol's handbag lay on the coffee table. He opened the clasp and raked around inside. An address book, nail varnish, three tampons, two packs of cigarettes, three hairbrushes, four combs, tweezers, lip gloss, more nail varnish, another comb, pencils, small purse containing some change and a credit card, powder compact, a couple of buttons, cotton buds, plasters, nail clippers, nail file, hair band, spool of black thread. Fuck. You'd think a woman with her mental history would have the decency to carry some drugs in her bag.

He closed the bag gently, and put it back on the table. As he started towards the bathroom, he trod on a creaky floorboard. He held his breath, but there was no acknowledgement from the policemen outside. No shouting. No cries of, "We know you're in there." It probably wasn't that loud. After all, how loud can a floorboard creak? Nonetheless, he walked the rest of the way as if broken glass layered his shoes.

In the bathroom cupboard he found a packet of Nurofen caplets. Just in time. A pair of thumbs was trying to scoop his eyes out from the inside. He swallowed four of the pills and pocketed the rest. Treading carefully, he made his way back to the sitting room.

It took almost a minute to slink along the length of the sitting room wall. He paused for a moment before poking his head around the frame of the doorway. At the end of the corridor the letterbox was a closed dark slit in the blue-white door. He took a deep breath, placed one foot over the threshold and stepped into the corridor. A pale golden light leaked through the frosted glass panel above the door. Creeping along the carpeted floor, he heard muffled voices. As he drew closer he held his breath. From here he could distinguish the odd word. Two more steps. Better. They were discussing a television program one of them had watched last night. Loud and clear now. He flattened himself into the corner and listened.

"This guy's a member of SO10, right, undercover, posing as a money launderer for the IRA. He's liable to drop one in his pants, 'cos he just found out last night that the guy picking him up at the airport in Belfast is a multiple murderer who's just got out of the slammer. So, the guy's there, waiting for him, card with his name on it and all that crap. Big guy, shaven head, goatee. Prison tatts on his arms, backs of his hands, neck. The undercover cop's a bit unconfident, you know. I mean, this guy's killed people. Loads of them. So he gets in the back. Car drives off. After a while he realises IRA's heading in the wrong direction for the meeting. He leans forward and taps him on the shoulder. Asks where they're going. IRA tells him there's been a slight change of plan. Nothing to worry about. Still, SO10's starting to panic. He's thinking somebody's talked, the game's up. He's going to be kneecapped, done over with a baseball bat, executed. He's wondering if he should dive out of the car or stick with it. Either way it looks like he's a goner. Anyway, after an age the car slows down and pulls into the gravel driveway of this isolated country cottage. Car stops. IRA gets out. Opens the door for him. SO10 gets out, clutching his little briefcase and quietly praying that he doesn't shite himself. IRA unlocks the door and steps into the cottage. Invites SO10 inside. SO10 enters the sitting room. It's covered in tapestries and paintings and stuff. Hardly an inch of wall space. IRA says, 'You look like a cultured gentleman. Thought I'd show you my work.' He's got a big proud grin on his face. He says, 'You wouldn't be interested in buying one at all, would you?'"

Don wiped his forehead. His hair was damp. The knuckles of a baby's fist were twisting in his brain.

"So he does. SO10 buys a painting from him. They haggle a bit over the price and eventually settle on a hundred quid. Turns out IRA developed a taste for art during his last stretch inside. IRA drives SO10 and the painting to the original rendezvous. And everything goes really smoothly. After what he's just been through, the meeting's a doddle. SO10 doesn't even break sweat."

Don wondered how long he could wait here. In fact, he wondered what he was waiting for. The end of the story? It was over. SO10 didn't break sweat. Great. That was it. Well then, what exactly *was* he waiting for? Maybe he should just open the door and turn himself in. The cops might be here all night, regaling one another with tales of police courage in the face of criminal adversity. They all wanted to be fucking heroes.

He had to make an effort.

Back down the corridor and into the sitting room. If only Robin was here to appreciate this. What a man will do for his brother, even if his brother refuses to acknowledge his existence.

She said, "LOVE". She would always say, "LOVE." He smiled at Carol's corpse. *This is love, Carol, and don't you forget it.*

Sometime in the past, a fire. Fast forward. Play. Ten years old. A winter morning in school. Power cut. Dark so deep you can bite into it. Miss Holt moves past him. He stretches out and grabs an arm. When she stops to see what he wants, he slides his other hand under her skirt. She jumps. Screams. Keeps screaming, reminding him of the pitiful wailing of his poor frail mother. Fast forward. Play. Thirteen years old. Camping. Razor blades in Ruth Harris's sleeping bag. Sliced the soles of her feet. Fifteen. Razor blades left in a napkin after he and mum dined at a cheap restaurant. The manager complained, said that it wasn't the first time. Sixteen. A question mark cut into a whore's cheek with a Stanley knife. Seventeen. An L carved into his girlfriend's stomach while she was asleep. She woke up screaming. He carried on. Couldn't stop. Lots of blood. Ambulance. Police. *Since he died, I—I need help. A nightmare. I didn't know what I was doing. The trauma of my brother's death. Seeing it all. I can't control myself.* Smart boy. Cautious, thereafter. Keeping it inside. The tension building up for the last ten years. *They took me away. My father drove me there. Left me to rot. For my own good. Because he loved me. Nothing can hide the truth. Killers kill. It's what they do.*

Fast forward. Stop.

Don plucked the knife out of Carol's naval.

*H*e peered through the keyhole. Feet apart, hands behind their backs, the two policemen stood with their backs to the door. Bored now, presumably. Run out of stories to tell each other. Just doing their jobs, standing guard in front of an obviously empty flat where no sign of anything untoward had taken place. Yet another hoax call they'd had to check out. One of a dozen or so they probably got every week. And now all they could do was await further instructions. Or was it? Had they received those instructions already? Had they been asked to wait until Eddie arrived?

If it wasn't for Eddie, Don could have waited them out. But Eddie had eliminated that particular option, damn him.

So. Nothing for it but to face the music.

When Don turned the latch, he tensed, but the anticipated click never came. He relaxed. A modicum of good fortune was a prerequisite of every successful venture. He opened the door a fraction and sized up the two policemen through the crack. One was a six-footer. The other was a couple of inches shorter. Don heard radio static. Perfectly normal. At least, neither of the policemen acknowledged it. The taller one rolled forward slightly on the balls of his feet.

Don opened the door wider, just enough to squeeze through the gap. He slid behind the smaller of the two policemen, slipped the knife under his chin and whispered, "Stay still."

The policeman stayed still. Apart from his mouth. It moved when he said, "Oh, God, oh, shit."

His colleague turned and stared. A shaving rash stretched across his throat like a thick, pink chinstrap. His mouth fell open and his hand moved to his belt.

Don shook his head at him. "You too," he said in a loud whisper. Shaving Rash's hand retreated. "Now lose the walkie-talkies. Both of you."

After he'd repeated his instruction, they did as he asked. He invited them to remove their truncheons and CS spray canisters, and lay them on the floor. Policemen were great at following orders. They were trained for it. And these two looked straight out of training college.

"Take your handcuffs out of your belt," he said to Shaving Rash. "Turn round. Hands behind your back." He gave the shorter one a slap on the shoulder. The blow made him grunt. "Fasten his cuffs." Don eased the pressure on Grunt's throat. A smear of Carol Wren's blood glistened on the policeman's neck. Once the cuffs were clipped in place, Don reapplied the point of his knife to Grunt's throat. "Any sudden movement," Don said, "and you'll get a nasty puncture wound. Jugular. Very messy. Now, your turn." Trembling, Grunt slowly eased his handcuffs out of his belt and stuck his hands behind his back. With his left hand, Don fastened the cuffs.

"Inside," Don said. Shaving Rash turned his head to look at his colleague. Grunt pursed his lips and nodded and Shaving Rash led the way. Don followed, the point of the knife hidden in the indented, blood-smeared skin of the shorter policeman's throat. Don closed the door behind him with the sole of his foot. "Straight ahead."

Grunt came to a halt when he saw the body in the sitting room. He said, "Oh, God. Oh, shit." Grunt's voice was recognisable as the one telling the SO10 story.

Don spoke to Shaving Rash. "Not so funny now, is he?"

Shaving Rash didn't reply. He couldn't take his eyes off Carol Wren. He bent backwards, as if he'd been punched in the face and was trying to avoid a second blow. Grunt said, "Oh, shit. Oh, God."

"Yeah, yeah," Don said.

Shaving Rash's voice was thin. It sounded like an old man's. "Did you do that?"

Don lowered the knife. "Why don't you both take a seat?" Neither moved. "On the settee," he suggested.

Shaving Rash said, "Did you do that?"

Don said, loudly, "Sit."

Shaving Rash rushed over to the settee. Grunt's face was a shade darker than chalk and he looked like he was about to throw up. Probably never seen a dead body. Most policemen never did. Almost certainly, he'd never seen one with "LOVE" carved in its stomach. His lips were quivering. He looked even younger than Shaving Rash.

Don said, "Sit."

Grunt staggered towards the settee, sat down next to Shaving Rash and said, "I have to warn you…" He caught Don's eyes and stopped.

Switching the knife to his left hand, Don strode up to Grunt and slapped him on the cheek with his open right. "What's your name?"

Slippery hazel eyes stared at Don. They sparkled with fear. Grunt said, "PC Hood."

"And you?" Don asked Shaving Rash.

"PC Fairchild."

Don said, "I assume you pair aren't the rapid response team? Why are you here?"

Hood said, "Somebody reported a domestic disturbance."

"Ah," Don said. "That's disappointing. Who?"

"Didn't give his name."

Don said, "I wonder why he didn't report a murder?"

Hood said, "How would he know?" He looked away, dropped his head and stared at the floor.

"Good point." Don understood. It was Robin, not Eddie. These two were here because of Robin. Part of his half-cocked plan to eliminate Don. Robin's problem was that he couldn't report Carol's murder without incriminating himself. Not even the police were stupid enough to believe Don would have made the phone call. Which asked all sorts of questions about the caller. If the caller had witnessed the murder, he was either an accomplice or the killer himself. Unless he was an innocent bystander. In which case, why place the call anonymously? So Robin had reported hearing a scuffle instead. The little bastard.

Come to think of it, Eddie didn't have much room to manoeuvre either. Exactly what could he tell the police? Only that a man he hardly knew might be in the process of killing his lover. And that when he left him, this man was unconscious as the result of being pistol-whipped. It was unlikely Eddie would be bringing reinforcements, but Don couldn't be certain. He didn't know what

Eddie had found that made him suspicious.

Why the fuck was the whole world out to get him?

Fairchild asked, "Are you going to kill us?"

Don looked at him. "That's up to you."

Fairchild squirmed on the settee. "You can't." His voice cracked. "You can't kill us. We're policemen."

"Be quiet, Lew." Hood lifted his head to look at Don.

Don studied the three red finger marks slicing across the policeman's cheek. "Listen to your colleague, Lew."

PC Lewis Fairchild stood. "You won't kill us." He leaned forward.

Hood said, "Sit down, Lew." Saliva gathered at the edges of his mouth. "Sit the fuck down."

"He won't kill us, Hoodie." Fairchild stepped towards Don.

Don sighed.

PC Hood said, "What did you mean, it's up to us?"

Don ignored him. "How old are you, Lew?"

Lew stopped. "Nineteen."

"If you want to be twenty, then slam your arse back down on the seat."

Fairchild glanced at Hoodie. Then he took a step back and sat down.

"If you get up again without my authorisation it'll be for the last time." Don twirled the knife in his fingers. "Is that understood?"

Fairchild ran his tongue over his lower lip and nodded. His left leg was shaking.

Don said, "Brothers and sisters, Lew?"

He nodded again.

"How many?"

"Two brothers."

"How about you, Hoodie?"

"Three sisters and a brother."

"You got a first name?"

Hoodie grunted. "Kevin," he said.

"I'll call you Hoodie," Don said. He knew their names and he knew how many siblings they had. They knew nothing about him. They were handcuffed. He wasn't. He was in control. He said, "I don't have much time. I have to escape and I don't want to be followed. What do you think I should do?"

Neither policeman replied.

Don continued, "Lew obviously doesn't think I should kill you. That's understandable. Self-preservation is a keen instinct. Logically, though, it seems to me that killing you would solve my problem nicely. I can stab the pair of you and walk out the front door as if nothing's happened." Don caught Hoodie's eyes and Hoodie fidgetted under his gaze. "You want to say something?"

PC Kevin Hood said, "You don't need to do that. You could just walk out anyway. We're handcuffed." He turned sideways and wriggled his fingers. "We couldn't stop you."

"You're underestimating your own resourcefulness, Hoodie." Don smiled. "I can't imagine a pair of fine police officers like yourselves would be incapacitated by a minor inconvenience like wearing handcuffs. Think about it." He stared at the knife for a moment. "This isn't my flat. I don't have a key. I can't lock the door." He looked at Lew. "Handcuffs won't stop you reaching the Yale. You might need a stool, or something to stand on, but that won't be hard to find."

"Tie us up, then. We can't get very far if we're trussed up like—"

"Pigs," Don finished off for him. "Apt phrase, Hoodie. But you could still shout. Make a racket." He smiled. "Squeal."

"Gag us."

Don said, "Excellent, Hoodie. You're doing very well. What do you think, Lew?" PC Lew Fairchild did not look well. "You want to be bound and gagged? Hoodie thinks it's a good idea."

PC Fairchild said, "I don't know."

"Neither do I," Don said. "Problem with binding and gagging, fun though it might be, is that it takes time. Of which, as it happens, I'm rapidly running out." The painkillers were taking effect. His headache had dulled considerably and now he could think more clearly. He'd have to leave before Eddie turned up. "I'm expecting company any minute. More of your lot, maybe." He scanned their faces, but they were both so scared their expressions revealed nothing but terror. "Unfortunately, I don't have time to look for rope or ligatures or strong tape. And even if I did, tying you up would take too long."

The silence lasted seconds. Hoodie said, "What's that mean?"

"Tying you up is not an option."

This time the silence lasted a little longer. Hoodie said, "What are you going to do?"

"I'm going to have to kill you."

Lew said, "You can't."

"You're policemen, right?" Don turned and walked towards the bay window. "Tell you what." He slid the window open and looked down at the grass twenty-five, maybe thirty, feet below. "I'll give you a choice, but we need to be quick. Either you jump out the window or I stab you in the chest. You have fifteen seconds to decide. Starting"—he looked at his watch—"now."

Hoodie stood. "Take the handcuffs off."

Don said, "Fourteen, thirteen."

Hoodie said, "We're on the second floor. If we can't use our hands to break our fall we'll probably kill ourselves."

Don carried on counting. "Eleven, ten, nine."

Hoodie walked towards the window. "This is farcical."

Don said, "Seven, six."

Hoodie said, "There's nothing to hold onto."

Don said, "Five. Shout and I'll cut your throat. Four."

Hoodie slung one leg over the windowsill and sat down.

"Three."

Hoodie shuffled forward, pulled his other leg over and turned to face the drop.

Don said, "Two."

Hoodie said, "Push me."

Don said, "One."

Hoodie said, "Come on. Push me."

Don said, "Zero," and shoved Hoodie in the back. Hoodie yelled on the way down. He hit the grass on his left side and yelled much louder. Don listened to the policeman's cries. Couple of broken ribs? Broken arm, maybe? One thing was certain. Hoodie wouldn't be chasing him down the street.

And neither, for that matter, would his partner. PC Lew Fairchild was out cold. It seemed the agony of choice had proved too much for him. He had keeled over on the arm of the settee. When Don pulled up Lew's sleeve and stabbed him in the elbow, he didn't flinch.

Kill him, don't kill him. Kill him, don't kill him. Don couldn't make up his mind. He lowered Lew's sleeve and covered up the stab wound. Killing him would be pointless. It would waste precious time. On the other hand, Don had never killed a policeman and the prospect wasn't altogether unattractive.

Hoodie's howls drifted in through the open window.

Fuck it, I have to go.

It was Lew Fairchild's lucky day.

Don knew there would be no return to normality now. The dynamics between him and Robin had changed. Okay, he might spend the rest of his life trying to evade capture, but from now on he was free to impose his will on anything he desired, including his little brother. He hadn't heard a peep out of him for ages. He dropped the knife and started to run.

11:37 AM

*H*alfway down the first flight of stairs Don heard the front door open. Footsteps rushed towards him. The door slammed. There wasn't time to turn back. He had to hope the visitor was a resident, not Eddie or, worse still (unlikely though it might be), reinforcements from Lothian and Borders finest. He climbed down to the first floor landing and waited. A bandaged hand appeared on the railing and then he saw the blonde hair.

Don didn't wait to say hello. He ran towards his former assailant, his right fist connecting with Eddie's jaw. Eddie hadn't seen him, hadn't expected the blow. His knees buckled and he sagged against the railing, face raised in a look of surprise. Don hit him again. Same place. Eddie slumped to his knees. Don would have liked to stay for a while longer, but flight seemed the more urgent of his conflicting desires. Or maybe not.

Eddie had whacked him on the head with his gun and given him a savage headache. For which, Don decided to hang around for a while longer and kick Eddie in the stomach a couple of times. He took aim and belted him hard. He was about to kick him again, when Eddie launched his fist at Don's gut. He missed his target but managed to catch Don a glancing blow on the thigh. Don reeled backwards until the wall stopped him. Eddie was trying to drag himself to his feet when Don bounced off the wall and kicked him in the face. Blood spurted from his lip. Don nodded in approval.

He'd love to stay longer. Another time, though. It wasn't sensible to be here. Breathing heavily, he stumbled down the stairs.

When he opened the front door, the light hurt his eyes. His head was pounding and he felt dizzy. He jogged towards the end of the road before looking behind him. No sign of Eddie. He hadn't appeared in the doorway. Don stopped long enough to tear a couple of pills from the packet in his pocket. The cold air had helped clear his head, but it still throbbed. Swallowing the pills, he broke into a run. He sprinted fifty yards, looked behind him and eased down. Still no one there. But was he safe? He slowed to a fast walking pace and after a while his heartbeat steadied and his breath came easier. Just as he began to congratulate himself on his successful escape, he heard a shout behind him.

He froze. When he looked over his shoulder, Eddie was twenty-five feet away and gaining by the second. Blood was smeared across his mouth. His teeth were bared in a demented grin and he was bellowing like a distressed bull. "…killed her. You fucking killed her, you crazy fucking bastard." He was waving a gun in his bandaged hand.

So Eddie had dragged his beaten body upstairs and seen Carol Wren in all her posthumous glory. He was pissed off, armed.

Don's feet pounded the pavement with a force that jarred his brain. Wind whipped his eyes and made them sting. He dashed around the nearest corner, adrenalin surging through him. Couldn't give Eddie a steady target. Lungs bursting, Don took the first left. Straight on. Across the road. Left again and he was almost on Morningside Road. He clenched his fists in relief.

People. Safety. He looked over his shoulder.

Eddie was twenty feet behind now, blood-smeared face rigid. His hand was in his pocket, hiding his gun. Grief did strange things to people.

Which way? Don turned left, towards town. He walked as fast as he could manage without attracting strange looks from passers-by. Eddie's presence behind him was like a weight pressing between his shoulder blades. Every few feet, he snatched a glance over his shoulder. Eddie was matching his speed. The homicidal maniac was still grinning, crooked teeth pink. Pedestrians were stepping out of his way without having to be asked.

Past the Bruntsfield Hotel. Breathing evenly. Holding the distance. A sudden break in the crowd. Fewer pedestrians. Don speeded up. Broke into a jog. He didn't know how good a shot Eddie was.

Of course, Eddie had it all wrong. He wasn't thinking. Had the situation been reversed, had Don been chasing Eddie with a weapon, Don would have fired it, thereby causing the pedestrians to drop to the ground and give him a clear shot. That's what any man with a modicum of intelligence and a decent-sized pair of balls would have done.

Don heard the crack. It sounded like a firework. Somebody screamed and a chill spread through Don's bones. He turned and looked at Eddie. The crazy fucking bastard! What was he doing shooting in a crowd? He'd bring the cops—Jesus! A couple of feet to the left, a chunk of wall leapt into the air. All around, people were flattening themselves on the pavement. Traffic ground to a halt. *Shit, shit, shit, shit, shit.* Eddie had a clear shot.

Don ran. The skin on his back felt as if it had been bundled into a heap in the centre of his spine and twisted tight around a stick. Where it felt tightest, that's where he imagined the bullet entering. Bruntsfield Road led downhill all the way to Tollcross. He kept picking up speed until he staggered and almost fell. His legs were going to give way if he didn't slow down, but fear kept him moving at a sprint, weaving a path through countless shopping bags, prams, buggies, hurdling a suitcase, narrowly missing a post box, a rubbish bin, a kid in a wheelchair. Outside the

Cameo cinema, he barged into a small crowd and got an elbow in the stomach that sent him spinning, winded. Somehow he stayed on his feet. He heard laddish jeering but didn't dare look behind him. No more gunshots, though, and no police sirens. Where were the cops when you needed them?

Someone was knitting a jumper with his intestines. Just for fun, someone else was snapping his ribs with a bolt cutter. Eddie was going to pay. This wasn't enjoyable any more.

He had to stop eventually. He decelerated and came to a halt at a cash machine, bending over, resting his palms on its surface while he sucked in deep breaths. His lungs burned. He coughed. His nose was running. He coughed again. His stomach shook like a bag of loose stones. He wiped his nose with the back of his hand and spat on the pavement by his feet as sweat ran down his back. He puffed his cheeks out. Breathed in.

He was a sitting duck. Where was the crazy fucker?

He looked back up the hill. No commotion. No Eddie. Had he given up? Was he hurt? Had the police caught him? Was he hiding? Too many questions.

A bus pulled into a stop nearby. On shaky legs, Don walked over and joined the queue. He fumbled in his pocket for change. Eddie had left him exactly three pounds and eighty-five pence. Nice of him. Don dropped eighty pence in the coin slot, tore off his ticket and took a seat. He waited for Eddie to appear. Waited for him to flash his bloodstained, crooked grin. Waited for him to walk up the aisle to the seat where Don huddled. Waited for him to pull the trigger of that ugly, black gun. Waited for him to end it all. But Eddie never appeared.

The bus pulled away and Don carried on living.

Three squad cars drove past.

When Don looked out the rear window, he saw Eddie sauntering past the cinema entrance, hands stuffed in his pockets, head down, coat collar turned up, hiding his injured mouth. The police cars didn't stop.

As the bus pulled away, Eddie melted into the crowd.

12:56 PM

*P*earce held the door open for her. "After you," he said.

Ailsa ducked her head under his arm and he followed her inside, detecting a faint trace of paint fumes. The facing wall, sunflower yellow, looked freshly painted. A five-tiered chandelier hung from a high, stark white ceiling. A stained-glass window cast shimmering yellow and red lights onto the wide wooden staircase that wound downstairs.

She led the way, heels clicking on each scarred step. She had decided he wasn't dangerous after all. But that didn't mean she had become supportive. Not by a long shot. After he had explained to her how Muriel had died, how he'd found her too late to save her, how he'd killed Priestley, her dealer, Ailsa just shook her head and refused to comment. For ages, she said nothing. Didn't ask about prison. Nothing. Sat there with her arms folded, staring at the wall, scrutinising that stupid picture of hers, the one with the scrawled-on eyebrows. Occasionally, she shook her head.

Pearce wondered if he should tell her the rest. Chances are, he'd have killed Priestley anyway, but he would never know how much difference the police information had made to his subsequent actions. Muriel had been dead for two days when he found her. Dead and naked, lying on the floorboards of an abandoned flat in Wester Hailes. The door was open. The police told Pearce that his sister's body showed signs of recent sexual activity. When pressed, they said that recent meant, "within the last twenty-four hours." After ten years, it was still hard to put into words. *Somebody had sex with my sister after she was dead.* How could you chat about that?

He said, "Say something."

She looked at him. "Why? You need my approval?"

It wasn't the drug dealer who fucked Muriel's dead body. The piece of shit responsible for that particular act was never caught and probably never would be—luckily for him. No, it was too long ago now. Nonetheless, Pearce held the dealer responsible. Priestley had supplied the poison that killed her. She died to make him rich. His greed had slowly fucked her to death. Did Pearce need Ailsa's approval for killing him? He laughed out loud.

"You don't, do you? You don't care what I think." Her eyes looked glassy. "You're going to go ahead with this stupid plan."

He said nothing.

"What can I say to stop you?"

He remained silent.

"You're using me, Pearce. I don't know that I want to be used."

"I'm not forcing you to do anything." He resisted an urge to reach out a hand and touch her hair. Instead, he rubbed his chin with the back of his hand. "Give me the gun and you'll never see me again."

"Christ," she said. "You haven't got a clue." She got up, went through to her bedroom and returned with the pistol. "Here."

He slipped it inside his belt, the butt flat against his spine. He pulled his t-shirt out of his jeans and draped it over the gun. He took a couple of steps towards the door, the gun digging into his back. He nudged the barrel slightly to the left. It was far from comfortable, but it would have to do.

She said, "I'm coming with you."

"It's okay. You were right. I'm using you."

"Fuck off, Pearce. You're not meant to agree."

He narrowed his eyes. "I'm lost."

"You sure are," she said. "Never mind, I'm coming with you. But under protest, understand? I'm not happy about this."

He rubbed his chin. "Why don't you let me go on my own?"

"Joe-Bob won't give you the time of day."

"Call him. Tell him you can't make it. Introduce me over the phone."

"He won't buy it."

"Try it and see."

"I want to come with you." She looked at her feet. "If I don't, I've got no chance of changing your mind."

"You've got no chance anyway."

"Can't stop me trying."

He sighed. "So you don't think I'm dangerous any more?"

"Not to me." She looked at him, hands clasped together in

front of her chest, tears staining her green eyes. "I want you to stay around for a while. Is that too much to ask? I want to get to know you, I want you to get to know—"

"Get your coat," he said. "We're going to be late."

She'd been quiet during the subsequent bus ride. Eyes closed, palms pressed together, hands clamped between her knees, she'd pretended to sleep. He hadn't disturbed her.

As he opened the door to the cellar bar, she said, "Go easy on Joe-Bob."

"Can't promise."

"Try to remember that he's not a drug dealer any more."

The interior was dark and noisy. A long horseshoe bar split the centre of the room. Jammed against the wall, the snout of a small cannon protruded beyond the deep surround of a green marble fireplace. A coal-effect gas fire warmed the smoky air and above the fireplace hung a shield, a claymore and a kilt. Sketches of old Edinburgh were scattered along the walls.

They walked towards the bar across an uneven flagstone floor.

"Is he here?" Pearce asked. The place was beginning to fill up, the lunchtime crowd arriving in force. None of the few solitary drinkers looked like his vision of an arms dealer. Or, to be precise, an arms dealer's lieutenant.

"Patience," Ailsa said.

He shrugged. When they reached the bar, he placed his elbows on the counter. "You want a drink?"

She held up her hands and pushed her palms through a ribbon of smoke. "Let me handle this."

Two barmen and a barmaid looked busy behind the counter. A couple of minutes passed. The girl was first over. White blouse. Tartan skirt. Striped tie. Hair in pigtails. She said, "Can I get you?"

Ailsa said, "We're here to see Joe-Bob."

"Nice." She was chewing gum. "Can I get you?"

"Can you let him know we're here?"

She placed her hands on her hips and strolled over to one of the barmen and whispered in his ear. After a while, he came over. He said, "Can I get you?"

Ailsa repeated what she'd told the girl.

He said, "And you are?"

"Ailsa."

"Right. And your friend?"

"Pearce." Pearce held out his hand.

The barman looked at it, then held out his own. "Roy," he said, squeezing Pearce's fingers. He leaned over. "Follow me. Joe-Bob's waiting for you."

Roy led them through an arched doorway into a wide corridor. Laminated plastic signs indicated that toilets were straight ahead. Roy turned left. He ducked under another arch and stepped into a cramped space. Benches lined opposite walls, with only a couple of feet between them. The ceiling was low enough to force Pearce to keep his neck bent. He got a good view of the seven or eight flattened cigarette butts littering the floor. Somebody had been kept waiting. Roy fished in his waistcoat pocket, found a key and unlocked a door marked *Private*. One after the other, they stepped into a small, square, unfurnished room with a dark blue curtain draped along one wall. The other walls were white and bare. Roy pulled the curtain to one side and revealed a brass-studded oak door. He rapped on it.

While he waited for an answer, he said, "Just out of interest, I don't suppose either of you would be interested in buying a live lobster?"

"Not for me." Pearce looked at Ailsa. He said, "How about you?"

She thought for a second. "Nope."

Pearce said, "The fuck kind of a question is that, Roy?"

Roy said, "Mate of mine's got a couple of dozen lobsters he's trying to shift. Said I'd ask around."

The door opened inwards.

A man's head appeared. Shaved at the sides, a two-inch wide strip of dyed red hair running down the middle. A Mohican minus the spikes. His face had the well-fed look of a chipmunk and his stomach spilled out over his belt. He was breathing hard. Climbing the stairs had knocked the wind out of him. He took a handkerchief out of his shirt pocket and wiped his forehead. He said, "Ailsa," and smiled.

"Joe-Bob." She smiled back and stepped through the doorway into his arms. They hugged and pecked each other on the cheek. Ailsa said, "I like the Mohawk." Roy beckoned to Pearce that he was leaving them. Probably off to check on his lobsters. Pearce nodded.

Ailsa pulled away from Joe-Bob's embrace and said, "Joe-Bob. This is Pearce. Pearce. Joe-Bob."

Joe-Bob's fingers dipped once again into his pocket and surfaced with the handkerchief. He mopped his head, transferred the handkerchief to his left hand, and extended his right. "Any friend of Ailsa's," he said.

The correct response was, "Likewise." Pearce said, "Cut the crap, Blowjob. You got the ammo?"

"I see," Joe-Bob said, withdrawing his offer of a handshake. He dabbed at either side of the red strip of hair on his otherwise bald head "I see. Would you close the door, please?" He turned and began to walk downstairs, planting each foot securely before daring to shift his considerable weight.

Ailsa followed Joe-Bob. Pearce brought up the rear, quietly humming "Stand By Your Man." He began to see why Joe-Bob's progress was so slow. It wasn't the fact that he was a fat bastard. The steps were worn and narrow and weren't designed to accommodate Pearce's steel toe-capped work boots. Even with his feet placed sideways, the rim of his boots hung well over the edge. He couldn't help thinking that this would be a good place for an ambush.

"Is all this subterranean shit necessary?" he shouted downstairs.

Joe-Bob's voice floated up to him. "I was in prison once. Never again."

"Thought you'd have liked it. All those naked men."

"Pearce. Christ. Sorry, Joe-Bob. My friend has a thing about drug dealers."

Joe-Bob said, "I'm not a drug dealer."

Pearce made it to the foot of the stairs and looked around. A fold-up chair sat in front of a trestle table. On the table sat a half-full cafetiere, a mug, a saucer with two chocolate biscuits resting on it, a pearl-handled gun, and a light-blue box with orange and green borders. Behind the table, half-a-dozen more chairs were stacked against the wall.

Joe-Bob sat down and picked up the gun. "Help yourselves to a seat," he said.

"I'll stand," Pearce said.

"I see." Joe-Bob waved the gun at Ailsa. She flapped her fingers at him and gave a little shake of her head. "You going to kill somebody, Pearce?" Joe-Bob asked.

"None of your business."

"Fair enough. Ailsa said you wanted bullets for her Tokarov pistol. There they are." He pointed to the box on the table. "Hope you know what you're doing."

Pearce stepped forward and picked up the box. It said 50 naboju/cartridges. Bullet/Strela. Type FMJ. 7,62X25 Tokarov.

"Nice gun," Joe-Bob said. "You know the Tokarov's a dangerous weapon?"

"It's a gun. It fires bullets. Of course it's dangerous."

"I don't mean that. It doesn't have a safety. You have to half-cock it."

"Speak English."

"You got the gun with you? I'll show you." Joe-Bob laid his own gun on the table.

Pearce reached behind his back and extracted the Tokarov from his trouser belt. He hesitated for a second. Joe-Bob already had a gun. If he wanted to shoot Pearce he could have done so by now. Pearce handed over the Tokarov.

Joe-Bob demonstrated. "That's the slide and trigger locked. See?"

Pearce nodded. "And when I want to fire it?"

Joe-Bob showed him.

Pearce nodded again. "Okay. Load it for me."

Joe-Bob sighed. "Your mum never teach you any manners?"

Anger ballooned inside Pearce. He banged his fist on the table. The saucer rattled and Joe-Bob's pearl-handled gun spun a couple of inches anticlockwise.

Ailsa grabbed Pearce's arm. "Don't." Coffee sloshed from side to side in Joe-Bob's mug.

Joe-Bob said, "I'm loading it, for crying out loud." He popped the clip, opened the box and started shoving bullets into the clip.

"You okay?" Ailsa asked Pearce. He nodded and she let go of his arm.

"You got eight rounds," Joe-Bob said. The bullets clicked in place.

"More than enough," Pearce said.

Joe-Bob pushed the last bullet home and slid the clip back in the gun. "Happy killing." He offered Pearce the gun.

Pearce reached out his hand.

Joe-Bob snatched the gun away. "Money, first," he said.

Pearce dug in his pocket and dropped a pile of notes on the table. "That enough?"

"If you weren't Ailsa's friend," Joe-Bob said, running a hand along his single strip of hair, "I'd take exception to your attitude."

"Gee," Pearce said. "I don't think I'll sleep tonight."

Joe-Bob picked up the notes and started counting. He dropped two tenners on the table and put the rest of the cash in his jacket pocket. "Get the fuck out of here," he said.

Ailsa said, "Thanks, Joe-Bob." She turned to go. Pearce followed her.

Joe-Bob said, "The money on the table's yours."

Pearce didn't look behind him. He said, "That's your tip, Cowboy."

1:30 PM

*S*ince arriving back home, Hilda Pearce's stink had faded. When Robin held his face in his hands, it was Carol's White Musk he smelled. He shivered as he got off his bed, feet crunching broken glass. The pictures he'd destroyed earlier were strewn across the floor. He walked through the debris to his sitting room and banged on the wall with his fist. No good. The rumble of gunfire continued. Maybe he should go next door and kill the deaf old bastard. "Turn it down," he yelled.

Stuffed with money, the holdall lay on the table. Robin kept telling himself that having all that money was a good thing, but it didn't seem to matter. He didn't care any more.

Banging on the wall made no impression. He kicked the skirting board and a black scuffmark appeared on the white paintwork. He shouted, "Turn the fucking TV down." He was a bit sensitive at the moment and the constant racket was driving him mad. He couldn't live here any more. Home shouldn't be like this. He'd have to start looking for another flat. *Hang on a minute*. *Slow down*. Within the last twenty-four hours he'd killed two people. Why the fuck was he whining about a blaring television set? He laughed aloud at the ridiculousness of it all. He was losing his sense of perspective. Bad news. Loss of perspective led to bizarre acts like holding up petrol stations with water pistols. Anyway, if he moved, where would he go? Share with Eddie again? Fuck it. It wasn't important.

It didn't matter. Nothing mattered. Eddie screwing Carol didn't matter. Hilda Pearce didn't matter. Death didn't matter. Carol was dead and it didn't matter. He was a murderer and it didn't matter. Carol was dead.

Shit. His stomach was lined with ice.

He walked over to the piano, opened the lid of the piano stool and took out the envelope containing the PI's photographs of Carol and Eddie. He'd hoped Carol might have found them. But why would she? She didn't know they existed, so there was no reason for her to have looked for them. He set the envelope on the piano stand. The pictures didn't matter. He didn't care any more. He wouldn't look at them. He sat down and punched a G minor chord. He hit it again and found himself playing the opening of "Dido's Lament" from Purcell's opera, *Dido and Aeneas*. The chromatics and suspensions collaborated to produce harmonies likely to break the heart of any normal human being. Not his. Oh, no. His hands hurt, but he didn't fucking care. He sang along.

TWO-WAY SPLIT | 159

"*No trouble.*" The tension in the D/E$^\flat$ false relation was agonising. Didn't mean anything to him. Remember? He repeated the bar. "*No trouble.*" His hands were on fire. *NO*. "*In my soul.*" He brought his fist down on the keyboard. Dissonance clogged his eardrums. He slammed the lid shut.

Lifting the envelope off the stand, he ripped it open. The photos fell out. Ten of them. He picked up the top one, which had landed face up. In it, Carol was holding hands with Eddie. Eddie was smiling for the photographer, crooked teeth displayed in his too-small mouth. She was looking into his eyes. Had she loved him? She was dead. What did it matter? He'd killed her. God help him.

What was Eddie going to do when he found out? Most likely he'd be philosophical about it. *Carol's dead? Hey, life goes on. This mean a two-way split?*

The holdall sat on the table like an ugly brown bag of conscience. A face with the fat cheeks of Hilda Pearce was starting to form on the fucking thing. Well, Robin had had enough. It wasn't going to distract him any more. He had to stop this, force himself to concentrate and come up with a plan to kill Eddie.

It was no good. He couldn't think with that thing staring at him.

He hid the bag in the bedroom.

Back in the sitting room he tried his hardest to focus on Eddie, but something else was starting to worry him. He'd done his best to avoid thinking about it, but it wouldn't go away. When he'd arrived home the door to his flat was open. Just as well, since he seemed to have mislaid his keys. For a moment, when he checked his pockets outside the main door, he had imagined he'd have to trek all the way back to Eddie's and get Carol's spare set. Of course, the police would have arrived by now, since the last thing he did before driving home was to call them and report a disturbance. It had taken him a hell of a long time to get home, though.

Thankfully, the old Henderson woman downstairs had buzzed him inside. When he got upstairs he found his door ajar. Nothing was missing. He struggled to remember if he'd locked up when he left, but his memory was hazy.

Luckily, he kept another set of keys in a drawer in the kitchen.

Shit. He needed to relax. All this thinking was doing him no good at all. Just making his headache worse. There was a lot on his mind and it was no surprise that he couldn't remember leaving his flat. He must have forgotten to close the door behind him. That was all there was to it. Had to be.

Relax. Let it rest.

He lay on the floor and started humming Mozart's A minor Piano Sonata. After the first movement, he fancied a change of mood. Mozart was too camp. He sang some Bach. A couple of fugues followed by a two-part invention. Then Beethoven's "The Tempest" Sonata. Impossibly hard for an untrained voice like his, but he gave it a damn good shot.

When the phone rang, he'd just reached the end of the first movement and had filled his lungs to begin the slow movement. Getting up off the floor required a huge effort. He contented himself with raising his head. The phone continued to chirp. Eventually, he uncurled himself and sat up. His muscles ached. He felt like he hadn't slept for a week.

Slowly, he got to his feet and walked over to the phone. When he picked it up, something crawled out of the receiver and dropped to the floor. He jumped on the disgusting, black thing. Crushed it with his heel. Ground it into the carpet.

He guided the phone to his ear. "Hello," he said.

"It's me. Please don't hang up. I have something important to tell you."

This was not good. This was not good at all. "Who are you?"

"Stop pretending you don't know."

"Go away. I don't know you."

"Play it your way. How about Carol? You know her?"

"Leave me alone."

Robin dropped the phone. It lay on the floor but he could still hear the voice. He picked up the phone and placed it on the cradle and the voice disappeared. Clever. He picked up the phone again and listened. Two voices. Pure sound, communicating by maintaining a constant interval of a major third. *Dial tone*. The words sprang into his head. He shook the phone and was surprised when nothing fell out of it. He placed it to his ear again and listened. Same story. Dial tone. He placed the receiver back in its cradle.

It rang instantly.

Don was back. "Please don't hang up."

"What do you want?"

A short pause. "You think you killed her."

"What do you mean?"

"You didn't. It was Eddie."

Robin's fingers formed a gun. It was a familiar shape. Someone else had done that. He said, "Bang. He's dead."

"Not when I last saw him."

"As good as. Why do you say he killed Carol?"

"I saw it with my own eyes."

"You're wrong."

"I know why you might think that. After all, he told the police it was me. But he'd be unlikely to admit it to you. I tell you, Robin, I'm a witness."

"A witness?"

"I can confirm that Eddie killed Carol."

"But he couldn't have. I did."

"You have to help me, Robin. We have to help each other. The police think I killed her. God, this is such a mess."

"I killed her. Not Eddie."

Silence.

Then Don said, "Try covering for him all you like, but you know you didn't kill her. Think about it. You saw her breathe just before you left. Remember? Eddie came back. Eddie killed her. Listen to me. I was there. I saw his fingers wrapped around her throat. He was choking your wife, Robin."

"Why are you making this up?"

"Why would I lie? Look, she was still alive when you disappeared. Do you believe that much, at least?"

"Suppose it's possible."

"Well, she's dead now and the man responsible is the same man who hit me on the head and knocked me out. Eddie."

"What did you see?"

"She wasn't making any sound, but her legs were moving. She was kicking. I tried to stop him." He sighed. "I failed, sorry. In the end, I thought he was going to kill me, so I ran away. He chased me and fired a couple of shots. I think he told the police I killed her. It's my word against his and I can't take the risk. I'm a fugitive. But you can help me, Robin. Together we can destroy the man who murdered your wife and tried to frame us for it."

Robin licked his lips. Was it possible he hadn't killed her?

Don said, "Will you meet me somewhere? Let me convince you I'm telling the truth."

Robin said, "I'm going psychotic cooped up here. A minute ago I saw a leech crawl out of the telephone."

"I hate when that happens."

"I need to get out of here."

"Sounds like it. Meet me for a beer?"

"Never touch the stuff these days."

"Coffee, then."

"Okay, but you have to promise me one thing. You'll help me kill Eddie."

"My pleasure."

"Okay. Where do you want to meet?"

"Filmhouse café?"

"When?"

"Soon as you can get there."

When the phone rang again, Robin thought Don had forgotten something. He was surprised when Eddie's voice said his name. "Who do you think it is?" Robin asked him.

"There's a fine fucking question. Look, you're ill. I don't blame you. I got rid of her handbag. Hopefully, the police will take a while to trace her and it'll buy us some time. We've got to run. I need my money."

"I've no idea what you're talking about." *Right. Pretend you're my pal, take the money, and then kill me.*

"I'm talking about Carol, you fuckwit."

Robin didn't answer.

"Can you meet me somewhere with the money?"

Robin said, "Carol's dead."

"She meant a lot to me. But if you just give me the money, I'll keep my mouth shut."

"Did you kill her?"

"The fuck are you saying, Robin? That won't wash. Your prints are all over her. You got the money? I'll settle for my share and Carol's. You can keep yours."

Silence filled Robin's ear. It hurt.

"I'm coming for the money," Eddie said. "You got it?"

"Did you try to kill Don? Did you try to shoot him?"

"Of course I didn't try to shoot him."

"Why not?"

"Because I wouldn't do that to you."

"You saying you didn't try to kill him?"

"That's exactly what I'm saying. What makes you think I did?"

"I'm going out, Eddie."

"Stay where you are. I think I should come over."

"The money's not here." Robin had to think quickly. "It's somewhere safe. I've got to fetch it. It'll take a couple of hours."

"I'll come with you," Eddie said.

"You can't. There's a dead body in your flat, Eddie. You have to stay out of sight. Did you kill her?"

"What's going on in your fucking crazy head?" Eddie sighed. "About three o'clock?"

"Three thirty. And phone me first to check that I'm back."

"Robin, you sure the money's stashed somewhere safe?"

"Every penny." Robin put the phone down.

2:00 PM

*P*earce dragged the heel of his boot across the gravel. The pistol was digging into his back again. He looked across at Robin Greaves's flat. If he waited until dark he could climb the scaffolding. It looked easy enough. Just above head height, a metal ladder was tied horizontally across three standards. Once he managed to pull himself up to the platform, he could free the ladder and use it to get to the second floor. He didn't need a ladder, really. He could probably climb up the lugs. The problem wasn't getting up there. The problem was what to do when he got there. You see, he'd have to shoot Greaves through his sitting room window, and he wasn't sure what effect glass had on the trajectory of a bullet. He could smash the window first, but that would warn Greaves and Pearce doubted he could hit a moving target. To be realistic, the only way he could be sure of killing Greaves was to have the Tokarov's muzzle pressed against the scumbag's forehead when he pulled the trigger.

Scaling the scaffolding wasn't an option. He needed to find a way to get inside the building.

Robin Greaves wasn't at home. Or if he was, he wasn't answering his door. Ideally, Pearce would pick the lock and wait in the empty flat for Greaves to return. Then he'd grab him and unload a couple of shots into the murdering bastard's skull. Unfortunately, Pearce had no idea how to pick a lock. It was the sort of topic that had often come up in jail, but Pearce had never paid much attention. No, the best he could do was break down the door. He knew how to do that all right. But if Greaves returned home to find his front door kicked in, he'd take one look and run.

Pearce considered whacking him in the street. That would work. Wait until he saw Greaves strolling along the road, then head towards him. When he was close enough, reach behind his back, yank the gun out of his belt, and bang, bang, one dead motherfucker. A great plan, were it not for its single fatal flaw. In the post office, Greaves had worn a balaclava, so Pearce didn't know what the little shit looked like. Pearce knew his general size and shape, knew what he sounded like, but he could pass him in the street and not know it. So much for that idea.

Perched on a low wall on the opposite side of the street, Pearce had detected no movement from inside Greaves's flat. He was pretty sure Greaves had gone out. Pearce had buzzed his entry phone several times. No response. He'd dialled directory inquiries and got Greaves's phone number and tried that too. Several times. Again, no response.

Pearce fingered the pistol through his t-shirt. The gun was awkward and clumsy and uncomfortable. He nudged the barrel over to the right. When he moved forward, it slipped back again. If only he could wait inside, hide somewhere and ambush Greaves as he unlocked his front door. That was the answer. And if nobody could see him, he could take the damned gun out of his belt.

It was going to happen. Sorry, Ailsa.

She had given it her best shot. They left Joe-Bob in his dungeon hideout and snaked their way back to the bar. Roy, the barman, had left the big oak door unlocked and it had been a fairly simple matter to retrace their steps. Within five minutes they were back in the bar area, where thick smoke singed the air.

Ailsa spoke over the hubbub. "I'll have that drink now."

Pearce gave her a long, hard look. "You trying to delay me?"

She leaned close and said in his ear, "This might be our only opportunity to have a drink together."

He grinned at her. "What do you want?"

When the barmaid bounced over, still dressed like a schoolgirl, still chewing gum, and still saying, "Can I get you?", Pearce ordered a pint of Guinness and a coffee. He followed Ailsa to a table in front of the fireplace.

Ailsa said, "You're not fooling yourself that you're doing this for your mother, are you?"

He peeled the lid off his individual UHT milk portion and poured it into his coffee. "Revenge is something Mum understood."

"She applauded what you did to your sister's dealer?"

"I didn't say she approved. I said she understood."

"And your mother's approval is of no consequence, I suppose?"

He picked up the teaspoon. "Bit late for that." He stirred the coffee.

"You don't think she's *up there* watching you make yet another huge mistake?"

He laid the spoon on the saucer. "Not a chance."

"Actually," Ailsa said, "I don't either. I just want to—"

"Save yourself the trouble. I know you think I'm a fool." She opened her mouth to interrupt him, but he held up a hand to silence her. "I'm sorry you think that. But maybe you're right. Maybe what I'm about to do is a mistake. And maybe I'll regret it for the rest of my life." He paused. "But I know this." He took a sip of coffee. "Most people don't have to make a choice. They have it easy. For them, the idea of killing someone is nothing more than a concept, a fantasy. They never have to make a real choice." When he raised his cup again, his hand shook slightly. He sipped the coffee. Lowered the cup. It rattled in the saucer. "I'm a convicted murderer. I have a choice to make. I know I'm capable of killing someone. That's not a concept or a fantasy. It's stark staring reality."

"Just because you can, doesn't mean you should."

"Just because I can, doesn't mean I shouldn't."

She glared at him. "If you do, you'll ruin your life."

"If I don't, how can I live with myself?"

"I don't understand."

"Revenge," he said, "is an important part of my grieving process."

Ailsa drank some of her beer. She wiped foam off her mouth with the back of her hand. "You found out who this guy is, yeah?" When he frowned, she added, "Your mother's killer?"

"I know his name and where he lives."

She nodded. "Why not tell the police?" She tapped the table with her fingertips. "If he's the killer, they're bound to be able to collect enough evidence to put him away. He'll be locked up for a long time." She held a finger in the air as if testing the wind. "There's your revenge."

He shook his head. "That's justice. Not revenge."

For a further fifteen minutes, she tried to persuade him. When he left her in the bar, his parting words were, "You did your duty. There was never anything more you could have done." She squeezed his hand so hard it hurt.

The sooner it was over, the better.

Pearce looked up at Robin Greaves's sitting room window. He dabbed his eyes with his thumb knuckles and they came away wet. The wind was playing havoc with his tear ducts. He jumped down off the wall and headed towards Leith Walk in search of a florist.

2:27 PM

*O*nce again in front of Greaves's building, a bunch of tulips now tucked under his arm, Pearce scanned the list of names by the door buzzers. Surnames only. The occupants had taken care not to reveal their gender. He rang the top four buzzers. No reply. Good. His finger moved to the bottom and he began working his way up.

The third one got a response. A female. Elderly. "Hello?"

He said, "Delivery."

A pause. "I'm not expecting anything."

He read the name next to the buzzer. "Ms Henderson?"

"Yes."

"Flowers. They're for you."

"Why would anybody…" She stopped short. "Oh, well. Come in."

There were four flats on the ground floor. Ms Henderson lived in the first one on the right. He knocked on her door and she opened it a crack. When he held up the flowers, she slid the chain off.

"You sure they're for me?"

Trying his best to look annoyed, he dug in his back pocket and pulled out the *Eye Witness* business card. He held it to the side, covering the back with his fingers so Mrs Henderson couldn't see the message Gray had written on it. "Henderson, right?" Wisps of white hair trailed over the old lady's scalp and her eyes were wiggling from side to side behind Irn Bru-bottle glasses as her mouth made perpetual little biting movements. He hated to lie to the old dear. "Henderson's the name I've got here."

"I'm Mrs Henderson right enough. But who would be buying me flowers, son?"

He put the card back in his pocket. "There's a note." He handed over the flowers.

Mrs Henderson reached out with an arm like a stick wrapped in brown paper. She looked for the note and when she found it, she frowned at him. "Can you read it for me?" she asked. "The writing's too small."

Pearce turned the label towards him and read: "From a secret admirer." He winked at her. "Still turning heads, eh?"

"Watch your lip, son. I've been pig-ugly all my life and I know it. This a joke, is it?"

He lifted his shoulders. "Somebody paid for those flowers, Mrs Henderson, and asked us to deliver them to you. If you don't want them, I can take them away. But I don't think it's a joke."

"I'll take them." The flowers disappeared through the gap in the door. "Now bugger off." She slammed the door shut.

He stared at the door for a minute. For a while there he'd thought Mrs Henderson was about to ruin his plans. Well, she hadn't. He was inside, which was exactly where he wanted to be. What, now? First, he retraced his steps. When he reached the front door, he opened it and then closed it with enough force to convince anyone who might be listening that he had left the building. He waited for a while, then retreated, as quietly as his heavy boots would allow, towards the stairs.

His right foot was on the third step when his mobile rang. A cold sweat broke out on his forehead and down his back, but already his fingers were scrabbling for the phone. He just had time to recognise Ailsa's number in the display panel before the phone rang a second time. He turned it off and stood motionless for a while. From this angle he could only see the bottom half of Mrs Henderson's door. He kept staring at it, expecting it to open. But time passed and the door stayed shut. After a short while he carried on up the stairs.

The first floor was quiet.

On the second floor landing he felt free to tread a little less carefully. From the flat next to Robin Greaves's the sound of a television blared. Gunfire. Lots of it. Pearce went up another flight, which is where he was going to wait. When he tried the top buzzers earlier, nobody had replied, which implied that residents on this floor were all out. If Greaves returned home first, Pearce would be able to slip downstairs and do what he had to do. If, on the other hand, a top floor resident came home before Greaves, Pearce would pretend he'd been visiting, leave the building and figure another way of dealing with his mum's killer.

But he didn't think Greaves would stay out for long. In Pearce's experience, a man who's just murdered someone needs to be in a familiar setting while he adjusts to the magnitude of what he's done. And nowhere is more familiar than home.

Pearce sat down in the corner. He leaned forward, removed the gun from his belt and half-cocked it as Joe-Bob had shown him. He waited, feeling remarkably calm.

3:10 PM

*R*obin glanced at his passenger as the car sped down Leith Walk.

Initially, Robin had been confused, but now he thought he'd worked it out.

To begin with, he believed he had killed Carol. Retrospectively, it was clear that he was mistaken. When he saw her stomach move just before he left her flat, he thought he'd imagined it. But it was real. What he saw was Carol taking a breath. He hadn't killed her. She was unconscious, that was all. Then, when Eddie came back, instead of calling an ambulance, the bastard had strangled her.

There was no room for doubt. Don saw him do it. Over a cup of coffee, he'd described what happened. He kept wincing and putting his hand to his head, apologising for having a splitting headache, for which Eddie was responsible. Robin wondered if maybe Don was just trying to hide those nasty scars. Anyway, as a result of Don having witnessed Eddie throttling Carol, Eddie was now trying to kill the poor sod. Shot at him in broad daylight!

Don was scared. Changing gear, Robin looked at him again. He looked unusual. Not just the scars. It was something else. Like his body shimmered. He gave the impression that if you looked away, he'd disappear. The poor guy was out of his depth. Probably wished he *could* disappear. This wasn't the sort of situation a normal person could handle. He was struggling, you could tell. Paranoid, poor bastard. Not entirely surprising, after what had happened. And Robin owed him. Sure. A brotherly tenderness soaked through Robin as he listen to Don explain that he was a rep for a pharmaceutical company these days. He'd gone to check on Carol's reaction to Sulpiride. Looking for paradoxical side effects, apparently. Robin told him he'd never experienced anything like that. Sulpiride worked well for him. Did what any anti-psychotic was supposed to. Repressed the hallucinations. So effectively, in fact, that just under five months ago, the hallucinations had disappeared completely. Robin told Don that he'd stopped taking his medication. He still picked up his Sulpiride prescriptions, of course, to keep the doctors happy. But when he got home, he chucked the pills down the toilet.

Don was a good listener. When he spoke it was to say that the only person he could trust now was Robin. He wasn't prepared to talk to the police. They'd believe Eddie's story.

Eddie had gone off his head. He'd killed Carol, for fuck's sake, and set Don up to make it look like he'd done it.

Why the hell had he killed her? Maybe he'd seen an opportunity to get all the money for himself. Maybe he was planning on killing Robin next. Eddie was always a crazy fucker. Misogynistic. Brutal. He was chucked out of the police force for breaking a seventeen-year-old's collarbone. The poor girl had been pregnant and Eddie's assault on her caused her to lose the baby. His story is that she was resisting arrest. Eddie, the sick bastard, referred to the incident as a miscarriage of justice. The gear stick squirmed in Robin's hand. He squeezed it into submission. Once it was pulsing gently between his aching fingers, he let go of it and wiped the slime on his trousers.

The car rolled into a parking space and he killed the engine.

"Do we wait here or go inside?" Don asked.

Robin said, "Inside."

"What about the police?"

"I don't see any."

"They'll come. Even without Carol's I.D., they'll discover her name and connect her to you."

"We have different surnames. It'll take them a while."

"Suppose we go inside. Then what?"

Robin looked at his watch. "When Eddie arrives at three thirty, you'll be hiding. I'll invite him in as if nothing unusual has happened. After a while, you jump out and confront him."

"He has a gun. What if he shoots me?"

"I'll get it off him first."

Don said, "What then?"

"I'll kill him."

"No."

"Why not? Look, we can drive him at gunpoint to some secluded spot and get rid of him. We both benefit."

"I can't."

"Why not?"

"It just isn't right, Robin."

"You're an honest man, Don. I admire that." He tried to keep a straight face. "You want to beat a confession out of him?"

"He won't confess."

"I hope not." Robin saw Don's Adam's apple slide up and down. "Fucker killed my wife and set you up." Robin smacked the steering wheel with his palm. "We're in this together."

"Till the end." Don touched his head and grimaced. "Like real brothers."

Robin opened the car door. The wind instantly chilled him. He stepped outside and slammed the door shut. Seconds later Don closed the passenger side door. Robin led the way to his flat, apologising for the unsightly scaffolding. He looked up. Already the light was fading. He walked over to his doorway and talked about Edinburgh's problem with falling masonry while he jiggled his key in the lock. Don clapped his gloved hands.

Robin pushed the door open. The stair lights hadn't come on yet. Robin and Don slid through almost total darkness towards the stairs, where trickles of silvery light ran down the steps. On the first floor landing pools of dusk gathered in the corner. Up another flight, the light was brighter, a shade darker than the light of a full moon.

Robin stuck his key in the lock.

Footsteps rushed towards him and something heavy slammed into his back. His face smacked into the door. His nose hurt. His lower lip started to bleed. He nearly dropped the key. "Eddie?"

He heard Don say, "Who are you?" Not Eddie, then. They'd already met. Don said, "Okay, okay, okay."

Something cold pressed against the back of his neck. A voice whispered in his ear, "Open the door." The voice sounded familiar. He couldn't place it, though.

He expected Don to run, but he hadn't moved. Maybe he'd frozen. Poor old Don, getting into even more trouble. Whoever this joker was, he wasn't playing for fun.

Robin turned the key and the door swung open.

"Turn on the light," the voice whispered.

When Robin flicked the switch, bright light flooded the hallway and it took a moment for his eyes to adjust after the darkness in the stairwell. If there had been a chance of exploiting his assailant's surprise, Robin blew it when he turned to look at him. Recognition was instant. Hilda Pearce's son was hard to forget. Over-developed arms, cropped hair, boots, jeans. He'd changed the t-shirt. This one wasn't covered in blood.

He had a gun and it was pointed at Robin.

Pearce closed the door with his foot. "Be a good boy and sit down."

Don said, "Who the fuck are you?"

"You know who I am."

Robin said, "I don't know who you think I am but you've got the wrong person."

"You're Robin Greaves. This is his flat. You have his keys. I might not have been able to see your face behind that balaclava, but I remember your voice."

Robin's thoughts were flying around his head like a flock of swallows. He reached out and grabbed one by the wing. It almost got away. "I'm his brother. That's why we sound alike. Tell him, Don."

Pearce said, "Who are you talking to?"

Don said, "Me."

Pearce said, "Stop this shit. Are you Robin Greaves or not?"

"Why do you want to know?"

"Because I don't want to kill the wrong person."

3:18 PM

*K*ennedy stood on the planks that formed the lowest level of the scaffolding outside Robin Greaves's tenement building. His head was spinning and he felt sick. Having managed to shimmy up a pole, swing his leg onto the flooring and drag himself onto the first platform, he now wished to pish that he hadn't. He sat down, back pressed against the tenement wall, knees drawn up to his chest, and took regular, deep, slow breaths. There was no safety mesh. Not even a series of planks lying lengthways along the edge. Which would have been a very false kind of security, anyway. He guessed scaffolders lined up planks like that to stop their tools rolling over the side, because an eight-inch high wall of end-to-end planks of wood certainly wasn't going to stop a body plummeting to the pavement. Okay, it was only a seven feet drop, but when he'd glanced over the side earlier, seven feet seemed a hell of a long way down. And he had to get higher. Much higher.

He shouldn't be here. It was a bad idea. What was he thinking, climbing scaffolding outside a block of flats where someone was likely to be murdered? That was asking for shagging trouble. Jesus pish. Well, he'd handed in his notice, which was something to be positive about. Mind you, it was either resign or get fired. Immediately after the meeting with Pearce—where Kennedy had given the big twat all the information he needed and got absolutely SFA in return—Kennedy turned to his boss and said, "I quit." It felt good, for all of a couple of seconds.

His boss said, "See you."

Kennedy couldn't leave it there. He had to have the last word. "I'll be in touch. About my wages."

His boss had his hand over his nose. Well, to be accurate, his ex-boss had his hand over his nose. When he nodded, his eyes screwed shut and he shrieked in pain. After a moment he said, "I'll kill that bastard."

Kennedy laughed in his face.

He wasn't laughing now. He struggled to his feet, which was quite an achievement under the circumstances. Next task was to free the ladder, each leg of which was lashed to three separate upright poles. Only then could he risk climbing up to the next level. Trying not to look down, he started to work on the ropes.

They had been tied with a special kind of knot and it took him a minute to discover how best to unravel it. It didn't help that his fingers were about as dextrous as frozen sausages. It was hard, painful work, but, eventually, he sussed it out. After the first one, the rest were relatively easy. Nonetheless, it took a couple of minutes to untie all six bindings.

He dragged the ladder into position underneath the entry to the next level. Lifting the ladder, he pushed it until the top poked through the hole above him. Propped against the side, the ladder seemed steady enough. He let go and wasted a couple of minutes watching a young couple on the other side of the street. Eyes focussed on the pavement in front of them, they were lugging a dozen carrier bags homewards. They didn't take their eyes off their feet. Around here, to do so was to step in dogshit. They disappeared round a corner and Kennedy turned his attention to a Ford Escort van, back door tied shut with orange string. Well, it looked orange. Fifteen minutes ago, the sky had clouded over and the light wasn't too good. The colour had faded from everything and it looked like it was going to rain, maybe even snow.

He had to do this. And he had to do it now. He couldn't postpone it any longer.

The top of the ladder was solid enough. The foot of the ladder was a problem, though. There was nothing to stop it slipping when he put his weight on it and there was nobody around to ask to steady it. *Here goes.*

When he set his foot on the bottom rung, the ladder tilted to the right. Instantly he withdrew his foot. He repositioned the ladder until it felt more secure and tried again. This time it didn't budge under his weight. He moved his other foot onto the rung above. He was breathing rapidly now and his fingers were gripping the ladder far too tightly. He told himself to calm down. He wasn't that high, yet. Even if he fell, which he wouldn't, he couldn't hurt himself. Not unless he fell awkwardly and landed on his head or something, in which case he'd probably break his neck or his skull or his spine and probably die or live the rest of his life in a wheelchair.

He forced himself up onto the next rung. And then the next. A gust of wind lifted his hair off his forehead. It bounced back. Lifted. Bounced back. He no longer felt cold. Sweat was stinging his eyes. If anything, he was too hot and the wind helped cool him down. He leaned his head against the ladder. Two more steps and his head would break through to the next level. One. *Yes*. And two. *Come on*. He didn't look down. Why should it be such a struggle *not* to look? Yes. He'd done it. He was on the next level. Only from the neck up, admittedly.

He wondered if his boss, shit, ex-boss, had gone to hospital this time. Kennedy hadn't hung around to find out. After his ex-boss—fuck it, call the man by his name—Gray's ridiculous threat on Pearce's life, Kennedy had laughed all the way downstairs and out the salmon pink main door. Out on the street he decided to give himself one more shot at the money.

Which was why he was here, climbing a shaky ladder fifteen feet up in the air, with another twenty feet to go.

Greaves's address was the only information Pearce had been given. There was no need to tail him, since he'd have to turn up here at some point. It was just a matter of waiting and Kennedy had lots of practice at that. Sure enough, Pearce had made an appearance shortly before two o'clock. He tried Greaves's buzzer and made a few phone calls. He hung around for a while, disappeared for twenty minutes and returned with a bunch of flowers. Then somebody let him into the building and he hadn't reappeared since. Greaves had got out of his Clio just a few minutes ago.

This was Kennedy's big chance. He had to do it. He owed it to himself.

He dragged himself up the last step and fell onto the wooden planks. This high up, he knew he'd never get back down. He had to carry on. If he didn't manage to get into Greaves's flat, he'd be stuck up here forever. He turned round, grabbed hold of the ladder and pulled it through the opening. He half-carried, half-dragged it towards the gap above his head. He turned the ladder upright and placed it in position. Only when he set foot on the bottom rung did he notice he was directly outside someone's window. Fortunately, the light wasn't on. But could he assume that no one was home? He started to climb, fast. He got to the top, dragged the ladder up after him and lay still, panting like a dog on a treadmill. He looked over the side and nearly fainted.

He didn't remember those hardboiled private eyes ever having to climb scaffolding. But, in the hypothetical event of his fictional heroes having to do so, he was sure they'd do it gracefully and without any fuss. And, no doubt, without the aid of a ladder. Inspirational characters who met all challenges with a stubborn, arrogant self-confidence. Kennedy felt deflated and wholly incompetent in comparison. He thought he might just stay here for a while, at least until his bowels stopped feeling quite so loose.

What spurred him on was the sound of gunfire. It came from above. At first he thought it was Pearce. After a while, he realised it was unlikely that, supposing Pearce had a gun, he would have quite that many bullets. And supposing he had, at some point he'd need to stop and reload. The shots were from a TV, of course, and it sounded like they were coming from a room on the second floor, which was where Greaves lived.

One more flight. Quick sprint up the ladder and that was it. Easy.

Once again he positioned the ladder. Again it tilted when he put his foot on it. He repositioned it. Still it tilted. He countered the imbalance by placing his weight on the left side of each rung. Five steps up, the ladder started to slide backwards. It only moved an inch or so. Hurriedly, he stepped onto the next rung. And the next. The ladder slid underneath him. His foot missed the rung. He looked up and watched in horror as the ladder scraped away from the edge where it had been resting. He flung out a hand. His fingers grabbed cold metal as the ladder clattered to the floor below. He swung by one hand, slowly rotating. His legs kicked out in the hope of locating a solid surface with his feet, but all they hit was air. He launched his other hand upwards. Couldn't find the vertical pole his right hand clung to. He tried again. No joy. His wrist hurt. If he could hold on until he stopped spinning, he might be able to pull himself up, grab hold with his other hand, swing a leg up, maybe hook it over the pole. He just had to hold on. He kept spinning and his fingers were growing numb. He was slipping. *Don't look down.* He looked down. *Fucking hell.* He was dangling over the edge. There was nothing but space between him and the pavement. If he could just hold on a little bit longer.

He swung his free hand one more time and at last caught the pole. He stopped spinning. *Thank fuck.* He hung there and started to laugh. He was scared shitless. The temptation to let go and get it over with was hard to resist. He closed his eyes and prayed, which was no help. He opened his eyes, gritted his teeth and with one last effort managed to manoeuvre his hands into position. He raised his knees and hooked one foot over the pole. The other foot followed. Then everything went out of focus and his mind blanked for a second. He dragged himself back from the brink of unconsciousness and snapped into an adrenalin-charged alertness. He let go of the pole with his right hand and grabbed hold of the vertical pole just behind him. He pulled, the muscles in his arm about to tear. He tensed his legs, twisted his body. He let go with his left hand and quickly clasped the bar underneath his stomach. Straightening his elbow, he fumbled with his other hand for the edge of the platform. When he found it he held on and dragged his leg across. After a moment he moved his hand along. Ignoring the sound of the blood pounding in his ears, he pulled his body further onto the planked flooring inch by inch.

When only his left foot dangled over the edge, he lay still. After a while he turned on his back and wiped the sweat out of his eyes. He felt light-headed. He'd done it, though. No motherfucking scaffolding would mess with him again. Maybe Max and Johnny weren't that special after all.

3:19 PM

*P*earce examined the man who claimed to be Robin Greaves's brother. He was wiping his palms on his trousers, nervously. But Pearce expected that. If somebody waded into your home uninvited and stuck a gun in your face, you'd be nervous too. Nerves proved nothing.

"I'm getting tired of waiting," Pearce said. Patches of dried blood matted the man's hair. Somebody had hit him hard. And fairly recently, by the look of it. He was a sorry fucking state. "You going to answer my question?"

"You've got it wrong. I'm not Robin. I'm his brother."

"Right. Let's see your wallet and I'll tell you who the fuck you are."

Greaves's eyes darted all over the place. The rest of him didn't move. Not the tiniest bit.

Pearce said, "Now." He didn't take his eyes off Greaves. "Wallet, please."

Greaves put his hand in his pocket. "What's the point?" He removed his hand. It was empty. "You want to shoot me?" He thumped his fist against his chest. "Go ahead. Shoot me."

Pearce said, "Okay." He stepped closer and aimed the gun at Robin Greaves. Pointed the gun at the man who killed his mother. Held the muzzle directly over his left eye.

Greaves stared into the barrel, eyes wide. His moment of bravado had passed. He mumbled something as a stain spread on his crotch. Urine leaked out of his trouser leg. "My hands hurt," he said. "I've got sore hands." He sank to his knees. Pearce kept the gun pointed at his eye. Greaves clutched his hands together and started rubbing them gently, as if he was washing them. "Really bad." He unclasped them to show Pearce his palms. "They don't work, you know?"

"I don't give a fuck about your hands," Pearce told him. "Why are you telling me about your fucking hands?"

"They're everywhere, now," Greaves said.

"What?" Pearce shook his head with impatience. "Who?"

"They came from your mother."

"What the hell are you talking about?"

Greaves rolled forward onto the floor and adopted a foetal position with his hands tucked between his knees. "They're everywhere," he said. "Leeches. Crawling down my leg right this minute." He started humming. "Tell him, Don."

Pearce said, "Stop it." Greaves didn't stop. The humming grew louder. Greaves opened his lips and started singing. No words. Something classical. Whatever it was, it sounded painful. His tenor voice drowned out the noise of next-door's television. Pearce didn't know what to do. He'd come here to kill a man, not fuck with this headcase who lay in a puddle of his own urine belting out some classical ditty and claiming that leeches were crawling down his leg and talking to somebody called Don who wasn't there. "Stop it." He shoved the gun into the flesh of Greaves's cheek. "Stop it." Greaves wailed all the louder.

Pearce walked over to the piano stool and sat on it. This was complicated. He needed to think. He looked at Greaves.

Greaves said, "I don't know what's happening any longer."

"Which member of the Greaves family said that?"

"Me. Don."

"Well, Don. I thought that choirboy called Robin stabbed my mother in the neck. Now I'm not so sure. Was it you?"

"Certainly not. And I find it hard to believe that Robin would do something like that."

Pearce said, "So do I. If this is all an elaborate con..."

"It's real."

Pearce hesitated. He nodded. "I can see that. Has Robin gone?"

"For the time being," Don said. "Are you going to shoot me?"

The door buzzer sounded before Pearce could reply.

3:26 PM

"*E*xpecting somebody?"

Robin's throat hurt. He stopped singing while he tried to sit up. He fell back and tried again. This time he succeeded. His eyes felt sore and puffy and strangely wet, as if he'd been crying. The buzzer sounded again. He blinked and wiped his eyes with the heels of his hands. Blinked again. His nemesis was sitting on the piano stool, a gun in his shovel-like hand. The buzzer sounded once more. The phone rang. Counterpoint. Bach.

"Don't answer it," Pearce said.

Something moved along Robin's thigh. He thought they'd all gone, but he could see its dark outline through his trousers. He slapped his leg as hard as he could. The thing stuck there. He pinched it between finger and thumb and squeezed. Pain sang in his fingers, creating harmonics. Perfect fifths and major thirds floated on top of the tide of sound. He pulled the damn thing off his leg, but it slipped through his fingers and he couldn't find it again. Maybe that was the last one. He hoped so. He stood and shook his trouser leg.

Pearce said, "Leave it."

Contrapuntal ostinatos. Robin remembered. They thought he wasn't paying attention. They thought he wasn't lucid. Ha! "The phone?" he said. "Or the door?"

Pearce didn't reply.

Robin said, "That'll be Eddie. I arranged to meet him at half three. He won't go away, you know." Robin took a step towards the door. He seemed to have wet himself. He felt himself blush.

Pearce said, "Leave it."

Robin stood still. His face was hot, but from the waist down, he was feeling very cold.

After thirty seconds the phone stopped ringing. Ten seconds later Eddie, or whoever was downstairs, pressed the buzzer again and left his finger there. It emitted one long continuous buzzing sound. It went on. And on. And on. Then the phone joined in.

Robin shivered. He wanted to play something. Something fast. Maybe a Chopin study. He looked at the piano keys and started to hum.

Don said, "For heaven's sake."

Pearce shouted, "Okay, answer the phone."

Robin looked at him.

"Go on."

Robin hobbled towards the phone and picked up the receiver.

Eddie said, "Fuck you playing at?"

Robin put his hand over the mouthpiece. "It's Eddie, like I said," he said to Pearce. Eddie had killed Carol, hadn't he? Robin could imagine how she'd looked, blouse unbuttoned, stomach bared, a single letter cut in her skin. How could he do that? You thought you knew someone and... Well, it just went to show. "He wants in."

Pearce said, "Tell him it's not convenient. Come back tomorrow."

Robin removed his hand from the speaker. "It's not convenient. Come back tomorrow."

Eddie said, "Are the police there?"

"No. It's just not convenient."

Eddie said, "I've got your keys, remember? I'm coming in."

Robin covered the mouthpiece again and passed on the message.

Pearce said, "Shit."

Robin told Eddie, "Shit."

"Who's with you?"

"Nobody."

Eddie hung up.

Robin stared at the receiver. Nothing crawled out of it. He set it on the cradle.

They waited, listening to the cowboys on next-door's TV. Pearce got to his feet and started prowling. Don leaned against the wall, looking sick. His face had a greenish tinge. He kept swimming in and out of focus and at one point seemed to disappear completely for a split second.

The doorbell rang.

Pearce said, "You might as well answer it. He'll let himself in if you don't."

Don said, "It's not a good idea for him to see me. He's already tried to kill me today."

Pearce rubbed his forehead with the back of his wrist. "Answer the door."

Robin started walking towards the door. Don crossed to the other side of the room.

"One last attempt." Pearce closed the gap between himself and Robin and pressed the gun into the small of Robin's back. "Tell him you're ill."

Robin stepped up to the door. "Eddie, can you hear me?"

"Let me in, you twat. Carol's—look, let me in."

"I'm not feeling well. Go away."

"Mother of frigging Christ. I'm coming in."

Pearce whispered, "Just open the door."

Eddie's lip was swollen. He had a dirty bandage on his hand and something long and black poked out of it. His cornflower blue eyes looked over Robin's shoulder. Without hesitation, he raised his arm and the thing in his hand spat. The noise it made was terrifying.

The pressure of the gun against Robin's back disappeared. When he turned, Pearce had collapsed on the floor. Something had hit the man in the shoulder and the force of the impact had knocked the gun out of his hand. He was groaning. Robin stooped and picked up the gun.

He looked at Eddie. "Why did you do it?"

"That's the lunatic from the post office." Eddie stepped into the room and closed the door. "The one whose mother you stabbed. I just did you a fucking favour, you mad fuck. Probably saved your poxy life. You get the money?"

"Why did you kill Carol?"

"Fuck you talking about?" Eddie glanced up, face twisted into crazy lines. He spoke through clenched teeth. Spit flecked his lower lip. He was staring through Robin, staring straight at Don.

Robin stood where he was and pointed Pearce's gun at Eddie. "Confess."

Without taking his eyes off Don, Eddie said, "What?"

"You killed Carol. Admit it."

"You're fucking crazy. Get the money."

"Confess."

"Fuck off and get the money."

He would never confess.

Robin fired. Eddie slumped against the door and slid to the

floor. One cornflower blue eye stared into space and where the other one had been was now a bloody hole. The black thing slithered out of his hand and lay still.

Don said, "Robin, give me the gun."

Robin grinned at him. "Just a minute." He turned round and bent over Pearce. "How's the shoulder?" he said.

Pearce flashed out a hand and grabbed Robin's wrist. Robin yelled as Pearce's fingers tightened. The man's strength was awesome. Robin was going to have to drop the gun. He couldn't hold on any longer. If he could only squeeze the trigger. He felt faint with the pain shooting through his wrist.

If…he…could…just…squeeze…the…

Pearce bucked and let go. A second red spot stained his t-shirt. Lower down. Central.

Robin let the gun fall and nursed his crushed wrist.

Don picked up the gun. "Where's the money?"

Robin couldn't move his hand. It had seized up. Maybe Pearce had broken it. Well, he'd sorted him out, hadn't he? Given him an extra bellybutton. The bastard was bleeding almost as much as his mum had and making just as much noise about it, too. Don was saying something.

"What did you say?"

"Where's the money you stole?"

Before Robin could answer, Eddie fell sideways. His head struck the wall. His neck bent and his ear stuck to the floral wallpaper. He looked like he was listening to next-door's TV.

Don walked over to Eddie and started rummaging in his pockets.

Robin said, "I think I've broken my wrist."

Don said, "One more time, you fucking hypochondriac. Where's the money?"

Robin glanced at Don. He was easing a wallet out of Eddie's trouser pocket. His face was an unusual colour. He looked a lot like Dad.

"You don't look well," Robin said. Don found a bunch of keys and slipped them into his pocket. "You should sit down."

Don said, "Last chance."

Robin turned away. He watched a bubble of blood pop on

Pearce's lips. He faced Don again. "Why do you want my money? I thought we were in this together. I thought we were helping each other."

Don switched the gun from one hand to the other and back again. He scratched his chin with the muzzle. "You're too trusting, Robin. I need the money to get away."

"He's dead." Robin gestured towards Eddie. "You can tell the police how it happened. He killed Carol. You're safe now."

"But he didn't."

"I can back you up."

"You're not listening, Robin. Eddie didn't kill Carol."

Robin hesitated. He heard the words repeating in his head. *Eddie didn't kill Carol.* Not possible. "You're confusing me. You said that Eddie killed her."

"I lied."

The room grew dark. In the silence, Apache war cries whooped through the wall from next door. Robin smelled piss wafting up from his crotch. He looked around him. A dead body sprawled in front of the door, one of its eyes missing. His wife's lover, Eddie. Another body lay at his feet, hands pressed to its bleeding stomach. Robin looked up at the man who had lied to him. Don had the face of a ghost.

Robin spoke quietly. "If Eddie didn't kill her, then it must have been me. Like I thought in the first place. Isn't that right, Don?" He leaned his head back and closed his eyes. "I came to believe I'd imagined it. It looked like she took a breath, just before I left." He turned his head sharply and opened his eyes. They probed Don's. "I wanted her dead for a while. Now I wish she wasn't. We were married, you know. We made vows to each other." He turned his head away. "Thing is, our marriage was never consummated." He flexed his fingers. Some feeling was gradually returning to his hand. "Yeah. We never fucked, me and my wife." He chuckled. "She couldn't bear to be touched. She couldn't bear for anyone to touch her." He paused. "I know what you're thinking." He shook his head. "One time we were visiting her mum," he said. "Her mum had M.S. Had it for a while. Her eyesight was deteriorating." Robin rubbed his wrist. "She lived with her boyfriend in one of those new houses. Wimpy or Barretts. One of those soulless places. Anyway, the point is, it had stairs, which she found hard to cope with. On this occasion, she got stuck. Scared, I suppose. Scared of falling. If she'd been on her own, she'd no doubt have overcome the fear. Or waited until her boyfriend came home from work. But we were there, so she asked Carol to help. Carol climbed halfway to meet her, then just stood there and called my name. She couldn't do it. Her physical revulsion was so powerful she couldn't bring herself to touch her own mother just to help her get down the stairs. Isn't that fucked up?"

"Sounds like my kind of woman," Don said. "I should have talked to her before I strangled her."

Robin's stomach shrank. "For a moment, I thought I was lucid. Are you real? I find it hard to tell."

"I'm as real as you," Don said. "How much money do you have?"

"About thirty grand."

"Lovely," Don said. "Go get it."

"Tell me again," Robin said. He cradled his sore hand in the palm of the other. "About Carol. Then I'll get the money."

Don sighed. "There's nothing to it," he said. "You thought you'd killed her. You hadn't. After you disappeared, she came round. I finished off what you started. That's it."

"You strangled her?"

"Yeah. And I carved LOVE on her stomach."

"But why?"

"It's what I do."

"You?" Robin stared at him. "You don't look like a killer."

"I do. I look exactly like one."

"Why Carol?"

"I wanted to help my little brother. He's such a fuck-up, you see. Can't do anything on his own. Listen, you wanted her dead. You tried to kill her. You thought she was dead anyway. What the hell are you complaining about?"

Robin said, "Had you planned on killing her?"

"To be honest, you put the idea in my head. I was actually trying to contact you."

"You mean, I could have stopped you?" Robin paused. "I could have stopped you." He stared at Pearce. His hand rested on his stomach, dripping blood. His eyes were open and he looked confused. "Carol would still be alive and she'd have me to thank," Robin said. "She'd owe me her life. Don't you know what that would have meant?"

"That's not what happened."

"It was a possibility."

"Not in this lifetime." Don grabbed Robin's elbow. "Enough chitchat. I'm a fugitive and I need cash. Fetch the money."

3:42 PM

Pearce read a lot in prison. He read all sorts of rubbish. For instance, he remembered reading somewhere that it was impossible to experience pain in two parts of your body simultaneously. Well, that was bollocks. Right this minute he had proof, if ever it was needed, that you should never believe what you read. The pain in his shoulder was the lesser of the two pains he very definitely felt, but it was still pretty fucking bad. It was as if someone had taken a knitting needle and pushed it all the way through the top of his arm. The pain in his stomach was in a different league. It felt as if he'd swallowed a hot coal, which lay in his gut burning like a motherfucker.

What bothered him most was the taste of blood in his mouth.

If he didn't get to a hospital soon, he would die.

If he did get to a hospital soon, he might still die. Like Mum.

When Greaves or Don or whoever the fuck the crazy bastard was that was talking to himself left the room, Pearce tried to sit up. The pain in his stomach kicked him back. He swallowed his scream enough for it to come out of his lips as a whimper. Okay. Sitting up wasn't an option. He stretched his arm out towards the body by the door. The gun that had shot him in the shoulder lay by the dead man's feet. Pearce's reach fell about three feet short. He fumbled for his mobile, thinking that as a last resort, he could phone the police. He heard a noise from across the room and raised his head. It hurt to hold it there. He let it drop. *One, two, three.* Lifted it once more.

That noise again. Yeah. Someone was opening the window. It slid up with a choked rattle. A leg poked through. A body. A white face.

Pearce recognised him. Kennedy. The kid from *Eye Witness.* He looked like he wished he was somewhere else.

He crept over to Pearce and whispered, "You okay? You don't look so good."

"Neither do you," Pearce said. "I'm dying. What's your excuse?"

The boy looked shaken. "I've got a problem with heights."

"You're here now," Pearce said. "You going to help me or what?"

"I'm here for the money."

"By the door," Pearce said, ignoring him, "there's a gun. Take it and shoot him."

"I'm here for the money."

"Greaves is a psycho and he's very fucking dangerous. I underestimated just how much. If you don't kill him, he'll kill you."

Kennedy stepped over Pearce and picked up the gun. "I've never used one of these before," he said.

"Neither have I. My advice, get as close as you can before you pull the trigger."

"I told you, I'm here for the money. I'm not shooting anybody."

Pearce licked his lips and tasted blood again. "Give me the gun, then. I'll shoot him."

"I'm here for the money."

"Everybody wants the money." Pearce raised his voice. "You can have the fucking money. Just give me the gun."

3:45 PM

*D*on said, "What was that?"

Robin handed him the leather holdall he'd buried under a pile of jumpers behind one of the sliding mirrored wardrobe doors. "I didn't hear anything."

"Shhh. Listen."

Photographs of Carol lay on the floor among broken glass and picture frames. Robin bent down and picked one up. He said, "You killed her." It was a statement, not a question.

"Shut up."

"You had no right to kill her."

"And you did?"

Robin said, "I need a smoke."

3:45 PM

"I—I don't think so," Kennedy said. "Nobody has to die."

"You can't be as naïve as you look," Pearce said.

3:46 PM

Don said, "Shhh." He shoved the gun into the flesh at the side of Robin's neck and held it there.

Robin moved forward. As quietly as could, he led the way back to the sitting room. Don followed, one hand jamming the gun into Robin's neck, the other gripping the holdall.

The room was freezing. Robin glanced over at the window. It was wide open and a young man stood in front of it.

Robin thought he'd keep his mouth shut. If Don saw the stranger, fair enough. When Robin turned his head, the muzzle of Don's gun scratched his neck. Robin swore.

Don said, "Shut it," and jabbed the gun upwards.

Robin's eyes watered briefly. When they'd cleared, he scanned the room. Eddie and Pearce lay where they'd fallen. Nothing had changed there. Robin's gaze returned to the young man, who was hopping from one foot to the other. Maybe he was about to dash back out the window. Maybe he needed the bathroom.

"Don't do it," the young man said. "Don't shoot yourself."

Don said, "I'll shoot whoever the fuck I want."

Robin breathed a sigh of relief. Don had spotted him too. The young man was real. Robin stared at his feet and said nothing further.

Don said, "Answer me or I'll blow your head off. What's your name?"

Robin felt the gun slide down his neck. It appeared over his shoulder, pointed at the stranger.

The stranger said, "Kennedy."

Don said, "What are you doing here?"

Kennedy shuffled his feet. "Nothing."

Don let go of Robin and stepped forward.

Robin said, "I need a smoke."

Don glowered at him. "Have a fucking smoke."

Robin's right hand was swollen, his wrist at least a third bigger than it should be. He reached into his shirt pocket with his left hand and took out a packet of cigarettes.

Bees swarmed in his skull.

Don walked towards Kennedy.

Robin flipped the lid open and, pulling out a cigarette, dropped the packet. He bent down to pick it up. Then flicked his lighter. The bastard was empty. "Anybody got a light?" Everybody ignored him. He tossed the useless lighter onto the floor. Out of the corner of his eye he saw Pearce's hand move. He held the black creature Eddie had brought with him. The creature was shaped a bit like a gun. Like the black Brocock they'd used in the robbery. Was he hallucinating? No, guns didn't writhe in your hand. This thing was pulsing. It had a heartbeat. Or was he imagining it? That was the worst thing about being ill. Not being able to trust what you saw. Almost as bad as not being able to trust what you heard. But he knew that, and he could compensate. Was it a gun, then? Had Eddie shot Pearce in the shoulder? That would explain the blood. And if so, that same gun was now pointing at Don.

Pearce's arm was far from steady.

Kennedy said, "Now would be a good time."

Don followed his gaze, turning his neck until he was looking over his shoulder.

Pearce pulled the trigger. The gun screamed and the bullet punched a hole in the wall about five feet to Don's left.

Don grinned and took a step towards Pearce. "Haven't I been careless?" he said, dropping the holdall.

Robin blocked his path. His left hand shot out and his heel struck Don on the nose. Something popped. Don's face registered shock and his nose splattered blood onto the carpet. As he lifted the gun, Kennedy grabbed his arm from behind and twisted it. The gun fired a bullet into the ceiling.

"Hold him," Robin said. With his good hand, he prised Don's fingers off the gun. Once he had it in his grasp, he pressed the muzzle into Don's crotch. "You can let go, Kennedy."

Kennedy said, "Let go of what?"

"Just move," Robin said. "Get out of the way."

Don tensed. He stood on tiptoe.

Robin's unlit cigarette still dangled from his lips. He pulled the trigger.

Don bounced backwards into the open window. He landed on his back against the windowsill and made gurgling noises. He looked like he was pissing blood. He probably was.

Robin walked over to him, seized hold of his legs and tipped him over the ledge. Robin climbed through the window after him.

Don lay on the plank flooring, the remnants of daylight dimly lighting his face. He spat a mouthful of blood. When Robin grabbed his coat, he didn't resist. Robin dragged him towards the edge of the platform. "Long way down," he said.

Don spat more blood. Turned his head towards Robin. "Can't feel my legs," he said, shivering.

"Good to know." Robin grabbed Don's ankle and lined his leg along the edge. He grabbed the other one and moved it alongside. "You killed my wife, right?"

A sudden grimace wiped the smile off Don's face.

"Sore?"

"Payback, baby brother," Don said. "But you know that, don't you? Same as you know I'm not here. All you've shot just now is a piece of your psychotic imagination. I'm not hurt. I'm not really bleeding. I have no flesh, no blood. I'm just your fucking crazy creation. That's all I am, little brother. Shit. Nobody else sees me. It's just you and me. You want to know a little secret? I didn't kill your wife. You did. You just borrowed my personality to do it, cause yours doesn't have the balls."

Robin sensed the cigarette in his mouth. Still unlit. "Got a light?"

"Fuck you."

Robin patted his empty pockets, then sat down under the window and stretched out his legs. He took the cigarette out of his mouth and threw it over the side. No flame, this time. No paraffin. He'd have to improvise. His feet touched Don's arm. Don grabbed hold of his trouser leg. Robin braced himself against the wall and pushed his legs straight. Don started to laugh. Robin pushed again. Don let go of his trousers and grabbed hold of a piece of scaffolding, knuckles whitening around the pole.

Robin got to his feet. He took a step towards Don and kicked his hand. His fingers stayed wrapped around the pole. Again, and they loosened, then tightened once more. Third time, Don screamed. But still he didn't let go. Robin kicked him again and at last Don's fingers fell away. Robin lay down beside him, trapping his arms at his side. For a moment they lay side by side. Immobile. Then, raising himself onto an elbow, Robin lowered himself on top of Don. Don tried to push him off, but Robin pressed his head into Don's chest, wrapping his arms around his back. He started to hum "Dido's Lament" from Purcell's only opera, rocking from side to side in time to the music.

He opened his lips and sang, "No *trouble, no trouble in my soul.*" Stopped. Spoke. "Sure you don't have a light, Don?" He didn't wait for an answer. He had built up enough momentum to roll onto his back. He flipped over and there was nothing but air underneath him. Don didn't exist? Not for much longer, he wouldn't. Robin gazed into Don's bloodied face. He stared into it all the way to the ground.

3:54 PM

*R*ubbish bins heaped on his left only a few feet away. The soft landing he never had. He turned his head. Stared at Robin. Landed on top of the suicidal fucker. Bounced off on impact. Probably broke every bone in Robin's crazy body.

And his own.

Don feels nothing from the waist down. His right arm is twisted under his back. When he tries to move his other hand, only his little finger twitches. Someone reaches inside his head and squeezes his brain. Steel fingers sink into his chest. Bright lights pop in his skull.

An odd thing happens: Don is unable to breathe.

A pair of birds circle overhead. One named Donald, one named Don.

Donald's in the garage messing with parfin and he knows Mummy doesn't like it. He did it one time before and she said it was very, very dangerous. She hit him with her hairbrush on the bare backside until her arm was sore and she had to stop.

Robin tugs Donald's arm and Donald says, "Go away."

Donald is eight years old. Robin is six. He pulls Donald's sleeve again and says, "What you doing Donald? Can I see?"

Donald sighs like it's a big deal and says, "Go away." He swings his elbow and catches Robin on the chin.

Robin says, "That hurt." If Mummy was around he'd cry. But he knows there's no point. Donald'll just laugh. Maybe even do it again.

Donald says, "Sorry," in the silly voice he uses that Mummy tells him off for. He pulls a face.

Robin peeps over Donald's shoulder and sees him soaking one of Mummy's old knickers that she uses for dusting. Donald's tongue's sticking out of his mouth like when he has a fit. Donald's pleptic, you know.

"Mummy's going to smack you if she finds out."

"Well, she won't, will she?"

"What you making with it, Donald?"

"A torch."

"You need batteries."

"Not that kind of torch, stupid. A fire torch."

"A fire torch? Wow. Can I have one?"

"You're too young."

"Show me how to do one."

Donald screams at him, "Leave me alone."

Robin waits until Donald's face has gone normal again and then he plucks at his jumper. "Can I smell?"

With a sigh Donald lets him move closer and sniff the soaked rag.

"Can I smell the bottle now?" The parfin is in a plastic water bottle that Mummy keeps hidden in a high cupboard in the kitchen. She doesn't know Donald can reach it by standing on top of the microwave.

"All right." Donald unscrews the top and Robin takes a deep breath. It makes him feel a bit dizzy. He takes another breath. Donald puts the top back on and sets the bottle on the bench next to the box of long matches.

Donald drops the rag. His eyes go funny.

"Stop it, Donald."

Donald falls on the floor and his legs start twitching.

"You having a pleptic fit?" Robin asks him. Donald carries on kicking. Robin knows he should get Mummy from Mrs McRobb's next door. But he wants another sniff of the parfin first. He grabs the bottle and takes the top off. It smells really nice and he thinks Donald might want to smell some too. But Donald can't smell anything at the moment. He's too busy twisting about on the garage floor.

Robin has an idea. He splashes some parfin on his big brother's face. He aims for his nose, but some gets in his mouth and mixes with the spit at the edges of his lips. Robin pours some in his hair. "Shampoo." He pours more. "For you." Mummy makes him laugh when she says that. He pours lots more. He bends over to sniff it. He rubs his fingers in Donald's hair. It doesn't foam up like shampoo. His fingers smell of parfin. He wipes his hand on his trousers. Shakes the bottle. There isn't much left, so he dribbles it over Donald's jumper and empties the rest on his jeans. It looks like Donald's peed himself. Ha, ha.

He's lit matches before. These are easy. Big ones. He opens the box and takes one out. The end is red. Sometimes they're brown. And once he saw a blue one. He strikes it on the side of the box and nothing happens. He tries again and the flame goes whoosh. He lets it burn for a while and then holds it next to Donald's head. His brother's hair glows blue and goes flickery orange and starts to crackle. He drops the match and puts the parfin bottle and box of matches back on the bench.

Donald is screaming. He's dancing on his back like a beetle and screaming. His hair is a big flame and the skin on his cheek is on fire. One of his eyelids looks like it's melted. Robin claps his hands and giggles. He gets the matches off the bench and lights another one. He drops it on his brother's chest and watches the jumper catch fire. He lights another one and drops it. Then he drops the whole box.

He waits and watches. He gets scared. He says, "Donald. Stop it now." When everything apart from Donald's shoes is burning he starts yelling, "Mum." He runs outside and into next-door's garden and up the steps and bangs on the door so hard that his fist hurts. Tears stream down his cheeks. He keeps yelling, "Mum. Mum."

She comes to the door and sees his face and says, "What is it, love?"

He grabs her hand and drags her along the path, back through the garden and into the garage.

She says, "Oh, love." Her hand clamps over her mouth. Her face is white. She says, "Oh, love." She runs over to Donald, who has stopped moving. "Love." She starts batting the flames with her hands. The smoke makes her cough. She chokes. Tears stream down her face. She shrieks, "Love."

3:54 PM

*P*earce heard the singing. Heard the scream. He watched Kennedy clamber through the open window and return a short while later, hand covering his mouth.

Pearce said, "Okay?"

Kennedy raised his eyes and gave the slightest of nods.

Eyes closed, tiredness swimming in his veins, Pearce said, "Dead?"

Kennedy moved his hand from his mouth and said, "I think so." He closed the window.

Pearce said, "You better get out of here." His mum's killer was dead. He'd killed himself and saved Pearce in the process, in a strange kind of way. Pearce felt cold. He was never cold.

The young man picked up the holdall and opened it. He said, "Jesus," and closed it again. He walked over to Pearce. "Give me the gun."

"No fucking chance." Pearce raised his arm. It took more effort than fifty press-ups. The gun wobbled in his hand. "Take the money and piss off out of here or I'll shoot you where you stand."

"That's all the thanks I get?"

"You were a big help," Pearce said. "Now fuck off."

"I don't believe this. You're only alive because of me. If I hadn't climbed up the scaffolding and got in the window and set up a distraction, you'd be dead." The bag swung in his hand. He looked about fifteen years old.

"What do you want? A kiss?" Pearce sighed. Bad idea. It made his stomach burn. He screwed his eyes shut. The pain was extraordinary. It made him want to laugh. "I *will* shoot you." He opened his eyes and searched Kennedy's.

"Who are you trying to kid?" Kennedy said. The muscles around his mouth gradually slackened. "You couldn't hit a barn door if you were standing right in front of it."

Pearce couldn't keep his hand raised. He let it drop, still clutching the weapon. "What do you want?"

Kennedy said, "The gun."

"What for?"

"Never had one and it's no use to you. You think I want to shoot you?"

"Maybe," Pearce said. "You might think I'll tell the cops about the money."

"You won't."

"You prepared to take that gamble?"

"It's not a gamble."

Pearce frowned. "What do you mean?"

"You're taking some of it, too."

"The money? I am? What about your boss?"

"I don't have a boss. I resigned earlier today. All this," Kennedy gestured with the holdall, "was my idea. He knows nothing about it."

"And your bright idea is to split the money with me?"

"Two ways, right down the middle."

"I don't want it."

"That's irrelevant."

"I refuse to accept it."

"Then maybe I will have to kill you."

"Don't act so tough," Pearce said. "It doesn't suit you."

"The only way I can trust you is if you're involved. Can't you see that?"

Pearce thought for a moment. "My word isn't good enough?"

"I can't make that decision. I don't know you."

Pearce said, "Okay. Go see this guy. His name's Cooper. He's got a first name but nobody knows what it is. You should call him mister." He gave Kennedy the address. "I owe him some money. He'll tell you how much."

"Roughly?"

"Less than a grand."

"You have to take more—"

"Doesn't matter if it's ten quid or twenty thousand. It's a two-way split however it's divided." Pearce paused for a moment to fight the pain. He carried on, "Either it's stolen or it isn't. Now, help me." His hands were covered in blood and he couldn't get his mobile off his belt.

Kennedy helped him detach the phone. "You want anything? A blanket?"

"Just piss off before the police get here."

"Can I have the gun?"

"Fuck off."

3:56 PM

*P*earce felt cheated. Revenge was sour. He licked his dry lips. They tasted metallic. He dialled 999. They told him an ambulance was on its way. He hung up.

He was exhausted. He dialled her number.

She said, "Hello."

He didn't know what to say. After a moment he said, "Hello."

"You're breathing strangely."

"Am I?"

"You okay? Pearce, what's happened?"

"You want the good news?" He paused. Coughed. "Or the bad?"

"Don't be flippant."

"Dread—" he said, "—fully sorry."

"Don't be cheeky."

"Right." He paused. Closed his eyes. Cold. Fuck, it was cold. "He's dead."

She screamed in his ear. "Christ Almighty!"

He dropped the phone. Still heard her screaming. No words. Just a long agonised scream. His fingers fumbled for the phone. Got it. Lifted it to his ear. It weighed as much as a fat baby.

She said, "Why are you telling me this?"

"That was the good news."

"Stop it."

"Stop it?"

"Stop it."

"Stop it." He paused. His eyes welled up. He fought back the tears. What was happening to him? His voice cracked when he said, "I didn't kill him."

"Oh, God," she said. "Oh my fucking Christ, thank God."

"Ailsa, I might," he said, "pass out."

"You what? What's wrong?"

"Tired." His voice was weak. "The bad news." He licked his lips. "I got shot."

"Christ. Where? Where are you shot?"

He tried to laugh, but couldn't. He heard the sound of a siren and felt an overwhelming sadness spread inside him. It thickened his blood. Lined his skin. Cloaked him from head to toe. "I'll be fine," he said.

She said, "Pearce. You okay? Pearce, you still there? Pearce. Answer me, you fucking bastard."

about the author

ALLAN GUTHRIE was born in Orkney, but has lived in Edinburgh for most of his adult life. He is married to Donna. He has published several short stories in a variety of magazines and anthologies. *Two-Way Split*, short-listed for the CWA Debut Dagger award under the title *Blithe Psychopaths*, is his first novel. His second novel, *Kiss Her Goodbye*, was short-listed for an Edgar Award. His website, Noir Originals, is at www.allanguthrie.co.uk.